Lorelei's Lyric

Southern Elemental Guardians 1

D.B. Sieders

FIRST EDITION

ISBN: 978-1-937996-80-2

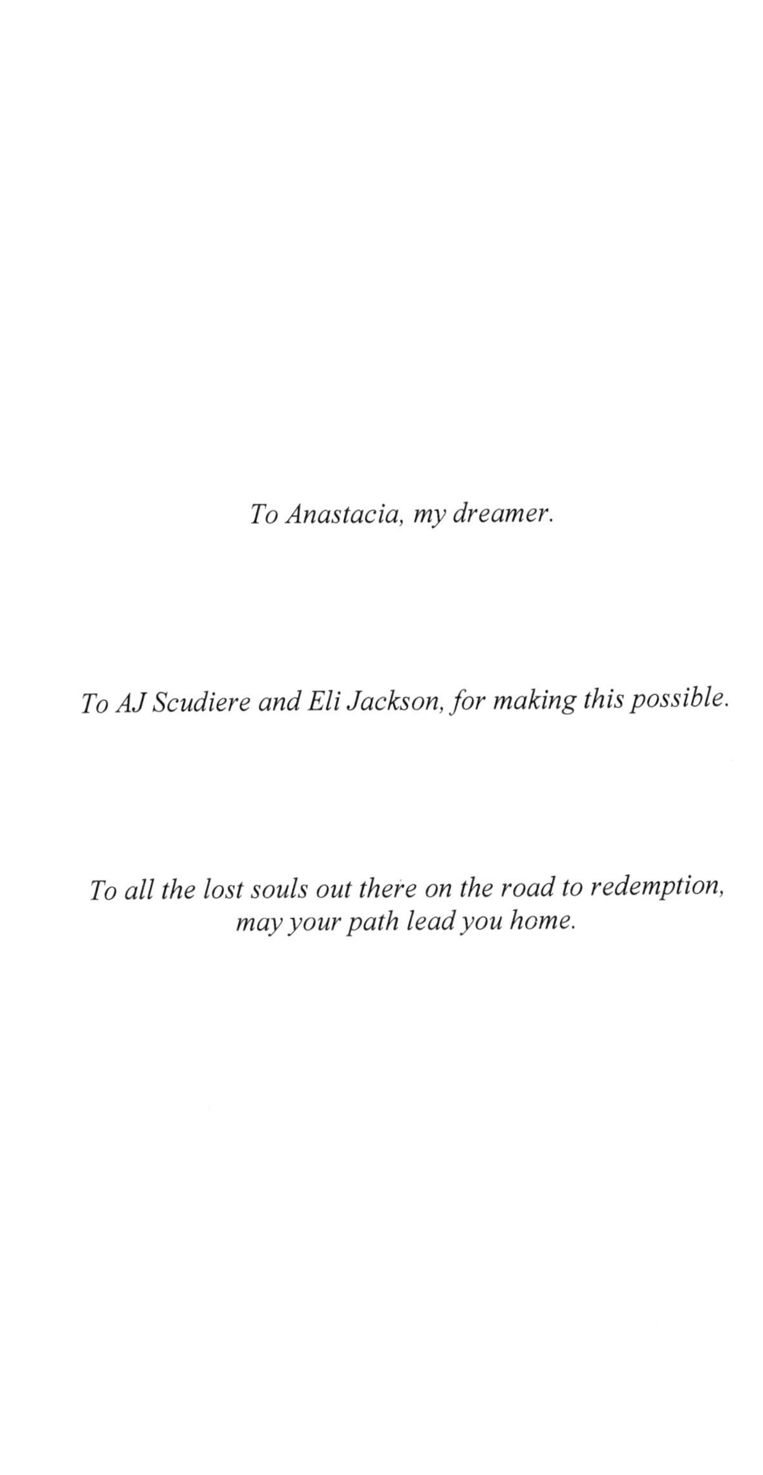

To Anastacia, my dreamer.

To AJ Scudiere and Eli Jackson, for making this possible.

*To all the lost souls out there on the road to redemption,
may your path lead you home.*

Acknowledgements

Thank you first and foremost to my dear friend/critique partner/partner in crime, Sophia Jones. You were there from the beginning and have been with me each step of the way. I could not have done this without you. I am profoundly grateful to Jenna Bennett, my mentor and RWA sister by way of Music City Romance Writers, for her unflagging support over the years. Thanks also to Caitlin Fryer and Jody Wallace for all things world-building. Thanks to my agent, Victoria Lea, for her faith in my work.

Thank you, Mark Steinwachs, for being my source for behind-the-scenes music business research. Any errors are my own and not his. He's awesome! I'm grateful beyond measure to Jeffrey Getzin for tearing apart my battle of the elementals scene and making it better.

Special thanks to Debbie Herbert and Jeri Smith-Ready for their kind endorsements, and I am eternally grateful to my amazing editor, Trish Milburn. Thank you to AJ Scudiere and Eli Jackson of Griffyn Ink for giving this story a chance and for loving Lorelei, Vance, and Catfish Jack as much as I do. Thanks to Julie Schroeder for the absolutely gorgeous cover!

And as always, thank you to my dear hubby and Kids 1.0 and 2.0 for letting me disappear behind the computer so I can turn the voices in my head into something I hope my readers will enjoy. I have the best family a writer could ever wish for!

Lorelei's Lyric is brilliantly clever with its unique blend of Southern humor and poignant mermaid mythology. Modern-day Siren, Lorelei, traveling to The Music City of Nashville? One helluva great premise that hooked me at page one! I fell in love with this shape shifting Siren and her romance with aspiring rocker Vance Idol. One of those rare books that will have you laughing and sighing and crying, touching your heart just as great music touches your soul. A must read!

—Debbie Herbert, *USA Today* bestselling author of the Dark Seas series (*Siren's Secret*, *Siren's Treasure*, and *Siren's Call*)

Lorelei's Lyric made me swoon! A perfect blend of mermaid magic and rock-star grit, Sieders' charming, irresistibly sexy tale gives us a love story to believe in. I can't wait to read more!

—Jeri Smith-Ready, Award-winning author of *Requiem for the Devil*, the WVMP Radio series, and the Shade Trilogy

"I asked you nicely. Once. I won't do it again."

The woman didn't flinch, but her gaze turned hard and held his without faltering. "You didn't, Vance."

"I didn't what? By the way, what's your name, *sugar*? Guess it must've slipped my mind since last night," he added, smirking.

"I'm called Lorelei," she said as she stood, forcing him to take a step back lest she knock him over. "And what you didn't do was ask me nicely, but it doesn't matter. You won't find your phone, clothing, or the means to leave until I'm sure you're fully healed."

He maintained his glower but found himself at a bit of a loss. Though she was tall for a woman, he still outweighed her by at least fifty pounds of muscle. Most men he'd faced down during his time on the road would have cowered, but she clearly didn't fear him.

Since he couldn't persuade her by fear, he shifted tactics again, reverting to his preferred method of persuasion when faced with a difficult woman. It hadn't failed him yet. He allowed his gaze to wander down her face to her full lips, and from there down along the slender column of her neck. Her audible swallow and the bob in her throat made him smirk with satisfaction. When his gaze fell to the swell of her breasts, he grew hard again and knew she'd read the heat in his gaze when it returned to her face.

He definitely saw heat in hers.

He moved past her, taking care to brush his skin against her bare arms, and sat down on the bed. He reclined and stretched his body, allowing the towel that covered his lower half to come loose. Plastering a smile on his face, one that charmed most women right out of their panties, he said, "Well if you *really* want to make sure I'm healed, Lorelei, I guess you'd best get on with your examination."

Chapter 1

"You'd think the water would be cleaner over here," Ilsa said, plucking a slimy plastic straw out of her hair.

"Oh, stop whining," Lorelei chided, flicking her tailfins and splashing her sister. "Honestly, you're a five-hundred-year-old mermaid, not a hatchling. Act like it for Neptune's sake."

"But it's really disgusting. *Humans* are disgusting." Ilsa pinched the straw between thumb and forefinger, arm extended to keep the offending object as far from her body as possible. To her credit, she vanished the straw with a flash of magic instead of tossing it back into the river.

"That's not what you said about the hu*man* you hooked up with last night."

Ilsa smiled, that dopey "I-got-laid-and-it-was-good" grin plastered wide across her face. "That's the whole point of this trip. And, I'll grant you the males of the species do serve their purpose, some very well, actually. But that does not excuse them for using our sacred waterways as dumping grounds."

"Here we go again," Lorelei muttered, hoping to avoid another hour of non-stop droning. "Give it a rest, already. You've done nothing but complain since we hit the Mississippi."

Ilsa flashed her a wide-eyed look of mock indignation. "I most certainly have not!"

Lorelei snorted. "You, my dear *Flosshilde*, are what the mortals would call a real diva."

Mentioning Ilsa's "old-fashioned" Old World name never failed to put the feisty Rhinemaiden into a fury, and she rewarded Lorelei's jab by dunking her under the murky waters of the Cumberland River. Lorelei emerged sporting her own expression of faux outrage, which made Ilsa dissolve into giggles. Warmth and affection surged through her at the sight, melting away the last traces of annoyance.

She was so glad Ilsa agreed to come along on her American adventure and much-needed holiday before she began her training. It was her last chance to enjoy the freedom of youth. Once in possession of her full powers, Lorelei would ascend their mother's throne as ruler of the Rhine.

Her favorite sister always managed to lift her spirits, pulling Lorelei out of the sea of her own melancholy and easing the ache she carried deep within her heart. It was a good sign. She hoped to finally put the past and its pain to rest with the change of scenery.

"No fair using my old name. *Some* of us weren't graced with lyrical names that stand the test of time," Ilsa said, still pouting. "But you've made your point. I'll try to maintain an acceptable level of maturity." Then she grew serious. "Or maybe not. You know, it's been ages since I've seen you so full of joy, my sister."

"Of course I'm happy. This is our first vacation, after all. Come on, we're almost there." She tried to stop her smile from faltering as she waded farther downstream. Though most in their circle of high-ranking water elementals regarded Ilsa as little more than a shallow, thrill-seeking beauty, she was no fool, as the shrewd look she flashed Lorelei proved.

Good thing her sister was also easily distracted.

"Wow, look at that," Ilsa said as they came around a bend.

Lorelei stared in wide-eyed wonder at the breathtaking vista downstream. Naturally, she'd witnessed the rise of mortal civilizations over the centuries, since they tended to pop up along the earth's waterways. The bright and bustling cities along their native Rhine had long served as personal playgrounds. But the vibrant lights of this foreign city still took her breath away. Just beyond the bridge lay downtown Nashville, world famous Music City USA. When she'd learned the city's nickname, she knew they just had to see it, experience it, and hear it.

Even from their comfortable distance, her supernatural hearing caught the sweet sounds of music, and she couldn't help but smile. Ilsa grinned right back, swishing her tailfins in anticipation. Lorelei understood the urge. She was eager to explore, too.

Too bad they'd have to wait. Their great-grandfather, the river god Eridanos, had ordered them to check in with the American water guardians at each of their stops for briefings on local customs and possible dangers. Just a little formality, he'd said, and an extra measure of protection.

He hadn't fooled either of them.

No, he wanted to keep tabs on his wayward girls, probably at their mother's request. Having had her heart broken by their mortal father, Melusine guarded her daughters with near-pathologic devotion. It had taken four centuries and promises from a series of chaperones before she allowed the two eldest Rhinemaidens to leave home and see the world. She feared her daughters would succumb to the same misfortune that befell her: mortal men.

Of course, should they fail to heed her overbearing maternal warnings, the nixie curse would stop any mortal man dead in his tracks. Literally.

"Well," Ilsa began, "how do you suppose we're meant to find our guide?"

Grateful to be distracted from thoughts of curses and annoying relatives, Lorelei answered, "If this place is anything like New Orleans and Memphis, our guide will find us."

"Fine, but can we at least go ashore and get ready? I can't wait to get out of this yucky water."

Lorelei sighed. "It's the same as the water back home."

And…cue the eye roll. "This is the New World! Hello? Should be fresher," Ilsa grumbled.

Lorelei resisted the urge to roll her own eyes. "We've been through this."

"Oh, for Neptune's sake—"

"At every single stop."

"But—"

"It's been going on at least a thousand years. More mortals, more damage to the elements." Lorelei said with finality. "They aren't going anywhere anytime soon. Get used to it."

"Okay, but I'm itchy, too. And I'm hungry."

And high maintenance.

Lorelei sighed louder. "Fine, we'll swim over to the river bank and wait on that log," she said, pointing out a felled tree jutting out from the shoreline. "But we keep the fins until after check-in."

They waded over and hoisted themselves up. Ilsa's turquoise tailfins shimmered in the moonlight as she stretched over the log's expanse. Lorelei wriggled her own silver fins, capturing the droplets of river water with her magic until they coalesced into a miniature waterfall that spilled to reunite with the source. While Ilsa set about untangling her long golden locks with a bit of magic and a finger comb, Lorelei breathed in the cool night air and enjoyed the view of downtown Nashville.

The buildings seemed to float above the shoreline. Bathed in the glow of the full moon underneath a cloudless sky, their lights reflected in the swirling waters below. It was just postcard perfect. Oh, New Orleans had enchanted her with riverboats and jazz, and the barbeque and blues of Memphis left her feeling fat and sassy. But Nashville, well, the magic of the musical energy captivated Lorelei as soon as they surfaced. It was almost as if the city was the Siren and *she'd* fallen under its spell.

So taken by the atmosphere, she was sorely tempted to give in to a bit of indulgence, something she hadn't done in a few centuries. A quick scan of the area with her keen eyes and ears told her it was probably safe. No humans were within earshot. Animals were much less sensitive to her call. And it had been so very long.

She could *sing.*

Eyes closed, she unleashed the sweet alto notes from Patsy Cline's mournful ode to lost love and let her heart soar along with them. Oh, she'd almost forgotten the rapture of song. Music was as essential to her kind as the waters they ruled and protected, as the bittersweet melody resounding through the night reminded her. Ending her long self-imposed silence was pleasure balanced on the razor's edge of pain.

"Looks like you've got yourself a captive audience."

"Oh no," Lorelei said after she opened her eyes. A host of bullfrogs, three muskrats, a snapping turtle, and even a blue heron surrounded her, their night-darkened eyes focused upon her with rapt attention.

One of the frogs released a plaintive croak. She hesitated, wondering how long she could serenade them before the spell became irreversible. Animals, like all mortal beings, were affected by the nixie call. While the wildlife in their home waters always recovered after an impromptu performance, as long as they weren't exposed for very long, she wasn't certain how the creatures in this part of the world might react.

And she knew all too well how humans reacted. Guilt twisted her gut and tightened her chest at the memory.

But it had felt so good to sing again, so *right.*

The heron spread his wings with a squawk. One of the muskrats waded closer, rubbing his furry little body against her fins. The other animals still had control of their faculties, too, and seemed to enjoy her voice. Figuring a few more bars couldn't hurt, she launched back into Patsy Cline and smiled as the creatures chirped, squeaked, and croaked their appreciation. After a verse and a chorus, she stopped. Her onlookers stared back at her with dazed expressions.

Ilsa took the opportunity to bust out Gretchen Wilson's ode to redneck women who say "hey y'all" and "yee-haw."

Lorelei covered her ears and looked in disbelief at her sister.

"What?" Ilsa asked, shrugging. "We *are* in Nashville."

The animals appeared unfazed, and still enchanted, despite the sudden change in both songstress and style. Lorelei clapped her hands twice and cast a bit of magic, willing the dazed wildlife back to their senses. When it became apparent the show was over, the crowd dispersed and left Lorelei and Ilsa to their waiting.

A deep, unearthly male voice silenced the nighttime river sounds and put both mermaids on high alert.

"Well bless my soul, I believe we got ourselves a couple of Nixies in Dixie."

Chapter 2

"Hey Vance, we're on in ten, okay?"

Vance Idol nearly jumped out of his skin. The sound of his bassist's knocking ricocheted through his pounding skull. Mark Rogen's voice, on the other hand, sounded muffled and distant though he stood right outside the bathroom door. Vance cradled his aching head in his hands, brow slicked with sweat underneath trembling fingertips, and let out a low groan.

"You okay in there, bro?"

"I'm fine," Vance managed to croak. He hoped he sounded more convincing than he felt.

"Look, I know it's been tough…but we can't blow this gig. Mags would've wanted us to go on."

"I know," Vance snapped. "Just give me a sec to get it together, okay?"

"Okay, but if you aren't out in five I'm grabbing Josh."

Heavy footfalls echoed down the corridor, and Vance's nanosecond of relief faded with them. He needed to get a grip. He couldn't afford to screw this up. The band had been working their asses off in every dive bar, shit hole, and roadhouse from New York to Cali and back again for the past five years. Nashville was one of their last stops on the long and winding road to discovery and a shot at the big time.

After all those years of paying dues, they'd wrangled a tour/production manager, a couple of regular crew, and plum gig at Marathon Music Works. Along with a loyal fanbase, Internet buzz, and a lot of self-promotion, The Rivermen, with Vance Idol billed as the frontman, managed to attract a sizeable crowd. The frontman bit happened on account of the small sliver of "fame" Vance garnered on a television talent show. He didn't make it to the finals but got far enough to be remembered. Yeah, that fame was about fourteen minutes, thirty seconds and counting, but it apparently still helped. Their lead guitarist, Joshua Rollins, had even spotted a couple of producers in the audience just before Vance excused himself.

I need a drink.

Okay, technically, he couldn't chalk his misery up to withdrawal anymore. That nightmare passed shortly after he'd quit drinking cold turkey. No, the oh-so-clinical term for this special brand of hell, according to the docs and counselors, was post-acute withdrawal syndrome. PAWS, they called it. Yeah, real cute and clever. Only there was nothing cute or funny about chronic insomnia, soul-sucking depression, or cravings that never went away. Then there was the joy of panic attacks and mood swings, though the latter fit with the surly rocker image. Good thing he'd picked a profession that allowed him to channel his inner black-hearted bastard.

He'd been warned, to be sure. His stint in rehab had been short, if not sweet, and the staff thought he'd left too soon. But hell, the band needed him and he didn't want to let them down by bailing for a few months, not when he was convinced he could deal with his problems all on his own. Now, faced with performance pressure and the ghosts of his past, he was on the verge of blowing it.

He stood and paced around the small room. Sweat seeped from every pore as anxiety pierced his gut like a thousand knives. His innards protested at the sudden change in equilibrium, forcing his left hand to grip the cool porcelain in front of him as his right strummed along the surface of the sink.

Perched on that sink was the key to oblivion, the bottle filled with amber liquid that would ease his pain and steal his soul. Again.

"Aw, hell!"

Everything had been fine. Scratch that, it had been shit, but the manageable kind of shit that still allowed him to drag his sorry ass out of bed, sleepwalk through his day, and pull himself together long enough for a gig. But then he'd walked into the dressing room and found a fifth of Jack sitting front and center on a small table, gift-wrapped with a damned purple ribbon. Someone must have sneaked it in while the crew was busy. Those guys knew alcohol was a no go on account of their lead's little problem. But hell, he should've been prepared for the possibility. For staff, groupies, sleazy execs—anyone on the scene who wanted to get in good with the band and grease some wheels with social lubrication—booze was the go-to. Just like the pills some skank out on the floor shoved into his palm, some kind of free sample as she breezed by, chilling him to the bone in her wake. He hadn't been on the wagon *that* long, and dealers knew how to sniff out desperation.

Not that he was into pills.

Yet.

Jesus, this was bad. Really bad. He should've turned around and bolted out the door as soon as he spotted the bottle. But no, he'd stuck around long enough to let his old mistress start whispering her pretty lies, tempting him to sneak off to the bathroom and take a swig. He was such an idiot for jeopardizing his recovery and his band's last shot at the big time, but a combination of nerves and grief had him clinging to his old crutch. He could have poured it down the sink, but then that sweet scent hit him, almost eased him. At first, he thought knowing it was there would be enough, buying into the delusion that he could always get rid of it as soon as they wrapped up their show.

Instead, he now stood at the precipice of disaster, overlooking a downward spiral from which he might never emerge.

He slammed his fist against the sink as anguish, frustration, and shame forced the strangled cry from his throat. The pain of the blow might have made him throw up, but he hadn't eaten more than a bag of chips the entire day. He couldn't risk it. Three bottles of Pepto and a Dramamine over the past twenty-four hours served as insurance against the messier symptoms he could ill afford on stage.

Just one more time, and I swear I'm done with this. I gotta get through tonight and then I'm done.

Hating himself, Vance picked up the bottle and pressed it to his lips. He'd had the lid unscrewed by the time Mark started banging on door. His eyes were already bloodshot, and he could chase the hooch with a couple of uppers and still make it to the stage. He'd have to scarf down some breath mints if he didn't want Josh to find out he was drinking again.

No, damn it, this is the last time!

Staring in the mirror, he wished he could punch the guy glaring back at him. He still had his looks, but weight loss and insomnia had taken their toll. His already prominent cheekbones jutted out from a gaunt face he barely recognized, and the hard set of his jaw told of a life lived too hard and too fast. Though bloodshot, his green eyes blazed with all the rage and pain he carried inside. He looked dangerous.

Yeah, you're real fucking glamorous, asshole.

He took a swig, letting the sweet taste and slow burn assault his senses as the liquid filled his mouth, but stopped short of swallowing. He closed his eyes, and waited, savoring the sensation before shame could drown it. The sweet oblivion he craved wouldn't come, not without a lot more. But maybe he could get through the next few hours. The ache in his back and legs would ease, and his hands might stop trembling. All he had to do was let it roll down his throat.

A vision of Maggie flashed in his mind, smiling, healthy, and whole—so very different from the strung-out junkie he'd last seen at the morgue after losing her to her demons and a poison not unlike the one he was about to swallow. Different from the ruined man he saw every time he looked in the mirror.

He couldn't do it. He *wouldn't* do it.

He spit out the booze. Mopping the sweat off his face, neck, and chest, Vance screwed the lid back on the bottle and stuffed it into his travel bag along with his pill stash. Strange, instead of filling him with a sliver of hope or pride at his small victory, despair and emptiness threatened to swallow him whole. *Figures.* Deep down, he knew it was only a matter of time. His just-say-no bit was merely a temporary stay of execution. Settling for the lesser evil, Vance dry swallowed two Percocet to calm his body and mind. Donning a long-sleeved black tee, he finger combed his hair and did his best to look like a rock god.

"Five minutes, man! Time to get your ass in gear!"

Vance opened the door and pushed past Josh. He made his way to backstage, picked up his guitar, and joined in with the band's pre-show ritual. Thanking God for steady hands, he strummed out a few confident chords. Mark joined in, quirking a lopsided grin.

"This is it, boys. Hope y'all brought your A-game tonight," drummer Steve "Sticks" Mitchell said, like he did before every show.

"A-game? Shiiiiit! Just try and keep up tonight, and how about you don't drop your sticks for a change?" Mark countered, smiling at his buddy.

"I never, *ever* drop my sticks, bro. Don't believe me? Ask any of them fine honeys in the front row and they'll tell you how well I hold my stick."

Mark laughed. "No one's looking at you, man, and you know it. They've all got their eyes on Josh and Vance!"

"It's show time, assholes," Josh grumbled as he jammed his cell phone into his pocket. He grabbed his guitar from the stand, nearly knocking the damned thing over. Vance didn't even need to look at his right hand man's face to know he was royally pissed off. Disappointment and accusation sharpened his voice, and rage poured out of his reverberating warm up strokes.

"Change in plans. We're adding 'This is Home' to the set list," Vance blurted out.

The guys went quiet. Aside from the milling crowd just outside and the sharp echo of Josh's abandoned last note, the atmosphere stilled, the weight of silence nearly suffocating. Fresh sweat beaded on his forehead and a familiar ache tightened his chest, but not from the pills.

This pain ran far deeper.

"Um, do you think that's such a good idea, man? We haven't rehearsed it. Hell, we ain't played it in eight months, not since…."

Not since we lost Mags.

"Sticks is right, Vance. I know you wanna, like, you know, make her a part of tonight, but we got a lot riding on this. You sure you're up for it?"

"I'm sure, Mark," Vance said, fighting past the tightness in his throat. "It's our best song. We still do "Road Rage" first, hard and fast. We move on to the ballad soft and easy and then segue into "Highway's Calling" full on balls to the wall. It'll knock them on their asses."

He twisted his face into a scowl as he stared down each of his bandmates. They would have trusted his instincts a year ago. There would have been no questions or hesitation back then. The guys would have followed his lead. Now, they glanced back and forth between each other with expressions of fear and uncertainty. And then Mark and Steve looked to Josh.

"To hell with it! I said we're doing Maggie's song and goddamnit, that's what we're gonna do!"

"Whatever you say, bro," Mark muttered.

Steve shrugged and nodded. Vance locked eyes with Josh and gave him a look that dared him to argue. It wouldn't be the first time. Maybe after the show they could finally work this out with their fists and be done with it.

Josh squared his shoulders and gave him a cold, hard stare. "Fine. I just hope you can get your head out of your ass long enough not to screw this up."

"This isn't just about us, J. She should be here, too."

"Yeah, she should be. But she's not."

Because of you, Vance Fucking Idol, he thought, finishing the accusation Josh hadn't worked up the *cojones* to voice out loud. He didn't have to, though. Vance had been living with the hell of it since the day she died.

While the rest of the band hauled ass on stage, Josh stood his ground, shooting eye bullets at Vance. With a muttered curse, he stormed onto stage while Vance stood frozen, wondering what in the hell had possessed him to tear open old wounds. They shouldn't change the set list, shouldn't do that song, but something deep inside compelled him. It had to be Maggie's song.

"Get your ass in gear, Vance! We're on!" Josh yelled, dragging him out of his wallowing and slamming him back to reality.

He walked on stage with steady legs, ignoring Josh, Mark, and Sticks, ignoring the audience, ignoring everything except his guitar and the pounding in his chest. Summoning his courage and whatever was left of the man he used to be, he poured his heart, soul, and pain into the opening chords, whispering, "For you, Mags."

Chapter 3

Ilsa almost fell back into the water in response to the deep, gurgling voice that boomed behind them. Lorelei jumped back into the river voluntarily, her power casting an eerie light across the water as she prepared to attack. Ilsa flashed to her side, the glow amplified as both water women braced themselves for fight or flight.

"Where is he?" Ilsa whispered.

"Don't know, but get ready to haul fins! I'll flush him out."

Back to back, tails looped around one another for protection, Lorelei and Ilsa spun slowly as they levitated out of the water, arms raised in preparation for battle.

"Who's there? Show yourself!" Lorelei's command carried authority, but inside she was on the verge of panic. This was bad. Friendly elementals followed protocol and made themselves known to visitors out of courtesy. The presence she sensed was powerful, to be sure, and he obviously knew what they were. Oh dear gods, what if they had stumbled into unfriendly territory?

"Yeah," Ilsa chimed in. "Come out on your own, or we'll call you out and drown you!"

The only response they received was a watery chuckle. Lorelei peered into the darkness, trying to locate the intruder, while Ilsa belted out a Wagner aria of such magic and volume it caused a couple of passing bats to plummet from the sky and into the water.

"Oh, no!"

Ignoring imminent danger, Lorelei panicked and dove in after the stunned creatures. She flung out a hand and sent a net of violet light weaving out to catch the first. After transforming the net into a cocoon of life-giving air, she cast her gaze about, frantically searching for the other. Seconds counted, and she wouldn't let these innocents suffer and die at the hands of their cursed call.

Heart racing and breath coming in shallow gasps through her gills, she faltered as memories assaulted her. Flashes of gold disappearing beneath the water's surface, lifeless eyes, a limp form in her arms. Cold, so cold.

Gone.

She couldn't lose another life.

Swooping downstream with the current, she caught up with the second bat. She grabbed it and clutched them both to her chest, praying to her kindred river gods she wasn't too late. She shot up to the surface, leaping out of the water and over to the adjacent shore. Lorelei placed the little masses on the log with gentle hands, willed them dry, and massaged their furry bodies and leathery wings until they revived.

Upon waking, the first one bit the tender flesh between her thumb and forefinger.

"Ouch! Well that's gratitude for you," she muttered, laughing through the tears that now spilled down her cheeks.

The bat blinked her inky eyes, and Lorelei swore she caught a flash of something in that angry gaze. A cunning and cruel intelligence seemed to lurk beneath the animal's diminutive exterior. Before she could look closer, the bat offered a parting hiss and took flight. Her companion followed, though at least he allowed Lorelei to scratch him behind the ear first before departing. He even did a few aerial loop-the-loops as if to show his appreciation. Relief and a deep satisfaction washed over her as the creatures took flight, knowing her power had restored and healed them.

"Lore! How about a little focus here?" Ilsa whispered from beneath the water.

When Lorelei finally spotted her, Ilsa's eyes and forehead were the only parts visible above the water's surface, and her gaze darted from side to side as she approached.

"Oh, right," Lorelei said, shaking off the distraction. Ilsa's attempt at channeling her inner alligator looked a bit ridiculous, but at least she'd kept her wits and avoided exposure. They could ill afford to be caught off guard outside of their home territory. Getting back with the program, she raised her arms in preparation for defense. Or attack. "Did you get him?"

"I don't know. I still don't see him. Either he fell in and washed downstream, or he's immune to our call. And if he's immune...we are in some serious trouble."

The laughter came again, louder this time and much closer.

"You two are as jumpy as a pair of minnows, and about as bright. Y'all go hop back up on yonder log and sit a spell. I'll be up directly."

"Catfish Jack?"

"The one and only, darlin'."

Lorelei breathed a sigh of relief. They had expected one of the lesser elemental guardians, or perhaps an emissary of the great king of the eastern rivers at most, upon their arrival tonight. That Catfish Jack himself met them surprised her, though his manner of greeting was on par with their reception in a few other cities. For reasons beyond her comprehension, the water sprites and enchanted river guardians of the Americas all shared a love of practical jokes. Apparently, irreverence was the norm in the New World. It delighted Lorelei, but seemed to annoy Ilsa to no end.

Of course, most of the jokes *had* been at her sister's expense. She was, after all, an easy target.

And right on cue, Ilsa opened her mouth and launched into a tirade befitting a thoroughly pissed-off water diva. "That was completely uncalled for, you rogue. We, who are known as Nixie, Naiad, Siren, and Mermaid rank among the highest water dwellers and are worthy of great respect. We rule the waters of the earth, great and small, salty and fresh. Our dominion extends from the mightiest rivers to the—"

"'Scuse me if I don't bow or curtsy, your majesties. We ain't so formal 'round these parts, and I'm a bit old to be bending so far."

Lorelei snorted, which earned her a scowl from her sister. She finally spotted the bearer of the voice, staring in awe as he waded in from the middle of the river to greet them. After hearing his deep chuckle and charming drawl, she looked forward to meeting the ancient river god who ruled this stretch of water even more.

In his current form, Catfish Jack was by far the largest freshwater fish she'd ever seen. Broad as he was long, he could've swallowed one of the speedboats they'd seen zoom by earlier in the day and still had room for a canoe. Maybe two. Rumor had it he'd been around since the birth of the Mighty Mississippi. He knew every river, stream, and creek east of it, though he made his home in the Cumberland River these days.

He lifted his great head from underneath the water and shook. Lorelei and Ilsa squealed as his long whiskers showered them with river water and debris. After his shake, Jack rested his head between the Nixies. Lorelei couldn't resist tweaking one of his whiskers.

"Hey now, that tickles!"

"Serves you right for getting mud all over us."

"Relax, darlin'. I hear it's good for the pores."

Lorelei cleared her throat and commenced with protocol. "I am Lorelei, and this is Ilsa. We are the daughters of Queen Melusine and keepers of the Rhine. We bring you good tidings from Eridanos, revered river god of the Old World."

"Pleased to meet y'all. It's always a pleasure to host my cousins from across the big pond, especially my old friend Erid's pretty little gals," he replied, winking at Ilsa.

Ilsa smiled, apparently charmed by the wink and flattery. No surprise there. Sliding a little closer, she leaned down and asked, "Speaking of the great and powerful Eridanos…I've been dying to know what he was like when he was younger." Ilsa ducked her head, feigning shyness as she looked through her lashes, the shameless coquette. "Did you really save him from an eagle when he came to visit?"

Oh, she was good! Lorelei nodded in encouragement, trying to disguise her giddy excitement as polite curiosity. Finally, after all of these centuries of wondering, they might actually get some dirt on their legendary elder. Rumor had it that he'd caused quite a ruckus during his youthful explorations, one that had caused a centuries-old feud between guardians of water and air in the New World.

Jack chuckled, clearly delighted with the opportunity to share a good story. "Yes ma'am, and not just any old eagle. It was one of them wily Air Spirits in disguise."

"You mean a Sylph?"

"You got it, and not just any old Sylph, either, darlin'. Sky Daddy is about the biggest and most powerful sky god around these parts, and not someone you want to cross. Your great granddaddy had turned himself into a big old bass so he could sneak through a stretch of open river without being caught and having to pay tribute, you see. Only he forgot that bass fish don't generally go jumping out of the water. Only river gods do that when they want to make good time. They also don't jump so high as to knock a passing bird off his flight path."

"And that bird Eridanos almost knocked out of the sky wasn't any ordinary bird, was he?" Lorelei asked.

"Nope, it was Sky Daddy himself out on patrol. Well, once Sky Daddy got back on course, he chased after Erid, figuring he could either have himself a good meal or catch a river god he could hold for ransom. So he swooped down and snatched him right out of the air on his next flying leap."

"Oh!" Ilsa cried in horror while Lorelei fought the urge to snort again. Not that Jack appeared to mind her sister's well-timed reaction. In fact, his great mouth split into a wide, fishy grin as he made the most of his dramatic pause.

"Now I'd been swimming along underneath him the whole time just to see what would happen. Y'all Old World cousins are right fools sometimes, forgetting your manners when you come calling in our home waters. Anyhow, as soon as I saw what was about to happen, I heaved myself up out of the water and swallowed 'em both!"

Well, well, well. Eridanos hadn't mentioned *that* part. Lorelei and Ilsa shared a look of agreement. They would most definitely bring this story up again when they got back home.

"What happened next, Catfish Jack?" Ilsa asked as she ran her hands over Jack's head and then reached down to tweak his gills. Jack shuddered in obvious delight.

Lorelei rolled her eyes but still smiled in spite of herself. She figured Ilsa would have their host wrapped around her little fins before night's end.

"Well, darlin'…ooh, that's it! That's the spot…." Ilsa scratched him under his chin, reducing him to a giant quivering mass of scaly contentment. Lorelei shook her head and laughed. Yup, her sister would have the old fish rolling over for a treat in no time.

After he let out a gurgle of a sigh and regained his composure, Jack continued his tale. "So, as I was saying, I swallowed them and dove down deep to the bottom of the river. Once they stopped wrestling with each other and giving me heartburn, I spit them out and gave them a little lesson in diplomacy. We did some haggling over tribute and manners, which ain't no easy feat with your great-granddaddy since he's a right stingy and proud old fool. Then I brought 'em back up, made 'em make nice, and let Sky Daddy go, though I'm afraid it started quite a feud between our kind and the Sylphs. Y'all would be wise to steer clear of them while you're here, and definitely don't go getting on their bad side by messing with critters under their dominion."

Lorelei shot a dirty look at Ilsa. "Nice going with the bats," she mouthed.

"How could I know?" Ilsa mouthed back. Then, turning her attention back to Jack, she asked, "So after you got him free, you kept our great-grandfather company for the rest of his trip, right?"

"Yes ma'am, I sure did. I must say, he's done pretty good for himself, if his sweet little brood is any measure."

"Why Catfish Jack, you say the nicest things," Ilsa said, wrapping her arms around him. Lorelei, who wasn't immune to a little flattery, followed suit and favored him with her own embrace.

"Now then, ladies, you should be all clear for a tour of my town. Once y'all shed your fins, I suggest you take a stroll along the riverfront. Go on down to the big brew pub on Broadway, get some good vittles, and then just follow your ears. You can't help but trip over some mighty fine music in this here city just about any night. But on a Saturday? Y'all are in for a treat!"

Lorelei shivered in anticipation. She couldn't wait to get busy exploring. Oh, to hear the music! It was the next best thing to singing for herself. Lucky mortals. They could sing and play with passion and wild abandon, never giving a second thought to death and destruction.

"Lorelei! Come on, let's go!"

She'd been so lost in her reverie, she hadn't realized that Ilsa had already hopped ashore and transformed. Long, shapely legs, visible beneath the hem of her super short skirt, stood in place of shimmering scales. Ilsa's golden locks flowed over her shoulders while her torso flashed with a dizzying array of colors as she tried to summon the perfect tank top to frame her ample bosom.

"Take it easy," Lorelei said, fighting not to giggle, "you don't want to use all of your magic on the first night!"

Ilsa waved a hand in dismissal, her top still flashing back and forth between crimson and turquoise. "We won't run out of magic long as we're near the water. Now hurry up and get ready."

Lorelei followed suit, her fins unwinding into a pair of long, lean legs as she strode ashore. Such a wonderful sensation, the transition from fin to flesh. It started with the elemental energy flowing within her. The power surged and then condensed into a single drop, creating a ripple at the heart of her true form that gained momentum as it traveled through blood and bone, forging and molding that fluid form to her will. It was if she became water, the force that was both her sustenance and her charge to protect. Indeed, the flash of light that followed shimmered in waves, reflected from vanishing scales before glowing skin emerged.

She charmed her raven hair into a braid and summoned dark, skin-tight denim over her new lower body and an iridescent silver tank top above. Smiling to herself, she willed a pair of gorgeous boots in chestnut leather over her feet and a matching cowgirl hat on top of her head.

Might as well go native.

Another wave of energy hit and nearly knocked her off her new feet.

"Ilsa, what in the name of the gods? I can't walk in these things!" Lorelei shouted in horror. Her sister had enchanted four-inch heels beneath her formerly sensible boots.

"Yes you can. You just have to practice. Oh my, don't they make her legs look luscious, Jack? We'll have to beat those country hunks off her with a stick."

"Careful now," Jack replied. "Don't want her losing her heart to one of them country hunks."

Lorelei really didn't see any reason for all the fuss. They'd traveled along rivers and streams throughout Europe and Asia for quite a few centuries. The men were always fun for a while, on those occasions when she chose to indulge, but she was a river maiden through and through. It would take more than a handsome face to capture her heart and lure her away from her home. Running off with a human could only end in disaster, as she'd learned the hard way long, long ago.

"Lore? You okay?"

Realizing Jack's crash course in local customs had come to an end, she blinked, shook her head, and snapped her attention back to the present. "I'm fine. Anything else we should know, Jack?"

"Nah, I reckon that's it. Y'all go on now. Come on back to the water tonight and I'll tell you more about your great-granddaddy's trip."

"And what if we find ourselves some company, Jack?"

"Well, Miss Ilsa, Union Station has some mighty fine accommodations, should you find yourselves in need. Not that I want to know about it," he added with a shudder. *Ah, so he* has *been told to keep us away from human men. Figures.* Once recovered, he added, "But I expect you two to find a little time for your Uncle Jack later on now, right? That'll serve as your tribute for safe passage and my protection."

"Of course," Lorelei replied. "How about we meet up on that stretch of shore over there near the street you called Broadway around 2 a.m. mortal standard time? We'll fill you in on our plans."

"Better make it 2:30, since we have to walk back," Ilsa said, looking down at her stilettos and half-sighing, half-whining. "Life would be so much easier if we could just materialize wherever we wanted to go."

Unlike their elders, the young Rhinemaidens had yet to harness the power of their element for long-distance travel. They could control water, change form to mimic water dwelling animals or assume land legs, and they could conjure clothing and other essentials. Dematerializing from one location and materializing in another wasn't within their repertoire. Yet. Such magic supposedly required maturity and wisdom, though legend held that it could be triggered in times of dire need or with proper tribute.

Other defenses could be triggered, too, and Lorelei shivered at the thought of dragon wings and serpent tales.

Shaking off those unpleasant images, she focused on consoling her sister. "It won't be long until we come into our full powers," she said, patting Ilsa on the back. "Probably less than fifty years. Besides, I thought you enjoyed our trek across the ocean."

"I suppose." Ilsa grumbled, but a small smile tugged at the corners of her mouth. "Cruise ship hopping has its benefits."

Jack quirked his giant head to the side, appearing confused.

"Plenty of lonely waiters, bartenders, and entertainers locked on a big boat and surrounded by the newly wed and nearly dead," Lorelei explained. "A veritable all-you-can-eat buffet for my fair sister. And since I'm sure she's hungry again, we'll take our leave and meet you back here at 2:30, Jack."

"Now there's a good girl. Go on now and have yourselves a fine old night on the town. Just be careful, you hear? I done been warned to keep an eye on y'all. Have a good time, and feel free to sample the local flavors, but don't go looking for trouble. Your mama will have my whiskers if anything happens on my turf."

Chapter 4

"I think I've found my new favorite drink," Ilsa exclaimed, staring at the glass in her hand with wide-eyed wonder.

"You say that every time you try a new cocktail."

"And I think I've found my new boy toy for the night."

"You say that about every bartender, too."

"But this time I *mean* it. Mojitos are delicious, and so is he."

Lorelei rolled her eyes. Every bar they'd visited between here and the Gulf Coast had been smorgasbord of the male variety for her sister, and it appeared that this establishment would be no different. She had to admit, though, they'd found some pretty tasty treats during their travels—of the culinary variety. Alcoholic beverages were definitely among them, not to mention chocolate milkshakes, real American hamburgers, and barbeque. As usual, both Nixies had opted for steak instead of fish at the brewpub, since they'd yet to meet the land dweller that could do justice to the fruits of river or sea.

"Everything all right for you ladies?" The waiter asked as he refilled their water glasses for the third time.

"Oh yes, everything is most excellent," Ilsa replied, flashing a bright smile. "Right, Lorelei?"

"Yes," Lorelei said absently. "May I have another margarita?"

"It would be my pleasure, ma'am," he said, brushing her fingertips with his when she handed him the empty glass.

"So, do we do dessert here so you can drool over the bartender some more, or are you ready to go catch a few shows?" Lorelei asked, turning her attention back to Ilsa.

"Our waiter is very good looking."

She glanced over in time to catch him smiling back at her.

"I thought you had your eye on the bartender."

Ilsa rolled her eyes and heaved a heavy sigh. *Here we go again.* "I do, but that's not the point. He's an attractive man and he's obviously interested in you, not that you noticed, apparently."

"So what's your point?"

"My point, dear sister, is that we're out on vacation, surrounded by hoards of attractive, red-blooded American males without Mother or our aunties around, and you've yet to sample any of the local flavors."

Desperate to change the subject, Lorelei joked, "Maybe it's because my gorgeous little sister captures their attention first. I hardly stand a chance with you around."

"That's not true and you know it. I've watched you turn away more than a dozen just between here and Memphis. What gives?"

Now it was Lorelei's turn to sigh. "Nothing. Now, are we doing dessert or a show?"

"Well, I don't think I could eat anymore right now if I tried. Food, that is," Ilsa replied with a wink. Uh-oh. She was up to something. "How about we take a little stroll? Mr. Cutie-Pie waiter tells me there's a pretty good band playing at Marathon Music Works tonight."

"I thought you wanted to hit The Wildhorse Saloon so you could try your land legs at line dancing?"

"We've got all week. Besides, it's a *rock* band," Ilsa said, sporting a knowing smile.

Her sister knew very well just how to entice her, the hagfish. She'd loved the raw power and energy of rock and roll music since its inception, not to mention the guitar gods who created it. It came as no surprise to her that mortal women often threw themselves at those guys. After all, if they could command their guitars with such confidence and stamina, there was more than a decent chance they could coax a few powerful notes out of a woman's body, or a mermaid in a woman's body.

"You know you want to," Ilsa singsonged.

"And I know you want to dance the night away with as many men in cowboy boots as you can wrangle, so what's with the pressure?"

Ilsa dropped the teasing expression and grew uncharacteristically serious. "I'm not trying to pressure you, Lorelei. It's just…"

"What?"

"I want you to have a good time and just let go for once. I mean, you're always so guarded. You've been that way ever since we grew into women. I always thought it was because of Mother, but even here and now, when we're finally out from under her thumb for the first time, it still seems like you're holding yourself back."

Lorelei dropped her gaze, cursing her own cowardice as much as her sister's powers of perception. Maybe Ilsa was right. She'd lived in fear of repeating the mistakes of her youth for so long, maybe she *had* forgotten how to really live.

"You're right."

Ilsa almost choked on her mojito. "Come again?"

Lorelei had to smile. "Yes, my sister, you heard me loud and clear. I'm *agreeing* with you."

"Really? You mean you'll go?"

"Yes, really. It's high time I "let go," as you put it, and I'd love to hear some honest to goodness rock and roll music. The real deal."

"That settles it, then," Ilsa said, delight painted across her fine features. "Off we go to chase rockers!"

* * * * *

"Anyone want a beer?" Mark asked. "We got fifteen minutes before we're on again."

"I'll take one if you're buying," Sticks replied.

"Lucky for you, they're on the house. Josh?"

"Nope. I stay sober for gigs," Josh replied, shooting eye bullets at Vance.

"Take it easy, man. Tonight's been a bitch for all of us," Mark whispered, probably hoping Vance wouldn't hear. He'd parked himself in the corner of the room opposite his bandmates so they wouldn't notice how twitchy he was.

"Hey, Vance! Want me to grab you a soda?" Mark yelled.

"Just water," Vance said.

"Sure thing, bro."

Just two more hours, man. Hold it together for just two more hours.

He wanted to believe the waves of nausea rolling through his body came from dehydration and an empty stomach. His twitching legs suggested otherwise. Gulping down some water and scarfing down a few chips could fix that problem and get him through the rest of the show. They'd done well the first hour. Even Josh had given him the nod of affirmation. He hoped it was good enough. Eddie Bends, their manager, was out schmoozing the producers in the audience. He'd give them a rundown after the show.

"I'm stepping out for a smoke," Vance said as he pulled himself back on his feet. "Come and get me if Eddie shows up."

Grateful for the cool spring air, he stepped out the back and walked around the corner before lighting up. He stood in the shadows where he could watch some of the crowd while remaining unseen. The snippets of conversation he was able to catch made him feel a bit better, laced with phrases like "awesome band" and "loved that ballad" and "that guitarist is hot." Had he and Josh been on better terms, he might have offered the gushing redhead who'd uttered that last bit a backstage pass. Then again, why should Josh get laid if he couldn't?

Well, it wasn't that he couldn't, really. He'd just lost interest.

"Hey there, baby. I've got just what you need."

He'd been so lost in thought he hadn't notice the petite brunette until her sultry, seductive voice jolted him back to reality. She slinked toward him, streetlights reflecting off her vinyl corset and piercings.

She flashed him a smirk. "Jumpy, aren't you? You still get nervous when you play?"

"Nah," he muttered, cursing himself and running his free hand through his hair. "I just didn't see you come up."

She moved in closer, enough to give Vance a good view of her cleavage and to feel the heat of her bare midriff through his T-shirt where she pressed up against him. He almost backed away, but the tightening sensation in his pants let him know that Mr. Happy had other ideas. It seemed his body was interested, or at least screamed with pure need.

Her porcelain skin was so pale it almost gleamed against the black fabric of her scant clothing. She was probably some mix of cyber goth, or Victorian goth, or whatever those who liked to flirt with the dark side called themselves these days. Plenty came to their gigs. Most of them didn't know jack shit about real darkness and God help them if they ever learned.

This one, though, she could be the real deal…

A mop of dark silky hair framed her oval face in a pixie cut, her bangs so long they almost fell over her pert little nose. That full, luscious mouth promised all manner of sinful delights and dark, inky eyes called to the deeper pits of his soul.

He couldn't have conjured a woman more suited to his current mood if he tried.

"So," he drawled, "what is it that you think I need?"

"He seems to know," she replied, hungry gaze fixed on the growing bulge in his jeans. She placed her small hands on his chest and traced light patterns with her fingertips. "Hmm, that's nice…very nice."

Vance agreed. Life on the road got lonely. He'd had plenty of offers from groupies, waitresses, barmaids, and even women in the grocery checkout line. But he just couldn't do it. Not anymore. No one else could replace Maggie, or take away his guilt.

But maybe this little vixen could take his mind off his cravings, off the lingering, all-consuming grief that…*no man, don't go there.*

"You got a name?"

"Maurelle."

"Well, Maurelle, I'm—"

"Vance Idol. I know. I've been to a lot of your shows. Saw you on TV, too."

"Have you now?" *Groupie. Figures.*

"Oh yeah. Been waiting for a chance to meet you. Alone. Guess it's my lucky night."

He fought against cringing at the cheesy line. How desperate *was* this chick, going after a wannabe rock star? Of course, given that he'd succumbed to the other excesses of the lifestyle, why not one more? If he was going to be a walking cliché, he might as well get some pleasure out of it.

Curling his lips into a smirk, he flicked his cigarette to the ground and ran his index finger over Maurelle's shoulder and down her chest until it hovered dangerously close to one perky nipple. She didn't seem to mind, based on her breathy sigh.

"You know what? It might just be your lucky night after all. Why don't you stick around after the show? I'll come and get you after we load out."

"Or maybe I'll just come and get you, big boy. See ya later."

She spun on one heel and walked away, giving Vance a lovely view of her swinging hips, luscious ass, and mile-long legs. He made a mental note to grab a condom, since she looked like a gal who'd been around the block a time or three.

Maybe a pack of condoms.

Chapter 5

"What'll it be, ladies?"

"I would just love a mojito," Ilsa replied with a giggle.

Shameless flirt. Guess she's not all that *sad about leaving the last bartender.* Not that he wasn't a cute bartender. Lorelei still fought a twinge of envy whenever she observed her sister in action. Ilsa could place mortal men under her spell without even opening her mouth to speak, let alone sing. Of course, footloose-and-fancy-free Ilsa had never suffered the consequences.

And she hoped to all the gods that her beloved sister would never have to.

"And what about you, cowgirl?"

Her cheeks burned. She'd worried the hat and boots might be overkill, making her look like a newbie tourist. Of course, she *was* a newbie tourist and very excited about this stop on her big American vacation, but still—how embarrassing.

Luckily, the barkeep just winked and smiled.

She forced herself to smile back. "I'll have one, too."

"Relax, Lorelei," Ilsa whispered once the bartender was out of earshot. "This is going to be awesome!"

"Maybe we should just stick with the original plan and hit the Wildhorse," she muttered, alarmed by the rush of heat brought on by the mere thought of a hot male rocker. Seeing and hearing one might prove too tempting, and therefore dangerous.

Before Ilsa had the chance to give her more grief, the bartender returned with their drinks. Nodding toward the stage, he said, "Looks like they're about to start. You ladies should have been here for the opening. They damn near brought the house down with a ballad of all things."

"You're in luck," said one of the servers as she filled up her tray with drinks. "I heard they got so many requests for an encore they're gonna do it again."

While Ilsa chatted up the bartender, Lorelei turned to face the stage and feasted her gaze on the luscious men donning guitars and fiddling with drumsticks. The venue was a large space, warehouse style, but it held the charm and aura of a more intimate venue. Nothing separated the slightly raised stage area from the floor, bathed in warm, comforting earth tones of brick and wood. Waves of crisp night air swirled around them, like a light breeze blowing in from outside.

Funny, she hadn't spotted any open doors or windows…

She shivered. Something else came in with the wind, something cold, dark, and menacing. Familiar energy. Elemental energy. Lorelei glanced at Ilsa, but her sister didn't seem to sense it. Perhaps it was nothing more than her doubts about being here in the midst of such temptation.

As quickly as she'd felt it, the energy disappeared. She shook her head and focused on the human energy around her instead, forcing herself to calm down and let go so she could enjoy this moment. The air buzzed with so much anticipation that goose bumps erupted on the flesh of her arms. Once they'd settled the bar tab, she dragged Ilsa closer to the stage. They had to push a bit, but managed to secure a spot right up front and to the left.

She had her eye on the man who appeared to be the lead guitarist, or maybe even the lead singer. With sandy blond hair that hung loose above his broad shoulders and well-muscled arms, she found herself hoping he'd sound as good as he looked. Instead of belting out a series of strong notes, however, he let loose an angry shout to someone off stage.

"Get your ass in gear, Vance! We're on!"

Well that wasn't very nice. Having experienced a heaping helping of Southern hospitality during their travels so far, the guitarist's angry display seemed especially shocking. Then again, mortal musicians tended to be a bit high strung. They didn't call the phenomenon "artistic temperament" for nothing.

Her thoughts stopped cold as soon as a tall man dressed in black strode across the stage.

Ignoring his bandmate, the man, presumably Vance, slung his guitar strap over a broad shoulder, nodded to the drummer, and then played a series of powerful chords that kick started the band into what promised to be a fast-paced rock-and-roll ride straight to ecstasy. Lorelei grabbed Ilsa's hand and squeezed it in gratitude. They'd sampled jazz, blues, and a fair bit of rockabilly country on their travels, but the music filling her ears and quickening her pulse—this was pure rock.

Then the man in black started to sing.

His powerful voice reached out through the microphone and wrapped her body in a commanding grip she felt all the way to her toes. His rugged, masculine features alive with passion, he sang with a tightly leashed fury that held the audience in a state of awe. And the way he played? His guitar strokes seemed to trail over her skin.

"Wow!" Ilsa shouted over the music.

Lorelei, still captivated by the man and his music, could only manage a small nod in response.

"Hello? Lorelei? Better close your mouth before you start drooling."

"He's amazing! He could be part Nix!"

"Well he sure seems to have cast a siren spell on *you*! You can thank me later when you're done gawking."

That may take a while, 'cause I think I could stare at him all night.

The band transitioned seamlessly from fast and furious to a slower, more sensual ballad that showcased the lead singer's sexy voice and sexier stage presence.

There's this place I go
When I'm feeling low
And the world's closing in around me
The place where we first met,
Oh, just one sweet sunset
And I can breathe so free and easy

When she managed to tear her gaze away from him and glance around the room, she realized she wasn't the only one affected. Almost every woman looked on with admiration, hunger, or outright lust. The men in the audience didn't seem to mind, since the music also made their ladies sway, shimmy, and gyrate to the seductive beat while they got to enjoy the view. Plus, they were all enraptured by the music.

It was pure magic.

She turned her focus back to Vance. He'd slowed his movements to match the pace of the music, which allowed her to get a really good look at him. Like the lead guitarist, his arms were well-muscled. His strong left hand held the guitar's neck in a powerful grip while the long fingers of his right stroked and caressed the strings. The tight black shirt he wore, now damp with sweat, accentuated a muscular chest and torso that tapered down to a trim waist. In truth, he looked a bit too thin, but that only added to the hungry and impassioned look that made his performance all the more compelling. A mop of jet-black hair framed his handsome face. Looks, charisma, and that amazing voice—the man had it all. And his words resonated with the deep longing within her.

The road's been long and lonely
I yearn to rest my weary head
The only peace I'll find,
Outside a box of pine
Is where we once shared a bed

The bittersweet twinge of envy she always felt in the presence of human musicians tugged at her just then. *Mortal man Vance, you don't know how lucky you are. Your songs are a gift of pure pleasure and joy.* Like all her Nixie kin, Lorelei possessed a stunning voice. She loved singing more than anything else in the world. She knew and could sing thousands upon thousands of songs in at least two-dozen languages.

And if she sang any of them long enough, someone would die.

"Wanna stay for the rest of the show? I'll just bet we could wrangle an invitation backstage if we work our way up front and center."

"Huh?"

Ilsa laughed. "I asked if you want to hang around and see about hooking up with Mr. Tall-Dark-and-Musical."

Probably not a good idea. This guy could definitely get me in trouble. "Nah, that's okay. How about we hit the Wildhorse next and see if we can snag a couple of cute dance partners?"

"You sure? He's checking you out."

She looked back toward the stage and locked her gaze with Vance's. For all the joy and passion he poured into his performance, the look in his eyes was…haunted. That soul-deep longing she'd heard in his first song shone through his blazing green eyes, calling to her and begging her to make it right.

Oh, this is home to me,
And you're the only thing I see
You may be long gone
But I still feel you there
Ever young and strong
And I'll find a way to go on and on
In the love we used to share

This is home.

While she still had the will to walk away, Lorelei tore her eyes away from him and turned back to Ilsa. "I'm sure. It's definitely time to go."

Chapter 6

"I got some good news, boys."

Their manager strolled into the dressing room sporting a shit-eating grin so big it even inspired a half smile from Josh and a grunt of satisfaction. Vance himself caught a small glimmer of hope at the sight. Even Josh couldn't deny it. They'd nailed this gig.

Vance offered Eddie his own subdued grin. Mark and Steve, on the other hand, almost tackled their manager to get details.

"The two major label execs were definitely interested and took your demo."

"That's freakin' huge!" Mark yelled.

"That's not even the best part. How'd you boys like some real studio time to work on a professional album?"

"Seriously?"

"You got Bob Louis from Whitewater Records hooked. It's a small label, but I've heard good things. He gave Velocity their start, and he's willing to polish your sorry asses up and make you shine."

The second piece of news inspired a lot of high-fives and handshakes between the men. A bite on their demo and the opportunity to put together a professional quality album would give them the shot they'd been dreaming of for years. Vance let the boys share congratulations and soak in all of the details from Eddie while he breathed a mental sigh of relief.

He'd made it through tonight. How he'd make it through the coming weeks was a matter he didn't want to ponder. Between arranging the music and lyrics they already had and polishing at least four more original songs they'd need for a full album, they'd be spending some long, grueling hours writing and rehearsing before they even hit the studio. He didn't want to fall back on booze and pills to get him through it.

He just didn't know how he could do without them.

Shaking his head, he tried to distract himself with something more pleasant, like the face of the woman he'd seen lingering up front during the second set. Like any showman worth his salt, he had learned how to work the crowd at live gigs, especially the ladies. He always made it a point to lock eyes with as many as he could manage. For a few verses or an entire song, he'd give each lucky woman his looks, his swagger, and his passion, making each one feel as though he sang just for her.

Of course it was all part of the image, though most of the time he enjoyed their reactions. At least he'd enjoyed them at first. But the flashes of bare breasts, suggestive to downright lewd tongue gestures, and drunken rebel yells from cheap groupies had gotten real old real fast. Besides, they didn't really want *him*. No, these women, groupies like Maurelle from the parking lot, they wanted the fantasy.

They'd never go for the reality.

Still, he'd noticed the dark-haired hottie in tight jeans after he'd hit the stage. Hell, any man with a pulse would have spotted her and the flashy blonde at her side. Hoping she'd grace him with a smile and just leave it at that, he finally caught her attention near the end of the last song.

Once he did, he couldn't look away.

Her eyes widened and her face flushed with excitement as he poured his heart and soul out to her through his guitar and vocals. When she parted her full lips into a sensual "O" and leaned closer to the stage, it drove him mad with the urge to give even more of himself over to whatever magic worked when man merged with music. Christ, he hadn't felt that kind of connection with his art in over a year. And she'd responded to his every effort with quicker breaths, rhythmically swaying hips, and those guileless, open eyes. Her reaction brushed over his body like a hot caress, a soothing balm for his wounded heart.

Watching her leave filled him with an unreasonable sense of disappointment. It was stupid. So she'd been into the music? Not surprising. Tonight had been one of their best performances. They'd received enough roaring applause and demands for an encore to prove it. He should just savor the moment for what it was: a beautiful reminder of why he'd become a musician in the first place.

"Hey Idol, care to join the conversation?"

Eddie pulled Vance back from his musings. *Time to get back to reality.* He ran a shaky hand through his hair and walked back over to Mark, Steve, and their manager.

"Yeah, sorry," he muttered. "So how soon do we get studio time?"

"However long it takes you to get sober or us to find a new frontman."

He spun around to face Josh, who slouched in the corner opposite his previously occupied spot. After taking a long drag from his cigarette, Josh stood up straight and gave Vance a cold stare while Mark groaned in the background to the tune of Steve's muttered curses.

Eddie looked back and forth between Josh and Vance, and then asked, "Someone wanna tell me what's going on here?"

"What was it tonight, Vance?" Josh asked, voice low, his gaze locked on Vance's the entire time.

"What the hell, man? I told you I quit."

"Your good buddy Jack Daniel's again, or are you finally sucking it off the pavement like the strung-out loser you are?"

"You wanna do this right here, right now? Tonight? In front of an audience?" He got up in Josh's face, a year's worth of pent-up rage and frustration tempting him to knock his former best friend to the ground. All that held him back was the gathering crowd of crew, bartenders, and lingering patrons milling around, drawn by the explosive mixture of tension and raised voices.

"Don't lie to me, asshole. You're twitchy as hell, sweating like a pig, and I'm guessing the only reason your sorry ass can stand is because you scored some uppers, am I right?"

"After what we pulled off on stage, you want to do this right now?" Deep down, he hated himself more than he hated Josh.

Josh just made an easier target.

"To hell with it." Vance growled, turning to walk away. "I'm outta here."

He made it halfway to the door before Josh's iron grip landed on his left shoulder. Before he had a chance to fight back, Josh had his right arm twisted behind his back and had wrestled him to the ground. He roared and bucked, but Josh held him firm.

"You lying sack of shit, I can smell it on your breath." Josh hissed in his ear. He pulled back and said louder, "Sticks, go get his bag."

"Aw hell, man. What the hell?"

"I said go get his bag! We deal with this *tonight.* And while you're at it, roll up his sleeves so we can see if he's hitting the hard stuff."

"I'll do it," Eddie said. He knelt down and yanked Vance's left arm out from under his body and rolled up his sleeve. Then he twisted his arm around and examined the flesh in the crook of his elbow.

"Son of a bitch," Eddie muttered. "Nothing, Josh. See for yourself."

Josh's muttered litany of curses let Vance know when he'd looked his fill. After Josh let him go, he groaned in pain, then rolled over and stood up, glaring at his guitarist. "Satisfied, asshole?"

"Not by a long shot," Josh said before he turned and stalked away toward Sticks. Vance rolled his shoulders and stood with as much dignity as he could muster. When he came back, Josh held Vance's bag in one hand and his bottle of Jack and bag of pills in the other.

"I didn't drink it," he said through gritted teeth, his gaze locked on Josh. He didn't look at Eddie or the rest of the band. Josh he could handle, but he didn't feel like facing the guys and seeing their looks of disbelief, disappointment, and betrayal.

"So now what?" Eddie asked.

"I'll tell you what," Josh began, hands on his hips and head hanging low. He'd tossed the bag aside along with the hooch and uppers. Vance almost cringed when the bottle struck the floor. Didn't break. Damn, he was so fucked. "We let the big shots hold onto the CD. They'll take their sweet ass time with it anyhow. We use the studio time we got now to lay down some tracks while Idol checks himself into rehab."

"Dude, seriously? How the hell we gonna cut an album without Vance?"

"We do the best we can and hope our boy's more interested in making music than killing himself. If he's not, we can always call B.J."

"Won't do you any good," Vance spat. He had one last ace up his sleeve. He'd hoped like hell that he'd never have to use it, but he'd be damned if he let Josh cut him off and replace him with a no-talent prick like B.J. Mitchell.

"B.J.'s available, interested, and he's worked with us before. We all own the music. We'll manage."

Vance laughed, the hollow, joyless sound of it echoing around them. "You really are stupid, Josh. We all have rights to the music, but *I* own the lyrics. You got jack without me, asshole."

He took perverse satisfaction at the look on Josh's face.

"Mags left all the songs to you..." Josh muttered in disbelief. "Fucking bitch gave them all to you?"

He punched Josh.

Eddie and Steve grabbed Vance, while Mark got hold of Josh, and they pulled the men apart before either could take another shot. Vance struggled to get loose. Hell, they needed to just take their business outside and be done with it.

"You got everything," Josh moaned in disbelief. "She wasted everything on you. She always did. First her life, and now her legacy."

"Josh, man, don't do this."

"Shut up, Mark! He knows it's true!"

"Josh, Maggie was sick," Sticks said. "She had the monkey on her back for years before the band, and you know damn well she's the one who drove our boy here to the bottle. We need to bury the past and focus on keeping Vance on track so we don't lose this chance."

Sticks turned to Vance and placed a hand on his shoulder. "Come on, let's go take a ride and start working on getting you well, brother."

"I need to get out of here," he replied, shrugging Sticks off. The walls started closing in as the cravings, Maggie's memory, and Josh's words pulled him further into his darkness.

"Vance, you need to come with me now so we can deal with this."

"I'll deal with it on my own. I quit on my own and I'll stay sober on my own. I don't need this shit."

"Don't go like this, man," Mark pleaded. "Eddie, help us out here."

"Just let him, go," Josh said, his voice breaking. "It's over. Hell, it's been over since Maggie died."

Vance grabbed his guitar and then walked back to his dressing room and packed it in its case to carry with him. He grabbed the Jack and pills on his way out, stuffed them into his bag and slung it over his shoulder. He pushed through the back door and stared out at the empty parking lot and road beyond.

"So, is it still my lucky night?"

He turned as Maurelle emerged from around the corner and sashayed in his direction. He could see her a little better this time under the street lamp. What he saw wasn't as pretty as he'd first thought.

Oh she had tits, ass, and swagger, but the dark circles under her bloodshot eyes, the slight tremors that accompanied her movements, and the aura of desperation overshadowed her assets. Vance recognized the signs. He'd seen them before, and lived them. The last thing he needed was another lowlife junkie to drag him down.

Well you're a damned drunk, asshole. And let's be honest—you don't have far to fall.

"Come on, baby," she said, moving closer and holding out her hand. "I told you, I've got what you need."

He glanced down and saw the bottle in her hand. And it had the same purple ribbon as the bottle he'd found in the dressing room.

What the fuck?

"That's right, Vance. I left you a present, but you didn't take it, did you?" She feigned a pout before flashing him a wicked grin and opening the bottle. Single-barrel JD. The good stuff. The sweet scent of smoky oak hit him and he froze, caught between the urge to snatch the bottle and down it and the urge to run like hell from the demon in front of him.

God, but he wanted it, needed it. Just the thought sent a tremor of hunger through his body and soul as dark images flooded his mind. Maurelle bending over his body, him sprawled and ready for her. Her delicate hands bringing the bottle to his lips, helping him wash down the pills and then kissing him hard—hard enough to bruise and biting down until their blood mingled with the burning golden liquid before going lower, leaving a trail of delicious pain as she bit into his flesh.

She'd know just what to do with that sinful mouth, teasing him and bringing him to the brink before the poison surged through his veins and sent him into oblivion.

"That's right, baby," she whispered, her breath a chilly breeze in his ear. When had she moved in so close? Moving her mouth to his, she inhaled deep and long, stealing his breath and his will. "Come with me. Give me all of that delicious darkness inside of you. I can take it all away."

Chapter 7

Hunger burned in her gaze, those dark eyes black with lust and something more sinister. Oh yeah, it would be so good. Too good to last. Somehow he knew if he followed her, it would be his last ride, and the darkest part of him was desperate for it. *You deserve it, too. After Maggie, you deserve it.* Hell, it wasn't like he had much left to lose, lowlife drunk that he was. He'd be among the greats if he joined Club 27. What a jam session that would be—Hendrix, Joplin, Morrison, Cobain. Damn, they'd all burned out too fast, but they'd made great music.

He hadn't made music that great. Not yet. Maybe not ever.

Another vision invaded his thoughts. The dark-haired woman from the audience, the one who'd been so into the music, *his* music, flooded his mind, washing away Maurelle's dark appetite with the longing in her gaze. Hers was a different kind of hunger. She yearned for the magic he created with his guitar and voice, the kind he longed to feed and that fed him in return. It was the kind that took all of his sorrows and transformed them into something beautiful, something that resonated with those who heard and connected him to other souls like nothing else ever could or would.

It was the connection he used to live for.

"Sorry, sugar. Guess I'm not in the mood after all," he said, stepping away from the dark temptress in front of him.

"Don't know what you're missing," she said with a smirk.

"Yeah, I do."

"Well, if you aren't up to the job, maybe one of your boys in there can show a lady a good time," she said, lips curling into an angry snarl.

"Go ahead," Vance said, calling her bluff. He even held the door open for her. *Lady, my ass.* "Knock yourself out."

With any luck, she'd give Josh a scorching case of the clap. The thought brought a wry smile to his face.

"You'll be back. Guys like you, they always come back to me."

She brushed up against his body as she squeezed through the door, then quick as a cat she reached up and dug her nails across his neck hard enough to draw blood.

"What the *hell?*" he yelled as he stumbled back, clutching his neck.

She propped herself against the open door and smiled, bringing her hand up to her mouth and gently sucking his blood from her fingertips. Her dark gaze flashed with cold calculation and malevolence.

She turned and walked through the door, turning to look back at him over her shoulder. "I'll be seeing you soon, Vance Idol."

Crazy bitch must have some kind of vampire fetish.

A cold gust of icy wind lashed at skin as the door slammed. *What the hell? It's supposed to be summer.* Weird, but maybe that was just Tennessee weather. The locals said it could change on a whim. He didn't quite catch the last bit of whatever nonsense flew out of Maurelle's mouth. She'd said something else, some other petty threat or insult, but he didn't quite catch it. Something about "being much worse."

"Whatever," he muttered. Not knowing or caring where he was headed, he turned and started walking in the direction of the downtown riverfront.

Aside from the occasional homeless wanderer, Vance had the city streets to himself. He gave a twenty and his last bag of chips to one guy who looked as bad as he felt, and received a toothless grin and a slap on the back for his generosity. He couldn't help feeling a kinship with the vagabonds of the night and made it a point to pass along a good chunk of whatever spare cash he had on him to the ubiquitous street dwellers that blended into the concrete landscape.

He didn't believe in much anymore, aside from karma.

There were plenty of hotels in the area. He could do with a hot shower and about ten to twelve hours of sleep. Beyond that, he had no plan to fix the monumental fuck-up he'd created. He'd wandered down to Riverfront Park when his cell phone rang.

Aw, hell. What now?

"Yeah." He barked into the receiver. When no one answered, he said louder, "Look, I'm not getting any younger here. What the hell do you want?"

"Hi, um, Vance? It's me. Katie." The voice, small and meek, reached through the phone and punched him right in the gut.

"Shit! Hey, yeah, um, hi Katie. What's up? How's school? Your parents know you're up so late?" *I'll just bet they don't know you're talking to me.*

He heard a nervous giggle and what sounded like the rustling of sheets. So she was in bed, as well she should be. Fifteen going on thirty, Katie Michaelson had made it a point to keep in touch with Vance and the band after Maggie died. He figured it was her way of holding onto her big sister's memory. The rest of the Michaelson clan had been happy to sever all ties well before Maggie succumbed to the excesses of sex, drugs, and rock and roll, but Katie never gave up. She hadn't given up on Vance, either, apparently, since she called at least once every couple of weeks to check on him. Not that he minded. He really liked the kid.

Plus, since he and the band had just parted ways, possibly forever, Katie was his only remaining link to Maggie.

"Of course Mom and Dad don't know I'm up. That's why I'm whispering. Anyway, school's okay. How did it go tonight? Did you guys get signed by a big shot?"

He couldn't help it as the corners of his mouth curled into a sad smile. So much hope and enthusiasm filled her voice. *Shit.* He really didn't want to let her down.

"How'd you know about tonight?"

"It's called the Internet, idiot! Your website lists all of your show dates."

"Oh, right. Well, it went great. *Really* great. We nailed it with Maggie's best song," he offered. The words were out of his mouth before his brain could stop them.

"Cool! Which one? 'River Queen'? 'Keep On Keeping On'?"

"No, it was, um…we did 'This is Home.'"

"Oh."

If hearing her voice had been a punch in the gut, Katie's reaction to her sister's prophetic final song credit was a bone-crushing blow. He cursed himself. Pain seemed to be all he brought anyone around him these days.

"You still there?"

"Yeah," he replied, coming back to himself. "I'm sorry, Katie. I didn't mean to—"

"It's okay. It really is a great song. I bet the crowd ate it up. Mags would've liked that."

"Yeah, she would have."

"So?"

"So what, shortcakes?"

"Hey! Don't call me that! I bet I come up to your shoulders by now!"

Vance laughed, surprising himself at how good it felt. He couldn't remember the last time he'd managed an honest-to-God chuckle. Katie had a knack for drawing out his sense of humor, much as her sister had back when they'd both been clean and sober.

"Well, to answer your question, some big shots picked up our demo."

"And?"

"And what?"

"You're holding out on me, Vance. I can always tell. Your voice changes."

"Oh, nothing really," he muttered.

"Tell me!"

Damn. "Well, there's this producer who maybe wants to record us—"

"AWESOME!"

Another deep chuckle rumbled from his chest as he listened to Katie, no doubt clapping a hand over her mouth. She told him to hold on in a low whisper. He could tell by the muffled rustling that she'd jammed the phone between the mattress and wall in her bedroom while she pretended to sleep. There was no way her parents failed to hear her enthusiastic outburst, and they'd probably be checking in on her in the next few seconds.

He stared out over the dark waters beneath him as he waited for Katie to come back. He had a decent view of the downtown riverfront. Lights still blazed on the L&C tower in spite of the late hour, as well as on the AT&T tower, better known as the Batman building on account of the twin spires jutting out of the top of the square "mask," and WKDF headquarters. He couldn't see the Ryman, but his musician's heart filled with reverence knowing she was nearby. Staring out at this city of music, the weight of his failures threatened to crush what little life he had left. He'd failed to fulfill his band's dream, his dream, and the dream Maggie would never realize.

He could do at least one thing to put it back on track.

Vance ended the call and sent Katie a text message telling her he'd call her back in the morning. He then fired off a quick text to his lawyer to see if he was up. It would only be around 10 p.m. in L.A., so odds were good.

When Lenny replied, Vance called and asked him to amend the terms of ownership for their song catalog, giving Josh and the other guys equal rights to the material. Though Lenny wasn't too thrilled about his decision, he promised Vance he'd notify Eddie first thing in the morning. Vance sent his manager a quick text with instructions to go ahead and lay down instrumental tracks, though he didn't mention vocals. They'd work that all out later. Or not.

At least now Maggie's songs would have a shot at getting some airtime.

Though he'd probably just pissed away his future, he felt like something other than a total prick for the first time in months. Some of the tight tension left his chest, and he managed to stand just a little bit taller. Walking back toward the street level, he took a last-minute detour and followed a path down to the narrow pontoon that ran next to the dock. Between the night air's coolness and the soothing flow of the river below him, he experienced an all-too-rare moment of peace. It wouldn't last. The cravings would soon begin to gnaw at his body, along with the deep ache the booze used to mask.

Vance took one last look at the view across the river. His gaze fell to the large sculpture between the stadium and the Shelby Street Bridge towering above him. Lights from the stadium illuminated the series of disconnected red ladders suspended over the water on the opposite shore. Some were twisted to mimic, or perhaps mock, old-fashioned roller coaster tracks. Shaking his head, he wondered at what passed for art these days, then laughed out loud. *Like I got any right to judge.* Sticking his phone into his travel bag, he turned to leave.

Then he froze.

A series of sweet notes echoing from somewhere near the water below traveled from his ears directly down his spinal column to his legs. The sound sent a jolt of pure energy and euphoria through his body and made him ache with joy and longing to hear more, to lose himself in the rapture of the music.

He took a step down the ramp as the song drew him closer to the river. It was familiar, one of Maggie's, the one they'd played just a few hours ago. Even through the fog seeping into his brain and chasing away rational thought, he recognized his own music. The songstress had transformed the fist-pounding intensity of the lyrics into a slower, sensual trickle of sultry verses that beckoned him.

He took another step.

Alarm sounded in one small part of his consciousness. He'd experienced a few near misses in his life even before he started hitting the bottle, enough to recognize the pull of oblivion. Those sweet notes would lead him to his doom. He should fight.

Thing was, he didn't much feel like fighting anymore.

Another step sent him stumbling farther down the pontoon to the dock. He dropped hard on his right knee, and the guitar case and his bag slid onto the concrete. No point in carrying his stash into the next life, and he figured he'd be able to find a new guitar in hell.

He sensed the music drawing nearer, swore it emanated from the water. Rather than satisfying, the proximity drove him mad with desire to get even closer. He stood, his boot kicking some loose stones over the dock's edge and into the river. One more step and he'd plunge into the water as well. He couldn't stop, didn't want to try. Then he'd find the music. It seemed fitting and beautiful, Maggie's song calling him home.

One more step.
And Vance Idol fell.

Chapter 8

"What was that?"

"What was what?"

"If you'd stop humming and singing that damned song over and over, like you have been for the past hour and a half, then maybe you'd actually hear something," Ilsa said. They'd surfaced at their rendezvous point just a moment earlier to wait for Catfish Jack.

"Good thing you can't drown fish. It looks like you've called all of them within a five-mile radius.

"Oh no, I'm sorry…I didn't even realize, I swear!"

Lorelei had been so wrapped up in her unintentional performance she didn't notice their shimmering entourage until Ilsa pointed it out. Gods, how could she be so careless? Singing out loud, and so close to the downtown area filled with mortals? A few quick splashes dispersed the fish, frogs, and other followers.

"Well, you'd better pay attention now that you've got your head above water."

"You're right, of course, though it *is* late by human standards. No mortal with an ounce of common sense would be hanging around the riverfront at this hour, right?

Besides," Lorelei added, her voice a soft whisper, "I really like the song."

"Uh-oh," Ilsa said, bringing her up short.

"What?"

"Don't look now, but I think you made some mortal without an ounce of common sense jump right into the river."

Lorelei's gaze followed Ilsa's pointing finger, and then landed on the figure bobbing up and down in the dark water. Between the moonlight, background city lights, and sharp nixie vision, she recognized the figure as a human man—a man in serious danger of drowning.

All on account of stupidity and her momentary lapse in judgment.

"Lorelei! Be careful, don't—"

She dove, her sister's voice lost as she plunged and then whipped her tail in a series of powerful, undulating strokes that sped her toward the man in the water. By the time she reached him, the current had already carried his body a good distance downstream. And he was face down. She flipped him, wrapped one arm around the broad chest underneath his arms, and pulled him to the shore. Transforming her tail into legs, she stumbled onto the muddy riverbank as she dragged the man's body out of the water, willing them both dry once they reached the shore.

She got her first good look at him then.

Lorelei shook off the shock of recognition and bent over him. He wasn't breathing. *What have I done?* "Oh no, this cannot be happening, this cannot be happening. Come on, Vance, you've just got to be okay!"

Ripping off his shirt and flipping him onto his side, she shook his body and pounded on his back until he began to cough, spewing river water out of his lungs. He convulsed, struggling to pull in life-giving air, but his breathing remained shallow.

Oh no, oh no, oh no!

Though some of their kind took perverse pleasure in calling mortals to their deaths, like the legends her mother perpetuated, Lorelei and her sisters enjoyed visiting the human world far too much to bring harm to its inhabitants. She found the notion of calling men for sport revolting. How could she have been so careless? Truth be told, she and Ilsa had been slipping ever since they crossed the Atlantic. This would never have happened back home, not after her first and only accident so long ago. The memory still haunted her centuries later.

That she'd called this particular man, a man who made such beautiful music, was unforgivable.

She wouldn't lose him, too.

She turned Vance onto his back and applied light pressure to his chest, conjuring her healing powers and drawing the water out of his lungs to make room for air. Taking in deep gulps of night air herself, she willed his body to follow suit. She soon felt the steady rise and fall of his chest as his breathing normalized.

Cradling his head in her lap, she indulged in the guilty pleasure of admiring him up close. She ran her fingers through his dark hair and then moved them down to caress his strong, square jaw. Light stubble tickled her fingertips and shot tingles down her spine and directly to the juncture between her legs, which remained as bare as the rest of her body. In her haste to save the mortal, it hadn't occurred to her to conjure clothing. Not that it mattered at the moment.

He wouldn't know flesh from fins or feathers in his current state.

She allowed her fingers to trail down his neck and over his broad chest. The delicious contrast between hard muscle and the soft skin and dusky hair covering it quickened her pulse and breath. His prominent ribs were a bit troubling. He could definitely stand a few good meals, but all in all he presented a fine example of the male form.

She smoothed her palms up and over his small, masculine nipples, eliciting a moan that jolted her back to reality as she jerked her hands away. Looking back at his face, she registered that he remained unconscious, though his dark, arched brows furrowed. When she placed her hands back on him, his face relaxed.

Looking further down his body, she found his manhood to be anything but relaxed, judging by the prominent bulge pressing against dark denim.

Though the urge to trail her fingers over his beautiful body was overwhelming, her primary concern remained undoing any damage she'd caused. She channeled her power into healing some fresh scratches on his neck and the bruises blooming on his torso. She winced at the dark circles under his eyes, as if he hadn't slept in weeks. The tremors racking his body disturbed her more. While clearly chilled, she sensed his shivering came from some deeper illness. Not fever from one of the common illnesses that still plagued humanity, though…

What on earth is causing him such torment? She was just about to channel her healing powers deeper when a voice from behind her interrupted.

"Oh dear. This cannot end well."

"Why don't you make yourself useful and conjure something to warm him?" Lorelei snapped, and then cringed as the sharpness in her voice echoed over the water. She needed Ilsa's help, but the idea of sharing this beautiful man cradled in her arms made her squirm with a jealousy she couldn't quite comprehend, or bring herself to admit aloud.

After letting out a very loud sigh, Ilsa picked up Vance's discarded shirt. Suspending it in the air, she transformed it into a large, dry blanket. She then bid it to fold and dropped it onto Lorelei's head.

"Ouch!"

"Maybe you'll remember to be gracious next time and say please. So now what?"

She didn't answer right away. Instead, she set about removing Vance's shoes and socks and then wrapping him in the warm blanket. Perhaps she should have removed his pants, too, and checked for additional injuries, but she didn't trust herself with any extra temptation.

"We can't just leave him here."

"Whoa, whoa, whoa.... Just what exactly *do* you plan to do with him then, besides the obvious?"

"What's that supposed to mean?"

"Don't play innocent with me, Lore. I've known you waaaaaay too long. I don't care how gorgeous and wounded he is, you can't just keep him."

Keeping him was exactly what she wanted to do, though. He'd already enchanted her with his music, his performance, and the deep yearning she'd glimpsed in his eyes when they'd locked onto hers during his performance. Now, holding him in her arms, she couldn't imagine abandoning him, not after her own foolishness had almost cost him his life. She'd nurse him back to health at the very least. She owed him that.

"Ilsa, please, I did this to him," she pleaded, gesturing to the helpless form in her arms. "I have to make it right."

"He'll be fine," Ilsa countered. "Look, he's breathing on his own now and you've wrapped him up all warm and snug. We'll just move him up to a park bench, let him sleep it off, and he'll either wake up and go along on his merry way or another human will find him in the morning."

"No."

"Oh for the love of Neptune, Lorelei, he's not some koi you can keep as a pet or a little woodland creature for you to rescue! He's a *man*. A hu*man*."

"Um, yeah, and I recall a certain blond pain in the tail mermaid who promised to meet a certain hu*man* from the Wildhorse tomorrow night for some private 'dance' lessons...hmm, who could that be? Let me think."

"That's not the same and you know it," Ilsa huffed. "You know the rules. We can play with all the mortal men we desire, so long as Mother remains blissfully unaware, of course. But we don't keep company with any *one* mortal man for very long. That's what we promised."

"Well that was before I made *this* mortal man fall into the river."

"Lorelei, this is not a good idea."

Ilsa was right and she knew it. She had tried to keep a mortal man. Once. She looked down at Vance, his head still cradled in her lap. His eyelids fluttered as he stirred, fighting his way back to consciousness. He began to tremble again. She smoothed her hands over his hair and whispered soothing words. Then his eyes opened and he met her gaze. The emotion reflected in those green eyes wasn't what she'd expected. Rather than surprise or fear, weariness and resignation seeped from his gaze.

"Go on, do it," he whispered.

She tried to still him, ease the deep ache she heard in his voice. "Shh, it's alright now. You're safe. Just rest."

"Get it over with…let me go," he replied, closing his eyes and drifting back into unconsciousness.

Lorelei sat dumbfounded. Did this beautiful man in her arms, with his amazing voice that enchanted droves of fans, actually *want* to die? She'd give almost anything for the ability to sing out loud for all to hear and enjoy. He had a gift and the freedom to share it. Why would he be willing to throw it all away?

The very idea confounded her. The more she considered the question, the sadder she became. Sorrow, however, quickly morphed into another, more powerful emotion.

Anger.

"Give me a week. Maybe two."

"What? No! You promised me a great vacation. You promised we'd go all the way up the Mississippi and back, eat fabulous food, listen to great music, and break a whole lot of hearts along the way. This," Ilsa said, looking down her nose and pointing at Vance, "was not part of the bargain."

"You can go on ahead. I'll meet you in Chicago, and we'll go on to Detroit and hit Motown together."

"But it won't be as much fun going alone," Ilsa whined. She also managed, as usual, to work in an impressive pout.

"You won't be," she said, plans already forming for the difficult days ahead.

Lorelei gently lowered Vance's upper body and head to the ground and stood. Walking back to the water's edge, she stooped down and placed her fingertips into the river and swirled. A glimmer of iridescent light flowed out from her fingers and into the depths. A few moments later, Catfish Jack's large head surfaced.

"Y'all are late. Must've had a fine time out on the town. Anything interesting happen?"

Lorelei took a deep breath and said, "Jack, I'm going to need a couple of pretty huge favors."

She stepped aside and gestured to Vance. Jack's black, unblinking gaze moved from Lorelei, to Vance, to Ilsa, and back again. He pulled himself halfway up onto land, placed one fin under his massive chin, and heaved a deep, gurgling sigh.

"Girl, your mama's gonna skin the both of us over this."

Chapter 9

"I think we've got everything covered, but let's go over this one more time to be sure."

Lorelei rolled her eyes. Part of her would miss the company of her sister, but a larger part would be happier once Ilsa stopped hovering and left her in peace. She hadn't hatched yesterday, for crying out loud. How difficult could it be to look after one human man until he was healthy enough to do it himself? Of course, she had no intention of letting him go until she was certain he wouldn't go out and deliberately seek his demise. That was the main reason she'd insisted on moving Vance to the sanctuary of Catfish Jack's lake house. But Ilsa didn't need to know that.

"Hello? Lorelei?"

"Sorry," she muttered. "What were you saying?"

"Food enough for two?"

"Check."

"Extra clothes for your patient?"

"Check."

"Good, because he smells pretty foul, between the river and being out cold for two days. You might want to bathe him before too long," she said, waggling her eyebrows.

Hmm, now that *could be fun.*

She really needed to stop that train of thought.

"Chocolate and booze stash?"

"Ah, yes. Leave it to you to think of essentials," Lorelei said, pouring as much sarcasm as she could muster into the comment. "I think you managed to clean out the candy aisle and the liquor store on my behalf."

"Good. Jack tells me the television has over five hundred channels. He has a computer with wireless Internet, and there's a fully stocked library upstairs, in case you get bored."

"Yeah, I saw that. This place is amazing. Is it really his, do you think, or does it belong to one of the local water nymphs?"

"They maintain shared residences near water and use them as they please, much as we do. Lucky for you, they're generous with guests."

"Yes, lucky," Lorelei agreed as she turned to survey the spacious living area. The secluded cabin, situated on several acres of private lakefront property surrounded by lush woods, would serve her purpose well. The interior consisted of warm cedar walls on two opposing sides with a rustic and welcoming stone fireplace in between, and floor-to-ceiling two-story windows on the remaining side that afforded an amazing view of the water.

The view filled her with a deep yearning, but it would have to wait. She needed to check on her patient.

She walked into the kitchen, running her fingers over the cool granite countertops as she surveyed the cooking implements hanging above the central island. Fine copper pots and pans reminded her of home, and she was also pleased to find the kitchen equipped with a gas range top and oven. She had no use for the Teflon variety she'd seen in the lower cabinets, but she was dying to try her hand with the cast iron skillet. Jack mentioned that she'd find a very old recipe book filled with the finest in Southern delicacies, among them one for cornbread. She'd get to that once the soup she'd started had simmered a few more hours.

If her patient couldn't handle the heartier ingredients, she'd coax him to take broth first in order to restore his strength. Then she'd work on getting a little more meat on his too-prominent bones.

Lorelei inhaled the rich aroma and smiled. Then she chuckled as she remembered the old mortal saying about the way to a man's heart being through his stomach. She figured it resided a bit farther south, but at least his stomach was a good place to start.

Not that she was looking for a way to his heart, of course.

"We're water goddesses, sweetie, not domestic goddesses. Why not just conjure something?"

"I like to cook."

"Yeah, you like to cook, and clean, and tend the helpless. Better take care, sister. If you fall for this guy and he falls for you, you could end up losing your fins forever."

Lorelei scoffed. "That rumor is older than we are, and I've yet to see proof that it's true."

"Auntie Ondine came close. Do you really want to find out?"

For once, Ilsa looked serious, so she considered the possibility. According to some ancient myths, a mermaid could escape immortality by accepting the love of a human, becoming human herself. While she couldn't imagine trading her beloved river home for a landlocked life, humanity did hold a certain appeal, as did the freedom to sing.

No, that joy was and would forever be denied her, thanks to her mother, and no amount of fairy tale wishing and dreaming would change that. There would be no escape. She'd learned that the hard way.

But maybe she could make amends by saving this mortal.

"I doubt it would actually happen," Lorelei said, waving her hand dismissively. Of course, the scenario was hypothetical and not at all relevant. She intended to restore his health and his spirit, and she intended to find out why such a talented and charismatic man would seek his doom. She also intended to hear him sing for her, and maybe share his bed for a time. Desire, and perhaps even affection, she would willingly give. But she'd not have her heart broken like her mother.

"But what if it does?"

"It won't, because I'm not going to fall for this guy and let it happen," Lorelei answered. Then she pulled Ilsa into her arms, holding her until some of the tension ease from her sister's body. She hoped it would shut her up, too, or at least get her to change the subject.

Naturally, it didn't.

"Well," Ilsa began after she squirmed out of Lorelei's arms, sounding resigned, "what do you plan on telling sleeping beauty when he wakes up?"

"Depends on how much he remembers. I thought I'd let him think I'm a doctor or something like that. Maybe I happened to be wandering downtown last night and saw him fall into the water? Figured I'd help him out?"

"Uh-huh. And how does your average mortal woman pull a big guy like him out of the water all by herself? Especially against the current?"

She groaned. Ilsa had picked a fine time to stop acting blond, but she was right. Passing for mortal while out on the town or during a one-night tryst with a human man was easy for a Nixie. Sticking around much longer than that often led to complications, not the least of which involved explaining her abilities.

"And, assuming you even get beyond that little sticking point, what if his friends or family come looking for him? What if he wants to leave?"

"No, He can't!" she blurted out. The strength of her conviction caught her off guard. She hadn't realized how much she wanted, no *needed*, to keep Vance here, with her, until faced with the possibility that he might want to leave.

Turning back to the counter, she leaned on the cool granite and placed her head in her hands. Perhaps she had bitten off more than she could chew. But she wouldn't back out now, not when his words still echoed through her mind and tore at her heart.

Go on, do it. Get it over with. Let me go.

"Here, this might help," Ilsa said, holding out a mobile phone. Lorelei took the phone and quirked a brow at her sister, waiting for an explanation.

"Read it."

She looked at the screen and noted three text messages. She had to fiddle with the blasted contraption a bit, cursing along the way about mortals and their ridiculous fascination with complicated gadgets. Finally, she worked out how to access the first text, received at 4:32 the morning before last, from someone called Katie.

IMS 4 not calling. PAW, CIL. Gratz on the show!

"What in the name of the gods is this gibberish supposed to mean?" she asked. Though she'd mastered many languages, along with modern vernacular, over the centuries, she drew the line at text speak on principle. "Oh. Do you suppose Katie is his wife, or girlfriend, or lover?"

She bristled at the very thought.

"Doubtful," Ilsa said. "Based on the text speak, I'm guessing she's too young. You know, you really should learn this stuff, Lorelei. Text and IM are all the rage these days."

She suppressed an eye roll and handed the phone back to her sister. "Just translate it for me, please."

"She says she's sorry she didn't call, but her parents are watching and she'll check in later. And she congratulated him on his show. The next message is from someone called Eddie, asking where he is and why he hasn't returned his calls."

"So someone *is* looking for him. How is knowing this supposed to help me?"

"Read the last one."

Lorelei took the phone back and read the last message, sent from someone called Sticks. Thank the gods he'd opted to text in full, comprehensible sentences.

I don't know where you are, brother, but I hope to God it's in treatment. Get help, get well, and get your ass back to the studio. We need you.

"Treatment?"

"Oh good grief, Lorelei, get with the new millennium! Humans these days are all about counseling and therapy. I'm guessing treatment means some sort of rehabilitation program, as in this guy must have an addiction. That explains why he's so thin and rough around the edges, by the way."

If Ilsa thought this bit of information would diminish her sister's interest in Vance, she'd just have to live with the disappointment.

Lorelei understood all too well why so many humans were willing to risk their lives and health by putting deadly poisons into their bodies. The thrill and euphoria of calling mortals to their deaths, feeding off their pain and ebbing life force, afflicted many of her own kin and were the root of many a mortal myth and legend. She'd been around long enough to understand that both immortals and humans who flirted with danger and death often did so to escape some other, deeper form of pain. She'd make it her mission to uncover the source of that pain and heal it for him as restitution for nearly killing him.

She just had to convince him to let her.

"Rehab. That's your cover, Dr. Lorelei," Ilsa said, handing her a stack of papers.

Glancing over them, she found information about rehabilitation programs, laws related to involuntary commitment, and counseling. Her jaw dropped and she looked back up at Ilsa, who blushed and looked down at the ground.

"When did you look into all of this?"

Ilsa shrugged. "While you were sleeping."

"But why? I thought you were trying to stop me from taking care of him?" She'd expected Ilsa to keep brow beating her until she acquiesced, or at the very least, to remain aloof in silent judgment. Lorelei hadn't been prepared to receive her blessing, let alone her help.

"Because I can see how much this means to you."

Oh honey, you don't even know the half of it.

She grabbed Ilsa, pulling her into a tight embrace. She held her in an iron grip, in part to express her gratitude, and in part to hide the tears that prickled the corners of her eyes and threatened to fall. It wasn't often that Ilsa surprised her, but when she did, she made it count. Lorelei figured it was time to return the favor.

"Thank you, my sister," she whispered.

Ilsa stiffened at first, but then acquiesced and squeezed her back. It wouldn't last long, as Ilsa shied away from anything serious or sentimental.

True to form, Ilsa sighed and muttered, "So, I suppose that means I should make the booze stash disappear."

"Probably for the best," Lorelei replied, smiling in spite of herself. "Now then, are you ready to hit the road?"

"No," Ilsa replied, a sour note in her voice.

Ah, now that's *more like my favorite sister.*

"Come on, you need to get your ample butt back downtown, find that handsome cowboy, and take him up on the dance lesson. And," Lorelei continued, grinning and beckoning over her sister's shoulder, "you'll have to find a couple more to keep these two little clownfish entertained."

Ilsa extricated herself from Lorelei's arms and gave her a puzzled expression. Puzzlement morphed into joy when the delighted squeals of Gisele and Gwen echoed through the room. Gisele ran into the kitchen and practically knocked Ilsa over.

Lorelei had the good sense to move out of the way, thus avoiding the blond whirlwinds.

"What are you two doing here?"

"Going on vacation with you," Gisele exclaimed.

"You aren't ditching us this time," Gwen said, doing her best to look miffed. As Lorelei recalled, Gwen, formerly known as the Rhinemaiden "Wellgunde," had mentioned loudly and often how unfair it was that her two older sisters were allowed to go traipsing across the sea while she and Gisele, a.k.a. "Woglinde," were stuck at home with Mother. Though Melusine agreed, after much persuasion and the intervention of Eridanos, to let her two eldest daughters travel abroad, she'd refused to let the twins go.

Fortunately, Melusine and their aunts had decided to take a little vacation of their own to China so they could enjoy celebrations in honor of the year of the water dragon. With Mother out of the way, it hadn't been too difficult to convince Eridanos to release the younger Rhinemaidens. He'd even used his divine powers to quickly transport them to the New World.

"See, I told you. You won't be going alone. I always keep my promises."

Ilsa gave Lorelei another big hug, whispering to her, "Just remember to keep your last promise."

"I will," Lorelei replied. She released Ilsa, who joined their two younger siblings. Then, addressing all of them, she said, "Now you three blond bombshells go on and have fun. Just stay out of trouble."

"We will!" the twins cried in unison, while Ilsa shouted, "Not a chance!"

A twinge of regret and longing twisted in Lorelei's gut as her sisters traded legs for fins and dove into the lake. They waved goodbye to her before disappearing beneath the surface. Following the complex network of above- and below-ground waterways back to the downtown riverfront should prove easy enough. If Jack could manage to squeeze through some of the tighter passageways, her lithe Nixie kindred should have no trouble.

And if they did, well…magic did have its advantages.

She took one more longing look at the water before heading upstairs to check on her mortal.

Chapter 10

Vance awoke with a killer headache and a belly full of bile.

He also awoke in a bed, a strange bed, and one he did not remember from the night before.

Then again, he didn't remember much of anything from the previous night, at least nothing after the confrontation with his bandmates and his walk downtown.

Shit, he'd walked out on them—and then he'd given away his songs.

Trying to sit up, and failing miserably, he fell back onto a soft pillow. After his head stopped spinning, he opened his eyes, lids fluttering as he adjusted to the brightness filling the room. He cursed the daylight, grumbling through the fresh pain unleashed by the rays of sunshine shooting through his skull, before taking in his surroundings.

In spite of bone-deep aches, his body registered the warmth and comfort of a luxurious bed. The crisp white sheets smelled fresh as they whispered against his skin, though his entire body felt and smelled decidedly less than fresh. The soft quilt above looked handmade. Both covered the large, king-sized bed he currently occupied.

He froze, and then slowly turned his head to the side, dreading who he might find next to him. He hoped it wasn't that groupie with the blood fetish. Though a bit rumpled, the sheets and comforter still covered most of the other half of the bed, and the pillow held no impression of another sleeping head. No, the other side of the bed was empty, thank God.

The fact did little to reassure him, however, after he realized he was naked.

Oh man, what the hell did I do last night?

He sat up slowly, managing to stay upright, and looked around the room. The wood panels and rustic furnishings screamed cabin, and a glance outside of the bedroom window gave him a view of woods and lake. He didn't hear any familiar urban noises, like passing cars or chattering voices of folks as they walked by along busy downtown sidewalks. Instead, his ears picked up on rusting leaves and birdsong. How did he get so far out of town? The nightstand clock read 4:27.

As in p.m.

Well, he *had* wanted at least ten hours sleep.

The rest must have done him some good. Aside from a few dull aches and a touch of nausea, which was already subsiding, he felt better than he had in months. No shakes, no sweats, no cravings. Hell, his arm didn't even hurt from where Josh nearly pulled it from its socket.

He was rubbing his neck when his fingers froze. He'd expected a sting from the scratches crazy groupie gal gave him, but aside from stubble, he didn't feel a thing.

How long have I been here? And where exactly am I?

Since he seemed to be in no immediate danger, Vance planted his feet on the ground and rose slow and easy. He had to fight a fresh wave of dizziness, owing more to hunger than the urge for a drink based on the roar from his stomach. Steadying himself, he padded to the *en suite* bathroom for a visit to the porcelain throne. After he finished, he walked to the vanity and looked in the mirror. Not a trace of those scratches. Weird.

His hair stuck up in ten different directions, dull and greasy, and he could stand a shave. The length of stubble decorating his jaw suggested he'd been out of commission for a while, longer than ten or twelve hours. A search through the drawers and cabinets provided him with some towels, soap, and frou-frou girly shampoo. Too bad he wasn't able to find a razor.

Or his pants.

After a few minutes of consideration, he decided to enjoy the large, multi-head shower. Most likely he'd lucked out and wound up going home with some local chick, one who would hopefully show up later with breakfast and his clothes. It wouldn't be the first time. Hell, he might get lucky again with his mysterious hostess *and* remember it this time if he smelled better.

Warm jets of water soothed his aching muscles and helped clear his head, though a noise from outside the bathroom interrupted his enjoyment and made him cut the shower short. He'd finished scrubbing his hair and body anyhow. Vance turned off the water, ran a towel over his head and body, and wrapped a fresh one around his waist while preparing to face the proverbial music.

In his experience, "morning after" conversations following one-night stands were awkward at best and could get downright ugly. Since he couldn't remember the particulars of last night's, or nights', encounter, he figured he'd play it cool and cautious until he could be certain of his hostess's mood. At the very least, he needed his cell phone to call for a ride. The pants would be nice, but he'd been kicked to the curb without them before. He'd survive.

Taking a deep breath and attempting to shake off any lingering effects of hunger and fatigue, he opened the bathroom door, plastered on his most winning come-hither smirk and said, "Borrowed your shower. I hope you don't mind, especially after I slept in and all—"

His first look at the room's other occupant made him forget the rest of his speech. Naturally he recognized her from the crowd at his last gig, but managed to keep his reaction neutral. He didn't want to offend her by letting his surprise show. He could have kicked himself for having forgotten a tryst with the most striking woman he'd ever seen or worse, passing out like a total pussy and thus missing the opportunity.

The tall woman wore the same tight jeans he remembered, though today she'd paired them with a blue halter top with freshwater pearls adorning the neckline and bodice. He couldn't help but notice how well it framed her cleavage. He'd always been a breast man. She'd dropped the cowboy hat and braid, too, allowing lush dark hair to cascade down her shoulders in enticing waves.

I'm such an asshole.

Her blue eyes widened in surprise and she asked, "What are you doing up?"

Before he could respond, she'd crossed the room, pushed him down on the bed, and set about examining his head and upper body. Acquiescing, Vance found himself enveloped in the sweet scents of a crisp mountain stream, wildflowers, and woman. Her touch would have turned him on had it not been so clinically detached. The hard set of her angular features conveyed deep concern, rapt concentration, and a quiet power he couldn't quite define. While a bit taken aback by her forwardness, he didn't care to mount any protest, at least not yet. In fact, he suspected she wouldn't tolerate any such objection.

That turned him on.

He sat up, reached out, and removed her hands from his shoulders before his response became a little too obvious. He didn't want to embarrass himself, or her, by pitching a tent in his towel. The softness of her skin beneath his hands didn't help.

"I'm fine, really. About time I got my sorry ass out of bed anyhow."

"No," she said, firm hands pushing back him down onto the bed. "You must rest to fully heal. And you need to eat."

He wouldn't mind food. Hell, he was hungry enough to eat an elephant. But her statement about healing gave him pause. He sat back up and scooted to the other side of the bed, out of her reach. "Look lady, I said I was fine. Now if you'd be so kind as to tell me where I can find my clothes and gear, I'll get dressed and be on my way."

"You can't leave. You must heal first."

"Yeah, you mentioned that, but trust me, sugar, I've been on much worse benders."

She furrowed her brow, but the woman didn't move. She didn't nod, speak, or get up to retrieve his belongings. A twinge of unease prickled up his spine.

"Where's the phone?"

The woman remained silent, though her furrowed brow turned into an outright frown. He wasn't sure if his tone or the pet name caused her expression. He told himself that he didn't really care, either.

Right. Time to shift tactics. Glowering, he leaned closer and said with a hint of menace, "I asked you a question. Where's the goddamned phone?"

"There is no telephone in this house, aside from the one in your bag."

"And where might I find that?"

"You won't."

"Like hell I won't," he said, snarling as he stood. Vance strode around to the opposite side of the bed until he towered over the obstinate woman. While he wasn't the sort of man who got off on intimidating females, her failure to comply with his requests pissed him off. He bent over and put his face about an inch away from hers, close enough to feel her breath against his skin.

"I asked you nicely. Once. I won't do it again."

The woman didn't flinch, but her gaze turned hard and held his without faltering. "You didn't, Vance."

"I didn't what? By the way, what's your name, *sugar*? Guess it must've slipped my mind since last night," he added, smirking.

"I'm called Lorelei," she said as she stood, forcing him to take a step back lest she knock him over. "And what you didn't do was ask me nicely, but it doesn't matter. You won't find your phone, clothing, or the means to leave until I'm sure you're fully healed."

He maintained his glower but found himself at a bit of a loss. Though she was tall for a woman, he still outweighed her by at least fifty pounds of muscle. Most men he'd faced down during his time on the road would have cowered, but she clearly didn't fear him.

Since he couldn't persuade her by fear, he shifted tactics again, reverting to his preferred method of persuasion when faced with a difficult woman. It hadn't failed him yet. He allowed his gaze to wander down her face to her full lips, and from there down along the slender column of her neck. Her audible swallow and the bob in her throat made him smirk with satisfaction. When his gaze fell to the swell of her breasts, he grew hard again and knew she'd read the heat in his gaze when it returned to her face.

He definitely saw heat in hers.

He moved past her, taking care to brush his skin against her bare arms, and sat down on the bed. He reclined and stretched his body, allowing the towel that covered his lower half to come loose. Plastering a smile on his face, one that charmed most women right out of their panties, he said, "Well if you *really* want to make sure I'm healed, Lorelei, I guess you'd best get on with your examination."

Chapter 11

She wasn't sure whether she wanted to kick him or kiss him.

Probably both, the smug bastard!

She liked Vance better singing or sleeping than she did now, when he seemed hell bent on bullying her one moment and seducing her the next. At least he seemed to have forgotten his fall into the Cumberland, and thus remained unaware that she'd caused it.

No, not going there. She refused to let guilt or the ripple of powerful muscle and naked flesh distract her from her purpose. She may be new to this man's world, but she was by no means inexperienced. Unlike many of her mortal counterparts, she'd always enjoyed holding power in the game of seduction when she chose to play, and enjoyed the pursuit as much as she enjoyed enticing her conquests to pursue her. Anticipation, calculation, and sparring with a worthy opponent always yielded the sweetest rewards. She had shared pleasure with many mortal men over her long existence, from strapping young shepherds to sword-wielding generals to mighty kings.

No way would she let some guitar-wielding jerk make her roll over and spread her legs with just a smirk and a flash of skin.

He did have nice skin, though, and it covered well-defined muscles that clung to his long, lean frame. She let her gaze drop lower to the towel that rested low around his hips, and imagined running her fingers through the silky hair below his navel and following it to the growing bulge that swelled beneath the fabric. The thought of exploring him with her fingers and tongue heated her body and dampened the space between her thighs.

Flashing Vance a sensual smile of her own, she leaned down and placed her hands on his bare chest, pushing him back and earning a wicked chuckle. His laughter turned into a deep groan when she hitched one leg over his body to straddle him. Running her fingertips over his flesh, she made certain to graze his flat, masculine nipples. She ground herself against his erection as she ran her short nails over the sensitive skin enough to thrill along with the sting. He swelled beneath her in impatience when she dug her nails in harder.

Lorelei, however, had an abundance of patience.

"So, doc, find anything interesting?"

"As a matter of fact, I did."

With supernatural strength, she yanked his right arm up and shoved the bag of pills she'd pulled from his duffle bag into his hand. When she met his gaze, all the heat and promise disappeared along with his arrogance. A twinge of regret burned in her chest, but she fought through it. Before she could help him, she'd have to make him face his darkness.

"Shit," Vance muttered. "Way to kill the moment."

"Care to explain these?"

Vance sat up and shoved her aside. He pulled the towel tight around his waist and stood, putting distance between them. He winced as he moved, and the rumble of his stomach was hard to ignore. He was hungry and clearly still in pain, though the anger rolling off him in waves almost masked his distress. She ached to soothe him, but she pushed those desires aside. He would never accept her help unless he acknowledged that he needed it.

He didn't appear to be ready or willing to do so…yet.

Please let there be a yet.

He turned back to face her, arms crossed across his chest. "What's to explain? Sex, drugs, and rock-n-roll, sugar. Isn't that what you wanted when you brought me home?"

"No. Is it what *you* want?"

He didn't answer. Instead, he gave her a cold, defiant stare. His body tensed and he squared his shoulders as if prepared to strike.

"Truth is I really just don't give a damn anymore."

"I'm not so sure I believe that. The man I saw on stage last night looked like the kind of man who gives a damn—about his band, his music, his audience. The kind of man who pours his heart and soul out when he sings. What happened to that man?"

Vance shrugged. "I stopped being that man back when…." He trailed off, shaking his head and running a hand through his still damp hair.

"When what?"

"Doesn't matter. And it's time for me to go."

He walked toward the door, stumbling a bit. He had no business being out of bed! She was tempted to sing a few notes so she could enchant him long enough to get him off his feet. *No, that's what got us into this mess in the first place.* She wouldn't take his free will again unless she had no other choice.

"Your friend Sticks is pretty worried about you."

Her statement brought him to a halt. He whirled around, almost falling in the process. "How the hell do you know Sticks?"

Panic flashed through her. She hadn't quite worked out the details of her cover story. Vance slammed his fist into the wall, the sound echoing through the room and slicing through her scrambling mind.

"I'm gonna kill that sonuvabitch!"

"Why?" she asked, cursing herself for the quiver in her voice. The display of physical power, even in the heat of anger, was dead sexy.

"For sending me to rehab! Why else? What did you do? Must've been planning it for a while. Did you slip me a mickey or something and then drag my ass out to wherever the hell we are? Great start to the whole detox thing."

Lorelei didn't speak, but she breathed an internal sigh of relief. She'd let him draw his own conclusions and play off them. It would probably be a lot easier than coming up with her own story.

Or telling him the truth.

"By the way, sugar, I've been through one treatment program already. As I recall, the docs and nurses aren't supposed to 'fraternize' with their patients."

Hmm, what a pity for your previous caregivers.

"I'm not a doctor, I'm a healer. And from where I'm standing, it seems like your previous experience with rehab didn't work out so well."

"Whatever. I didn't sign any papers. You can't keep me here."

"Of course not. But I would like you to stay. I want to help you."

"Sure you do, because you're a *healer*," he said, his voice dripping with sarcasm. "Well, I've got news for you—you couldn't fix me even if I wanted you to, and there's nothing worth fixing anyhow."

Any argument she offered would agitate him further, so she'd remain silent. It would keep him talking. The more he ranted, the more he'd reveal about himself whether he meant to or not. Plus, if she got him riled up and ranting, she could probably stop him from leaving, or at least delay any attempt. Not that he would get very far, if his posture and labored breathing were any indication. He looked exhausted, and his need to lean against the bedroom wall hadn't escaped her notice.

Great gods, she was responsible for that, at least in part. She'd harmed the mortal, damaged him, and she'd almost taken his life. Maybe Ilsa was right. She had no business meddling in his affairs. What if she made things worse?

Hadn't she vowed to never harm another mortal? After she'd done the unforgivable so long ago, had she learned nothing?

His anguished voice burst her bubble of misery and regret. "Aw hell, what do you want from me, lady? You don't even know me. I don't know what kind of little fantasy you've built for yourself after catching my act, but that ain't me, sweetheart."

She couldn't undo her past mistakes, but perhaps she could atone for them by helping this beautiful, troubled mortal.

She met his gaze and issued her own challenge. "So who are you, if not that man?"

"I'm just another asshole with a guitar. And tomorrow there'll be a dozen more assholes just like me waiting in line to be the new frontman for The Rivermen because I pissed away my song rights after I got my ass kicked out of the band."

The admission hit her like a tidal wave. "Why would you give away your songs?"

"They weren't *my* songs! They were Maggie's, and they deserve to be heard—"

He stopped talking and leaned harder against the wall. He closed his eyes, put his hands over his face, and slid his body along the wall to sit on the floor. "Ah, hell, just give me back my shit and let me go. Please, just let me go."

Chapter 12

Damn! Vance screamed on the inside, since he was too tired and strung out to yell his frustration out loud. The realization that most of his frustration resided in his cock surprised him. Of course he was far enough past his taste of Jack and pill-induced numbness to feel some major cravings, but craving the comfort of this woman's touch more than a drink? He didn't even know her. Yes, she was beautiful, and the way she'd handled him during her "exam" had been sexy as hell. He grew harder just thinking about it, so hard he ached. Accustomed to taking the lead when it came to sex, her initiative surprised him and, even more surprising, shot his libido straight into the stratosphere.

Only to bring him crashing right back down to earth with an unwelcomed dose of reality.

His mysterious hostess had been as direct with her interrogation as she'd been during her physical exam. And damn it all to hell, she'd loosened his tongue with her bold, in-your-face questions. Vance wasn't a talker, at least not off stage, and he'd spent the greater part of the past two years mastering the fine art of evasion. He was tempted to blame his distraction on those mile-long legs, luscious lips, and killer rack, but there was something more to it.

He was probably just too tired and messed up to figure it out.

But, he surprised himself again by realizing that he really wanted to figure *her* out.

Her soft sigh brought him from his wallowing.

"You have a choice," she said, leveling him with her gaze. "I won't stop you from running, Vance, if that is what you truly wish. All I ask is that you rest here one more night to regain your strength, after you've eaten of course."

"What makes you think I'm running?" The tightness in his voice pissed him off, though he struggled to clamp down on his response. What gave her the right to sound so disappointed and angry with him?

"I don't think you're running, I know you are."

He scowled and opened his mouth to protest, but she cut him off. "You said it yourself—there's nothing worth fixing. You gave away your songs, walked away from your band. What's that, if not running?" She spread her arms wide, inviting him to answer.

Vance kept the scowl, but had no defense against her argument. Must've picked up that little trick in headshrinker school, twisting his words around and using them as weapons. How else could she make him feel like a fucking coward just for wanting to go off on his merry way?

If he left now, she'd be right. If he didn't, she'd win and would own his ass while he stayed. Neither option was particularly appealing…unless, of course, she decided to keep up the routine physical checks.

His stomach chose that moment to mount another loud protest right after he picked up on a rich aroma wafting from downstairs. He raised his gaze to Lorelei and searched hers. While he couldn't quite define her expression, he didn't detect any judgment or challenge. She seemed to be waiting, her patience more powerful and persuasive than any ultimatum.

What the hell.

He could always decide after he ate.

Struggling to his feet, he straightened the towel around his waist and made his best effort to grin. "Well, what's for dinner, sugar?

*****

While the clothes weren't his style, they were clean and they fit. Lorelei had given him a decent assortment from which to choose once he'd agreed to stay and eat. He still hadn't found his bag or phone, even after shamelessly searching every room upstairs, but at least he could walk out dressed if he left.

No, not if he left. When he left.

He held tight to the railing as he walked down the stairs. He told himself it was the new boots, but the restlessness in his legs and the gnawing dread in his gut reminded him of the tough decision ahead of him. Oh, he'd been contemplating it for some time, long before he'd stumbled into Lorelei's house of wet dream rehab and before his last gig.

No, she was right. He'd been running from it, and the truth of it pissed him off.

"If you can bring yourself to stop fidgeting and frowning for a moment, I could use a hand."

Lorelei lifted an enormous pot of the range top and appeared to struggle with its weight. He crossed to the kitchen in a few long strides and relieved her of her burden, his fingers brushing hers as he took the handles. A familiar jolt of longing coursed through his body at the contact, and he didn't think he imagined the flash of heat in her blue eyes.

"Where do you want it?"

"Out there, on the table."

She gestured to the open door leading to a patio and then busied herself pulling a large cast iron skillet out of the oven. Vance carried the pot out and placed it on top of the trivet waiting in the middle of the bistro table just outside the door.

"Smells good," he said, an understatement of epic proportions.

His mouth watered when the scent of fresh cornbread reached his nose. Mixed with the rich aroma of what he guessed was some sort of soup, he had to resist the urge to dip the ladle into the stockpot and pour great spoonfuls into his mouth. If her story held true, he'd been out of commission for well over twenty-four hours. No wonder he couldn't wait to dig in. Still, the sudden return of his appetite surprised him.

"Thank you," Lorelei replied as she stepped outside. She carried a covered basket to the table along with a couple of bowls and silverware. After arranging their place settings, she returned to the kitchen. He followed. Might as well keep up the gentleman act and see if she needed him to carry anything else.

He stopped dead in his tracks when he came face to face with this mystery of a woman holding two wine glasses and a bottle.

Surely that's not…

He couldn't suppress a wry chuckle.

"What's funny?"

"Well, sugar, don't get me wrong, but this ain't exactly standard rehab fare." When he caught her blush and cringe, he quickly added, "All I mean is that it looks and smells a helluva lot better." *Way to go, asshole. She gives you clothes, offers to feed you, and this is how you say thanks?*

His breath hitched when she graced him with a bright, relieved smile. "A hearty stew paired with the finest sparkling grape juice money can buy," she said with a wink.

Relief warred with the cravings still clawing at him, but relief won. He wouldn't be tempted by alcohol or have to suffer through an awkward evening watching her drink while he battled the urge.

"You'll heal faster with better meals, and you need to eat more anyway. You're far too thin."

He stood up straighter, squaring his shoulders as his cheeks heated. "You're pretty direct, aren't you?"

"I suppose I am. You, on the other hand, are...how does the saying go? Kind of a tough nut to crack?"

"Oh, I get it," he said dryly, "This is the part where I lie down on the couch and spill my guts while you take notes? Try to work out if I'm a down-and-out drunk because of my lousy childhood, right?"

"Did you have a lousy childhood?"

God, did she have to keep leveling him with that direct gaze?

"No." He couldn't even bring himself to be flippant in the face of such a blunt question.

"Then why do you do it? The drinking and the pills?"

"Long story. And I don't anymore," he muttered, trying to forget how he'd nearly fallen off the wagon. "Not really."

"I've got time to listen. But first, let's get you fed."

She didn't even wait for him to respond. No, she walked right past him and headed outside as though the matter was settled. She just assumed he would follow, eat dinner, and voluntarily submit to whatever headshrinker bullshit she planned to pull on him later.

He was dumbfounded.

Well, damn it all to hell, and heaven help the both of them, but she was right.

With a muttered curse, he followed her out to the table.

Chapter 13

Lorelei breathed her first real sigh of relief after dinner, when Vance agreed to join her for a fireside chat in the living room instead asking for his gear so he could leave. He'd eaten two helpings of stew and cornbread, moaning in pleasure after every other bite. She found his appreciation flattering, though his throaty soundtrack proved more than a little distracting.

He'd insisted on clearing the table and cleaning up the kitchen. While she enjoyed watching him as he worked, still marveling at his willingness to participate in domestic tasks that were part and parcel of the new trend in modern mortal male behavior, she noticed his discomfort. His legs seemed shaky, and he kept running his fingers through his hair and fidgeting. The fingers of his right hand seemed particularly restless, though she doubted he was aware.

She gathered from the information Ilsa left for her that Vance was craving alcohol or medication, or perhaps experiencing symptoms of withdrawal. Oh, he claimed he'd quit and she believed him, but she'd also found the bottle of whiskey he'd hidden in his bag when she'd pulled out the bag of pills. He was obviously still thinking about them, likely in the throes of long-term withdrawal that he couldn't seem to shake.

His suffering was obvious, as was his craving for relief. The stress of his recent performance, not to mention nearly drowning on account of her gross irresponsibility, seemed to have triggered all of the physical and psychological symptoms of early withdrawal. According to the literature, it would only get worse unless he ingested more alcohol or pills. If he didn't, he would have to endure the agony and deal with the root cause, assuming he was willing to stay and try to rid himself of his dependence once and for all.

Addiction seemed as evil to Lorelei as any curse the ancient gods of land and sea could devise. It seduced desperate humans with pleasure and masked their agonies with oblivion, only to trap them in a state of constant pain and torment without it. Many a mortal had lost his life by indulging too often or too hard, and artists and musicians seemed to be the most frequent target of its spell.

She vowed she would not let it take this man's life.

If he was anything like other men, mortal or otherwise, he'd probably rather die than admit to his distress, though, which would make it difficult for her to help him. Of course, she wasn't sure he even wanted help, or if she could convince him to change his mind if he didn't. His earlier admission about giving up on his band and his music still filled her with shock and anger. To waste a gift like his was the most grievous sin Lorelei could imagine.

They had much to discuss, if she could get him talking.

"So what now, sugar?"

She almost jumped out of her seat. She'd been so wrapped up in her thoughts she didn't notice he'd finished his post-dinner cleanup and joined her near the fireplace. Gesturing to the couch across from the loveseat where she sat, Lorelei said, "Have a seat, or recline if you wish. That is protocol, from what you've told me. More juice?"

"I could use something with a little more kick."

"I would offer you wine, but that isn't really part of the protocol, you know."

He arched a brow at her and smirked, a habit she found almost as irresistible as infuriating. "Yeah, I guess this really is rehab, sugar, if one lousy beer or glass of wine counts, but I was actually thinking coffee."

She couldn't help grinning. "Of course! Since you must forgo wine, I would be happy to make some fresh coffee, or would you prefer tea instead?"

"Nah, I'll 'forgo' tea. By the way, where are you from? Haven't met any other folks around here who talk like you."

"I am from the Rhineland," she answered. When he furrowed his brow in confusion, she corrected herself. "Um, I mean I am from Germany. Land of the mighty Rhine River? And what about you, Vance? Where are you from?"

He plopped down on the couch and crossed his left leg over his right knee, which eased a bit of the restless movement in the leg below. "Ah, back to my lousy childhood, doc?"

She sighed. "I was just making conversation. If you don't want to talk about your childhood, then please feel free to choose another topic."

"Like what?"

"Like what compelled you to start abusing your body with too much drink?"

Vance's eyes widened and his jaw dropped, but he recovered quickly. He remained on edge and silent, though, and she ached to soothe him. Warring with her impulse to comfort him, however, was her own personal restlessness. She hid hers better than he did, owing to centuries of practice, but it clawed at her nonetheless, and centered at the juncture between her legs.

Legs she would have to shed soon. The water called and she'd have to answer. She only hoped Vance would give her a few answers first, along with an assurance that he'd stay.

As her gaze drifted to his fidgeting hands, she formed an idea that might help get him talking, as well as taking her mind off the lake.

"Wait here," she said.

Lorelei walked through the cabin toward the front door, stopping at the small coat closet. She opened the door and glanced over her shoulder to make certain he hadn't followed, not that it really mattered, and then conjured his guitar case. If he gave her any grief about sticking around, she could always use her nixie powers to hide it again. She lifted it with ease, but pretended to struggle with the heavy weight in order to keep up the pretense that she was a mere mortal female, and carried it back to the living area. Vance looked up at her in surprise, though he appeared pleased to see his instrument again.

"Will you play for me?" she asked, handing him the case.

He arched a brow and gave her a small smile. "Music therapy, doc?"

The corners of her mouth turned up in response. "Why not?"

"I guess I could. It's been a while since I've played unplugged...."

She stared in fascination at his long fingers, now calmer, as they pulled the guitar from its case and settled it between his legs. After adjusting the levers at the top, tuning machines he called them when she asked, he settled the instrument on his right knee and strummed a few chords. Lorelei had to look away from his hands, now busy caressing the guitar's strings and curves. The image of his hands running along her body with the same commanding strokes proved too distracting.

Looking at his face didn't help dampen those desires. His features had relaxed, yet the tension morphed into an intense focus on the notes he created. He furrowed his brow in rapt concentration, as if the guitar were his lover, whispering her secret desires that he would all too willingly fulfill with slow, steady strokes until she bid him to play her harder.

"I got my first guitar when I was twelve," he said, continuing to play. "It was part of a bargain I made with my mom. She'd let me pretend to be Kurt Cobain on my own time, and I'd be her good little choirboy and give her bragging rights in the parish. Pop died when I was pretty young, so she was all I had, and vice versa. I tried to make her proud."

"I lost my father when I was young, too."

She wished she could take it back as soon as the words escaped her. This was supposed to be about healing Vance, not about her baggage. Clearing her throat, she asked, "So the church, is that where you learned to sing, Vance?"

"No, that's where Jersey boy Vincent Violetti learned to sing, back before Vance Idol was born," he continued with a wry smile. "Vinnie was a pretty decent kid. Did okay in school and even thought about giving college a try, but he still wanted to be a rock star. By then he'd traded Kurt Cobain for Slash and Dave Kushner, even if he had more Scott Weiland in him. So he worked a few years, saved some cash, and wandered out to the West Coast to try his luck."

Lorelei smiled. She knew that mortal entertainers often adopted flashy stage names. "I think I like Vincent better than Vance. It suits you."

He gave her a lopsided grin that warmed her to her very core. "Anyway, he got some attention on one of those reality TV talent shows and then hooked up with a couple of guys who could play, too. They started getting some local gigs, cover band stuff really. Played the hell out of it though, me and Mark and Josh. Sticks came on board a little later, but we were all tight. That's when we got serious about writing our own stuff."

She didn't think he was aware, but his random chords had swirled into a cohesive melody, one she recognized from his show, only slower and smoother. The words seemed to come of their own volition as well. Though he sat only a few feet from her, his mind was clearly miles away. His voice deepened a bit as he became wrapped up in his recollections. She detected a healthy dose of nostalgia and the sharp twinge of regret, but less of the bitterness she'd sensed when she first broached the uncomfortable subject of his past.

"You must have meshed well there, too," she said soft and low, not wanting to throw him out of the moment. "Your songs and music are beautiful."

"That was Maggie."

She stifled a gasp at the change in his features. Whoever this woman was, she must surely be a big part of his pain.

He didn't speak again for a long moment, just strummed and plucked those gorgeous, haunting chords from the guitar with eyes closed and brow furrowed. He kept them shut when he started talking again. "When we found Maggie, she'd been living on the street for a little over six months. Happens a lot, especially in L.A. It made her hard, but when we heard her singing for change on a downtown curb, we knew we'd found the missing piece. She could write songs that made you wanna pound your fists to the beat, cry, dance, or make love in the moonlight."

A stray surge of jealousy rose in her chest, but she batted it away. She had no business feeling that way. He hadn't known her back then, and though he poured out the pain of his heart to her now, she remained a stranger.

Besides, he wasn't hers, and could never be even if this woman didn't present an obstacle.

"So she joined your band?"

He kept playing. After a few moments, he opened his eyes and answered. "Oh yeah. We had to clean her up first, get her off the heavy stuff, and get her head on straight.

She was the one with the lousy childhood. That's what made her turn to drugs. Anyway, it started out great. We all 'meshed well,' as you put it. Mags hit it off with everyone, especially me and Josh."

His tone changed as he said Josh's name, and a sour note rang out through the room.

"Sorry," he muttered.

"Did she sing with the band?"

"Yeah."

"I didn't see her onstage with you last night, Vincent. What—"

"Don't."

The flash of pain that crossed his face would have stopped her, even if his words hadn't. He turned away from her, eyes closed against the painful memories her question unleashed. She held her tongue and let him use the music to work through his hurt, those raw, haunting notes pouring out his heartache. Whatever happened had left a gaping wound in his heart that festered. That was clear now that he'd shed his cloak of swagger and bravado. Part of her wanted to press him for answers, pierce the wound so it could finally heal. Yet she feared if she pushed him too hard this soon that he might decide to run. She'd have to do this on his terms and work at his pace to earn his trust, in spite of her deadline.

"Vincent?"

He opened his eyes. "Hmm?"

"Stay. Please."

"I don't know if that's such a good idea, Lorelei."

She held her breath for a moment, and then exhaled it in a slow, shaky stream. Something about the way he said her name left her as breathless as the soft notes he'd been making. Oh, gods, she needed to pull herself together.

When she got herself back under control, she said, "I want to help you."

"Why? You don't even know me."

Because I almost made you drown? Because you play and sing so beautifully it makes me want to cry? Because when you look at me like that, with those haunted green eyes, all I want to do is hold you and make it all better?

"Because I'd really like to get to know Vincent Violetti better. He sounds like a pretty good guy."

He closed his eyes again and lowered his head, but she knew she'd said the right thing when he started playing in earnest.

And then he began to sing.

It was almost too much to bear, hearing the same ballad that had enchanted her when she'd first seen him. Only this time it was stripped bare, with just his guitar and voice pouring out all of that longing and passion. She already knew the words and notes, having a strong musical ear and memory. His soft voice whispered over her body and through her heart. Each note tingled through her spine.

Great gods, she'd already begun whispering the words along with him.

Just like back at the riverfront, where she'd almost killed him with his own song.

"Do you sing, Lorelei?"

"What?"

"I asked if you sing. Hey, are you okay?"

He put the guitar down, leaning it against the couch, then stood and walked to her chair. Crouching, he looked up at her, searching her eyes, and she became aware of the tears falling from them. He reached up and brushed them away with his fingers.

"You're shaking like a leaf. What's wrong?" he whispered.

"Nothing," she muttered. "I just—I really like your music."

He rewarded her with a genuine smile, one she suspected hadn't graced his handsome face for quite some time. After a long sigh, the smile disappeared and he said, "My life's not pretty, especially right now. I thought I had this…thing under control, but I swear I feel like I'm back in detox. I don't imagine this healing stuff you're throwing at me is going to make it easier or prettier, especially if I have to think about how it all started, and, you know, really deal with it."

"You won't have to go through it alone."

"Lorelei, I wasn't a very nice guy most days, even when I wasn't drinking. I haven't been for a long time, so I doubt I'll be better company without it."

She reached out and cupped his face in her palm. "I've got the guts to take it if you do."

Vincent closed his eyes and leaned into her touch. The dark circles under his eyes and hard lines etched on his face seemed to deepen in the waning light. He didn't answer, but the movement of his jaw as he nodded sent shivers through her palm as the rough stubble caressed her fingertips.

Lorelei was no stranger to battle. She'd witnessed plenty during her long existence, mortals fighting one another with bare hands, spears, swords, and guns. Gods and goddesses often fought alongside them, as well as in their own wars. She'd seen courage and conviction in the midst of tragedy then, but something about the quiet battles that raged within the individual, mortal or divine, had always touched her more deeply than any outside struggle.

She didn't have the words to capture her regard for him in that moment. His small gesture belied the tremendous courage it must have taken to stand his ground and face the coming battle against himself and his demons. She was convinced he had the strength and will, even if he didn't yet believe it. She could help him through the dark days ahead only if she could control herself. The realization of how close she'd come to unleashing her call on him again sent a jolt of fresh panic through her body.

"You should rest," she said, trying to keep the tremor out of her voice. "You'll need your strength."

"Yeah," he muttered, rising and stretching. "Mind if I keep my guitar? It…helps."

"Of course not. I had no intention of keeping it from you. You were made for this, you know—making music, with this instrument."

His gaze dropped to his feet. She couldn't tell if his discomfort came from the compliment or admitting the need for the comfort of his music, but her heart ached for him. She couldn't hold him, not yet. His pride had taken enough hits already. But she could be there. She would be there to ease him when he needed it and could allow himself to accept it.

"I can teach you to play if you like. Maybe you could sing with me, too."

His voice pierced the bubble of silence and sent a fresh lick of fear through her body and soul. Gods, she'd never experienced such a deep yearning mingled with terror. To make such an offer, inviting her to indulge in her greatest joy and share it? The urge to give in battled with guilt and shame at what her voice had almost done to him. He couldn't keep tempting her like this.

"Lorelei? You okay?"

"Oh, yes, it's nothing," she muttered, rising from the couch and putting some distance between them. His offer moved her beyond measure, but she could ill afford to forget who, or what, she was.

"Um, okay," he said, ignoring her brusque reply. Perhaps he hadn't noticed. "Well, I guess I'll see you in the morning. Goodnight, Lorelei."

"Good night, Vincent."

As soon as he disappeared up the stairs, she fled out the back door and ran straight to the water.

Chapter 14

She ran all the way to the shore and took a blind dive into the lake, entering as woman and emerging from the depths as Nixie. Her body flooded with relief when fins replaced legs, but restless energy still filled her, as did anger and frustration. She dove once more, plunging into the murky depths with unnatural speed and then launching herself back up and out of the water and performing a back flip that would've put all of the dolphins at Sea World to shame.

Using the momentum of the first dive-and-flip combination, she propelled herself once more through the water, down deeper, and then launched herself back up into a twisting summersault. When that failed to satisfy, she set about circling the lake at a dizzying pace, cutting through the water with sharp, undulating strokes and alternating between great gulps of night air for her lungs and great gulps of water for her belly and gills. The water fortified and restored her strength, and she imparted her power to the lake and its inhabitants in return.

After another ten laps and several leaps burned off her excess energy, she hauled herself up on a large rock in the shallows. She closed her eyes and savored the night air.

The early summer daylight had bathed the land and water with warmth during the day and left a pleasant chill in the evening when it retreated.

She didn't know if it was the peace of the evening or her nixie magic that started it, but she reveled in the symphony created by the local wildlife nonetheless. After tuning their striated wings, the crickets chirped in synchrony, accompanied by the rough three-note phrases of katydids. The deep bass notes of bullfrogs added to the mix. Not to be outdone, their smaller cousins croaked lighter notes from the trees above while a couple of owls hooted in the distance. One reclusive coyote even added his plaintive howl to the performance.

The beauty of the night music took her breath away, until her wracking sobs drowned it all out.

"Aw, darlin', easy now. It breaks my heart to see you cry."

"Jack?" she asked, lifting her head from the rock and looking through bleary eyes. "Is it really you?"

"'Course it's me, darlin'. Didn't think I'd just swim off and leave you here all on your own now, did you?"

Overwhelmed, she slipped back into the water and wrapped her arms and tail around the great fish's body. She couldn't help the fresh wave of tears, but at least some of them held a touch of gratitude.

"Hey, easy now, easy. What's wrong? Did your human up and leave?"

"No," she managed between jagged sobs.

"He not do right by you, then?" She couldn't see his face, but his tone and the rumble running through his massive bulk left little doubt of his feelings on the subject. A jolt of power surged through his body and the surrounding water, the likes of which she'd only experienced from the most powerful river gods of her home waters. Pity the poor mortal who dared cross Catfish Jack, or those in his care.

"No, no, he's been nothing but gracious, at least after getting over the shock of waking up in a strange place.

He says he'll stay, and he'll let me help him with his troubles."

She released Jack and heaved herself back up on the rock. He held his head out of the water and gave her a puzzled expression—at least, as best he could while wearing a fish face. "Well, that's what you wanted, ain't it?"

"Yes, but…."

"But what, darlin'?"

"He makes me want to sing."

"Aw, darlin', my poor sweet little Nixie," Jack murmured, patting her hand with his fin.

"And I almost did it, Jack. I almost sang with him tonight and if I had? Oh, I don't even want to think about it."

"But you didn't, right? That's something, ain't it?"

She supposed he was right, but she didn't want to think about the next time. Even without the danger of water, singing to a mortal and entrancing him with her spell would be deadly. Or worse.

Heaving a sigh, Jack asked, "What are you gonna do, darlin'?"

"I don't know, Jack. I can't leave him now, not until I can get him through the next few days and get him to go back to his music and his life, whole and healed. But after tonight...."

"You scared you might not be able to stop yourself next time?"

"Yes," she whispered, fresh tears falling.

"Aw honey, come here."

Jack held her for a little while, adding his own rich bass to the nighttime chorus. She wasn't sure if he sang because he meant to soothe her, or if he sang because she couldn't, but she didn't care. She was so grateful for the gesture and content to let the comfort suffuse her being and her heart.

After two late nights and long days, she couldn't quite stifle the queen-size yawn escaping her lips. Jack chuckled and said, "Why don't you go on back inside and get some shuteye, darlin'?"

"That's probably a good idea. I'm going to need all my energy and then some to maintain human form all day, take care of Vincent, and keep myself from slipping again."

"Now then, I've got some business with a few ornery water sprites over in Radnor Lake, so I'd best be off. For now. Don't worry. Things'll look better when the sun comes up. You'll see."

* * * * *

After bidding farewell to Jack, Lorelei took a few more laps around the lake to clear her mind and rejuvenate her body. She was just about to shed her fins when an unnatural breeze swirled over the lake. Coupled with the sudden surge in elemental energy, it signaled the imminent arrival of some unexpected guests. Wind was the purview of Sylphs, and given her family's history with their sky kindred, she braced for a less-than-friendly visit.

Now she *really* wished Jack had stuck around.

She waded back into the depths and waited. The wind and energy intensified, coalescing around a dark form that hovered over the water's surface. Like the Sylphs she knew back home, this one was short, though voluptuous, and sported a pair of gossamer wings similar to those of a dragonfly. Those wings, however, were black as pitch and matched her cropped raven hair and dark clothing. They made her porcelain skin appear even paler by contrast. She might have been beautiful if not for the cruel, twisted smirk of her lips and wicked scowl. The air of malevolence swirling around her sent prickles of warning up Lorelei's spine.

"*You*," the Sylph cried, her delicate little eyebrows shooting up until they disappeared beneath long black bangs. "I might have known."

"Have we met?" Lorelei asked, levitating out of the water in order to meet the Sylph eye to eye.

In a burst of light and wind, the feminine form disappeared and was replaced by that of a small bat. Her dark, inky eyes glinted in the moonlight as she fluttered around Lorelei. Then the bat dove down lightning fast and bit her between her thumb and forefinger before swooping back up and shifting into her Pixie form.

"Ouch!"

"Serves you right," she said with a sneer. "First you almost drown me and my brother. And then you steal what is rightfully mine."

Anger surged through Lorelei's heart, along with all-too-familiar guilt. She clamped down on both, remembering to tread lightly. She was outside of her home territory and had, it seemed, committed a grievous offense against a couple of local elemental guardians. This situation called for diplomacy.

"Ilsa meant no offense. She thought we were under attack and unleashed her call in self-defense. That is why I rushed to pull you and your brother out of the river and why I revived you. We would never deliberately harm a living creature with our call. Besides, you are as immortal as I am, so you weren't in any danger of drowning."

"Oh spare me, flashy fins. Your kind are all the same, coming to our lands uninvited, sneaking around without paying tribute, taking what is ours. My grandfather told me all about conniving *foreign* river folk."

Guilt disappeared and left her shaking with fury. "Look, Fairy Princess, my sister and I paid our tribute through Catfish Jack. We travel through *his* waters, by *his* leave and with *his* blessing. And I've stolen nothing from you or anyone else."

"What did you call me?" the Sylph asked, moving closer and pointing her finger in Lorelei's face. Her wings beat with a fury that whipped up a few small waterspouts.

"What? Fairy? Isn't that what the mortals call your kind, little air sprite?"

"If you know what's good for you, you'll never, *ever* use the 'f' word in my presence again, Pond Scum. You hear me?"

"Oh, is that a challenge, Pixie Pie?" Lorelei asked, tailfins twitching back and forth. The stress and guilt of the past two days coalesced and morphed into a boiling anger that left her itching for a fight. Sparks of elemental power burst from her fingertips as she called forth a series of whirlpools and bid them suck the energy right out of those annoying little waterspouts. She noted the glow surrounding the evil Fairy in front of her with satisfaction. Good. The little she-devil seemed just as eager to tangle.

Gale force winds burst from the angry Sylph. Lorelei conjured a shield of water to cocoon her body as storm clouds gathered overhead, rumbling with thunder. The Fairy even had the nerve to call forth lightning bolts. Their impact stung as they hit her watery shield. Great gods, the Sylphs in these parts must have an alliance with the guardians of fire! She could only imagine the havoc they wreaked on the creatures dwelling within the lake, not to mention the wildlife in the surrounding woods—creatures that were supposed to be in this horrible little Sylph's care.

Time to put an end to this. Right. Now.

She unleashed her voice, belting out a rapid series of notes imbued with just enough strength to temporarily stun her opponent. As soon as the last note echoed, the Sylph's winds ceased and her storm clouds dispersed a few moments later. Lorelei then dipped her fingertips into the water, releasing her healing powers. Dazed, the Sylph glared at her.

"So much for not using your call to deliberately harm another. That's the third call you've unleashed this evening alone, Nixie. Slow night?"

The accusation stung, but gave her pause. *The third call…* The horrid Sylph had been there for the first, of course, and the one she'd just unleashed, but not the one that called Vincent. "How do you know about the second?"

"Because, I tracked your victim here by his blood. The mortal musician? The one you decided to take for yourself and feast on, no doubt. He's *mine.* I saw him first, marked him first. But you stole him down by the river before I could claim him."

"It was an accident," Lorelei whispered.

"Oh, that's rich," she said, barking a laugh that echoed across that water. "Don't play innocent with me, Nixie. It won't work. Your kind are famous for calling mortals to their deaths. Only you didn't quite finish the job. Let me guess—you took one look at his handsome face and decided he was simply too delicious to dispatch right away. Thought you'd have a little fun with him first, did you?"

"No, it's not like that. I'm not like that—"

"Well, no one steals from me on my turf. Hand him over and we'll call it even."

"And if I refuse?" Lorelei replied, rising to the challenge. "You're no match for my call."

"And you're no match for my power without your voice."

Chapter 15

The air around Lorelei disappeared, her last breath literally sucked out of her throat as the Sylph willed her into some sort of vacuum. She dodged another bolt of lightning by diving back down deep into the lake's waters. Not to be outdone, she conjured a massive wave and pulled her opponent down under with her.

Switching from lungs to gills relieved her from oxygen deprivation, though it failed to return her most powerful weapon. Still, the Sylph was now incapacitated, unable to conjure any of her elemental forces underwater. Drowning another elemental wasn't possible, of course, but depriving the Sylph of air would hurt as much as keeping a Nixie from water. They were both breaking the rules. But she would rather face the wrath of all the gods than give Vincent to this creature.

Unfortunately, that left them both at a bit of a stalemate.

She surrounded the Sylph's head with a thin layer of air. It was enough to ease her pain but not enough to wield as a weapon. Perhaps the gesture would inspire a temporary truce. If not, then at least no immortal or god could accuse her of unsportsmanlike conduct.

Before she could even contemplate her next move, something large and powerful dove into the lake, latched onto the Sylph with its talons, and pulled her to the surface. Lorelei followed. She burst from the water in time to see a giant eagle carry the Sylph away from the center of the lake before unceremoniously dumping her onto the shore.

Lorelei waded back to the shallows and waited. No way she'd leave the water now, not with another powerful sky guardian on the scene. The eagle executed a series of dives and loops before careening toward the ground. Just prior to impact, this new Sylph transformed into a tall, masculine form in a burst of light as ostentatious as his aerial acrobatics.

This creature was definitely no Fairy.

He stood well over six feet tall, bare chest and arms covered with lean muscle. His lower body was clad in dusky, soft leather breeches. A helmet of blond hair so pale it almost appeared white in the moonlight covered his head and fell down below his shoulders. Sharp yellow eyes peered out from beneath a strong brow, alternating between the other Sylph and Lorelei. With his hooked nose, imposing height, and aura of raw power, he was one of the most impressive elementals Lorelei had encountered on either side of the world. Unlike his companion, his dark wings were covered with feathers and spanned at least twelve feet as he spread them, positively preening.

Well, perhaps he was a tad on the fairy side.

His gaze finally settled on the wet, angry Pixie. Crossing his arms over that broad chest, he chuckled and began to shake his head. "Making friends wherever you go, Maurelle. Always making friends."

"Not cool, Bruce. I had her right where I wanted her until you showed up. And anyway, she started it."

"I most certainly did not," Lorelei said, heat creeping over her face as Bruce focused his now amused eagle-eyed gaze on her.

"Now as much as I enjoy a good girl fight, and believe me, I do," he began, waggling his eyebrows in a way that made Lorelei's face flame, "those that involve my sister tend to be a bit of a buzzkill. And being in charge of the sky elementals in these parts, I'm obliged to keep inter-elemental disputes from getting out of hand."

"Sky Daddy?" Could this really be the legendary ruler who'd once swallowed Eridanos? He appeared big and powerful enough to be a sky god.

He threw his head back and laughed out loud, the deep, rich sound echoing out over the water. "Not quite, my little goldfish. I'm his grandson. But feel free to bow if you're so inclined. Or you could just give me another delicious scratch behind the ear. I'll be your Batman anytime."

Of course, he was the second bat she'd rescued from the water. The friendly one. He waggled his eyebrows and shivered in mock delight.

Cocky jerk.

"Well since you're here, why don't you make yourself useful and settle our dispute, brother dear?" Maurelle sneered. "She stole a mortal I rightfully claimed. Tell her to hand him over." She pointed an accusing finger at Lorelei like a petulant, tattling child.

Bruce cocked his head to the side as if confused. Then his eyes widened and he said, "Oh, Maury, please tell me it's not that dreadful musician you've been chasing. It is, isn't it? You've become a complete and total angst junkie. And here I was hoping this was just a phase. Honestly, you should try feeding off life and positivity for a change, like I do."

"I'm not interested in being a magnet for shallow, brainless males."

"Oh, and this ridiculous Emo succubus thing you've got going on is so much better?"

"I hate to interrupt," Lorelei said, trying and failing to rein in her impatience. "But I do have other more pressing matters to attend to. Can we wrap this up?"

Bruce gave her a measured look, a shrewd intelligence lurking just beneath the surface of his amused gaze. "Pressing matters, huh? Tell me, Nixie, what's *your* business with this human?"

"Isn't it obvious?" Maurelle said with a disdainful snort. "She called him for sport, but then decided to have a little fun with him before draining his life force and dispatching him."

Bruce's gaze turned hard. "Is that true?"

"No," Lorelei answered. "I didn't mean to call him. I was singing down by the river, and…I wasn't thinking. I didn't know there were any humans in the vicinity, I swear. Anyway, I pulled him from the water, tried to heal him, but…"

"But nothing! You don't honestly expect us to believe—"

"Enough," Bruce bellowed in a tone that invited no arguments. "Leave us, Maury."

"But—"

"The mortal was not in your possession when this Nixie called him, so by law he was still fair game. You know that. And attacking a fellow elemental without just cause is punishable by a thousand years' imprisonment and possible forfeiture of power. Is this guy really worth the risk?"

"I *do* know the law, and I call for charges against this water sprite and her sister. She attacked us without provocation by calling us into the river."

"Extenuating circumstances," Bruce replied with a wave of his hand. "They believed they were under attack at the time. It was actually Catfish Jack's doing, but I for one have no desire to tangle with him over a little prank. Besides, this Nixie rescued us from the river, if memory serves." Bruce flashed Lorelei a wink and a smile.

A sudden gust of icy wind surrounded them, no doubt a manifestation of Maurelle's fury. "This isn't over. Not by a long shot," she said before transforming into a raven and flying off into the night.

"You'll have to excuse my little sister," Bruce said, sitting down on the rocky shore and extending his hand in invitation for Lorelei to join him. "Maurelle's been on a bit of a rebellious streak for the past fifty years or so. I'm Bruce, by the way."

"I am Lorelei of the Rhine." She conjured land legs and clothing as she left the water and sat down a few feet away from him. "As for your sister's so-called rebellious streak, feeding off human suffering and attacking fellow elementals seems a little extreme, wouldn't you say?"

He shrugged. "It's no worse than the sport your kind enjoy, though I neither condone nor indulge in such pursuits." He slid closer and leaned in to whisper in her ear. "I prefer other, more life-affirming pursuits, with humans and immortals alike."

The wave she conjured soaked them both, but Bruce got the brunt of it, as was her intention.

"Hey! Talk about extreme," he yelped as he leapt to his feet, shaking the excess water from his head.

"Serves you right, you arrogant windbag," she said. "I'm surprised you don't favor peacock feathers. And Maurelle? Bruce? Those are the best modern names you could come up with?"

Flashing a wicked grin, Bruce transformed the dusky feathers coating his wings into a bright tangle of jade green and blue. Then he shook and flapped, pelting her with a fine spray of river water. She burst into giggles, levitating and donning fins once more so she could spin in the glorious shower he'd created.

"Hmm, they're pretty flashy, but I think I'll keep the eagle feathers. I look so much better in earth tones. As for the name, it's easier to pronounce than Tłanuwa, and sadly, the mortals who so named and venerated me no longer dwell in these parts." Bruce shifted his wings back to their former state while Lorelei took pity and willed the water from his trousers and boots. "Truce?"

"Agreed," Lorelei said, settling back down on the shore to sit beside him. She kept the fins, though, in case he decided to get frisky again and she had to summon a tsunami. "As long as you promise to behave yourself and tell me what your sister has against my mortal."

"Your mortal. Hmm, interesting. It's nothing personal, I'm sure. As I told you, this is her grand rebellion. She's fighting the whole sweetness-and-light sylph image. Joy, passion, and happiness are like nectar to most of us, but not Maury—I fear she's become addicted to the taste of anguish."

"So put her on a diet."

"Oh, what a saucy little nymph you are," he said, his voice low and sinful. "Alas, it's not so simple, and mortals are fair game for gods and elementals. You know that. I've tried to be a good influence, but perhaps I've done more harm than good. After all, with me as her older brother, she does have a lot to live up to."

"I see. Sweetness, light, and modesty."

"It's the truth, my dear. Care for a demonstration?"

"Not particularly."

"But you need it just the same." He inhaled deeply. The air around them charged with elemental energy as her breath rushed out under his power. It wasn't the awful choking sensation she'd experienced with Maurelle, though. No, this was something else, something healing. He coaxed a cleansing exhalation that carried the evening's distress with it and left her floating on a cloud of peace.

Bruce sighed. "If only I'd wooed you down by the river before you met him. Pity. Given my sister's attraction to abject misery, and what I've gathered from watching him, I fear this mortal will bring you nothing but suffering and grief. You may not be able to save him."

"I have to try."

He stared at her with those mesmerizing yellow eyes, and his piercing gaze softened. "I wish you luck, Rhinemaiden. You're going to need it."

"And what about your sister? Will she be giving me any more trouble?"

"Not if she knows what's good for her," he said, flashing her a wicked smile. "Which means you should probably watch your back."

"I'll do more than that," Lorelei replied, channeling her power through the roiling waves of the lake.

"And I'll do what I can to help." Bruce stood and stretched, flexing his massive wings in preparation for flight.

Yes, she'd have to watch her back and Vincent's, too. And speaking of, she wondered what could possibly motivate a Sylph to take the side of a water guardian against his own kin.

"Why?" she asked.

"Why what?"

"Why would you help me?"

He cocked his head and put on what she assumed was his thinking face. "Sweetness and light, positivity and life, my dear. That's what we Sylphs do. It's what feeds us," he said before sucking in another great breath that stole hers. "You could definitely stand a little more positivity, Nixie, because quite frankly, you taste terrible."

The cocky bastard took flight before she could hit him with a water ball.

* * * * *

Vance lay in his bed and gazed at the stars since sleep seemed hell bent on eluding him. In spite of lazing half the day away, he knew he needed more rest in order to face the next few days. The meal had helped, and the company even more so. Though he hardly knew her, the beautiful and enigmatic *fraulein* with her keen insight, blunt manner, and lyrical voice managed to get close to his heart in a single evening. Too close in fact, at least for his comfort and apparently for hers as well.

He couldn't get a handle on the woman. She'd gone from the hot little hellcat who straddled him in this same bed to the ice bitch who called him out on his pill stash in the space of a few minutes. And by evening, she'd transformed into a cross between Betty Crocker and Florence Nightingale, nourishing his body and comforting his heart and mind only to turn into a frightened kitten for no apparent reason.

Screw doctor-patient privilege, or healer, or whatever the hell she was, the way she'd handled him this afternoon had been much more than clinical. No woman could fake that kind of heat. His cock twitched just thinking about it. And she was so in tune with his music, just as she'd been as she stood in the audience at Marathon. Her reaction struck him as even sexier than their earlier bump-and-grind session.

So why in the hell had she run away from him?

He'd been racking his brain for over an hour trying to figure out what he'd done wrong. God knew he'd screwed up with most of the women in his past, as tonight's trip down memory lane reminded him. There had been plenty of heat with Maggie, so much that it damn near consumed both of them. It should have consumed him, too, instead of leaving him behind in agony after she finally broke free. He wasn't sure whether he'd given up after that, or had been seeking the same means of escape, but he never questioned that he deserved it. Hell, he would have welcomed it.

Until tonight—when Lorelei told him he was still good for something, something other than monumental mistakes and misery.

She didn't pussyfoot around his issues, either. Aside from his band, no one had ever confronted him about the drinking and the attitude. It had caught him off guard and pissed him off. Yet he had to admit, it was also exactly what he needed.

Wrestling out from under the covers, he decided to get up and draw the curtains closed. Between the light of the full moon and the damned racket the local wildlife decided to make all of a sudden, not to mention some sort of freak thunderstorm that had blown in and out, it was no wonder he couldn't sleep. Ignoring the way his legs shook and the first twinges of pain tingling through his body, he leaned his head against the window and looked out toward the lake.

A pale figure emerged from the water, her bare skin bathed in moonlight and casting a beauty that put Botticelli to shame. God, he must be hallucinating. No woman in her right mind would go skinny-dipping in icy lake water, and goddesses didn't exist outside of myth and legend. Yet there she stood in all her naked glory, filling him with desire and dread in nearly equal measure. He wasn't alone. When she turned to survey the lake and surrounding woods, all of nature stilled. It was a reverent silence, and also the silence of creatures in hiding as they waited for a predator to emerge and strike. Gone was the gentle woman who'd chipped away at the walls he'd built around his heart and soul. This creature would surely tear them down with a wrecking ball.

Definitely dreaming here, man. Might as well close your eyes.

He nearly jumped out of skin when a raven landed on his windowsill. Rather than flying away it stood its ground, staring at him with fathomless black eyes. What the hell? It flapped its wings and Vance shivered, chilled by a sudden rush of cold air swirling around him.

As quickly as it hit, the cold air vanished with his breath, as did the raven, disappearing into the night sky. Another deep ache swelled from his innards. God, it was going to be a long night.

He stumbled back to bed and settled into a fitful, uneasy sleep.

Chapter 16

It was still dark when the first real pain hit.

Between the sweats and restless anxiety, Vance had been unable to sleep for more than twenty-minute intervals. The dull aches didn't help, but they were nothing compared to the fire in his muscles and the waves of nausea that jolted him from the all-too-brief bliss of slumber.

He tried to stand and wound up on the floor instead. From there he crawled on hands and knees to the bathroom. It hurt like hell, and he barely made it to the toilet before losing the contents of his stomach. Wave after wave struck him until he finally could produce nothing more than bile.

Too bad. That was the first decent meal I've had in months.

His dark humor left him once a series of violent chills wracked his body. Too weak and in too much pain to remain upright, he fell back and hit his head on the corner of the vanity. Shivering on the cold tile floor, his mind wandered back to when he'd been struck down with a bad bout of the flu as an eight-year-old. Almost twenty years later and he still remembered the alternating hell of burning fever, teeth-chattering chills, and feeling like his insides had been torn out after vomiting more times than he could count.

It was as sick as he'd ever been until now.

His mother had stayed with him, wiping his brow and holding his hot little hand as he'd drifted in and out of delirium. He remembered being out of commission for more than a week. His father had already been dead three years, and he was sure the time off work put a pretty big dent in the family budget, but his ma stayed with him anyhow, offering love, and comfort, and safety.

So when's the last time you called her, asshole?

He chased away that thought. It wouldn't do him any good now, remembering what a worthless son he'd allowed himself to become in spite of everything she'd done for him. He couldn't shake the thoughts about Maggie slicing through his brain, though. In the eye of the storm, that beautiful and all too brief span of time between cleaning her up the first time and the final fall, she'd shared everything of herself with him. She'd entrusted him with her body, her soul, and her music. He was supposed to keep it safe, keep *her* safe.

He'd failed.

As much as he craved warmth, comfort, and ease for his suffering, Vance refused to call out for help. He'd survive, of course. Detox hadn't killed him the first time. It just made him wish he were dead for a few days. The phantom echoes triggered during the course of his long-term withdrawal weren't as intense, but they still hurt. *This* hurt. But he deserved to suffer this and more for what he'd done. And after he paid his pain debt, he'd either spend the rest of his miserable life atoning for his monumental fuck-ups or he'd follow Maggie's lead and take one last ride on the fast train to oblivion.

The way he felt now, the second option held a whole lot more appeal.

* * * * *

Lorelei woke up with a jolt and a sense of dread.

Something's not right.

She chided herself for neglecting her charge. After pouring out her sorrow to Jack and the water and dealing with the Sylphs, she'd come back to the cabin and collapsed in her own bed. She hadn't even bothered to check on Vincent. The pale light filtering from beneath his bedroom door let her know he was up. Her keen nixie hearing picked up his low groans.

Jumping out of her bed and jerking the door open, she ran down the hall to Vincent's room. His bed was a mass of tangled sheets, but she didn't see him in it. The light coming from the bathroom led her to him.

He lay curled up on the tile floor, covered in sweat and shivering violently. Blood pooled around his head. She crouched down beside him and tugged at his shoulder, trying to turn his body to face her. He flinched as though her light touch had set his skin on fire, or perhaps she'd frightened him in his delirium.

"Shh," she murmured. "It's only me. Let me take a look at your head."

"Go away."

His voice was a raw scrape, but she could hear the menace beneath it.

"You're bleeding. Let me help you."

"Don't want help," he whispered. "Just leave me alone."

She resisted the urge to bristle under his blatant hostility. Many human lifetimes worth of experience had taught her a bit about the male ego. Like most men, Vincent seemed to prefer licking his proverbial wounds in private as a matter of pride. She'd probably let him, were it not for the head wound.

"Let me look at your head first and get you back to bed. Then I'll leave you alone, if that is what you truly desire."

He didn't answer, but acquiesced when she tugged on his shoulder once more. She cursed herself when she saw the sizable gash on his forehead. Hesitating for only a moment, she ran her index finger over the wound to seal it. She spotted a towel draped over the side of the bathtub, one he must have left from his earlier shower. Grabbing it, she wiped the excess blood off his head with one corner, then folded it and placed it under his head. She scooted over to the vanity and started digging around for some more towels and cleaning supplies. He probably wouldn't remember the injury, and if she cleaned up the mess in the bathroom, she hoped he'd be none the wiser.

"Hey, how'd you do that?"

Oh no! He's more lucid than I thought.

She turned back in time to see Vincent prop himself on one elbow and run his other hand over the area that held the nasty cut only a moment ago. Moving back over to him and taking his shoulders, she eased him back down to the floor. She then tried to surreptitiously wipe the excess blood away from the area around his head.

"I didn't do anything," she lied. "It was just a tiny bump. Barely there, really."

"Damn, I must be hallucinating," he muttered, closing his eyes and grimacing, "I mean, I looked outside the window tonight and could've sworn I saw you out there taking a dip in the lake, bare-assed naked."

She didn't answer. Instead, she busied herself preparing a basin of tepid water and a cloth. After cleaning the residual blood on his forehead, she began running the cloth over his face, neck, and torso with slow, gentle strokes. Her fingertips grazed his bare skin from time to time, and she made a concerted effort to ignore the heat and softness of it and the resulting heat of her response.

He accepted her ministrations at first, but soon raised his hands to brush her aside. He even tried to roll away. She didn't understand. Between the sweat seeping from his pores and the heat rolling off his skin, he had to be in misery.

"I told you to leave me the hell alone."

"I only want to help you."

"You said you'd leave me alone if that is what I *desired.*"

"Why are you so stubborn, Vincent Violetti? You're sick. I'm a healer."

He barked out a harsh, humorless laugh. "Right. You're a 'healer.' Tell me, where exactly did you get your medical degree? Or do you do the whole third world tribal bullshit snake oil thing?"

Damn it! She should have taken Ilsa up on the offer to fabricate some sort of credentials. Shaking off the insult, she yelled her frustration. "I can ease your suffering!"

"I don't want you to ease it!" His voice was ragged and hoarse, but he still managed to put some volume and menace behind it.

Though she had promised to leave him if he wished, she decided to press a little harder. His outburst reminded her of his earlier plea the night she'd called him, when he'd asked her to get it over with and let him go. Something made him seek out pain and self-destruction, and Lorelei wanted to find out what manner of darkness drove him.

"Then tell me why, Vincent. Why do you want to suffer like this?"

"Just go."

"*Tell me.*"

"Because Maggie had to suffer. She suffered, because of me."

He turned away from her then, curling himself into a ball on the floor and wrapping his arms around his knees. After a moment, his body began to tremble again and her heart broke for him. She placed a hand on his shoulder. He flinched, but didn't pull back from her touch.

It's a start.

She held her hand still, fighting the urge to embrace him, or shake him until he couldn't see straight. Neither would help. Worse, pushing him too far while he was so vulnerable might destroy the thin threads of trust she'd woven between them earlier in the evening. Trust couldn't be forced, only earned.

Perhaps she could earn his trust by giving him hers.

"I hurt someone I loved once," she began. Her voice shook, keeping tempo with Vincent's quaking body. "His name was Gairovald. We met near the Rhine one day. I was swimming. He'd come to fish. I was a hun…ah, I was fifteen."

She stopped for a moment and allowed her mind to wander back to that first day, something she hadn't done for long time. The tall man—no, he'd still been a boy—with golden hair and laughing eyes dove into the river to save what he thought was a drowning maiden. At the tender age of one hundred and fifty, she was a very young maiden indeed, by nixie standards.

They'd hidden themselves in the tall grass by the riverbank while his clothing dried. Young and…curious, they'd traded innocence for passion, the warmth of affection, and had promised eternal devotion to one another. He vowed to return to her the next day. They would run away together, he from his village and her from her mother. They would live on love and fish, he'd joked, after Lorelei filled his basket with enough to feed a small army.

"What happened?"

She jumped in surprise at his words. She hadn't realized that she'd spoken aloud.

"He came back to the river. I was young and careless. I wasn't paying attention, and I…I didn't mean to—I couldn't—he never left the river."

She'd been singing. Foolish, young, and in love, she'd forgotten what she was.

And he paid the price.

By the time she realized the danger, it was too late to undo it. His body survived, breath, heartbeat, and the spark of life filling it. But it was only a shell. Whatever it was that had been *him*, perhaps what humans called the soul, had been forever lost to her call. Killing him was a mercy, but she'd even lacked the courage to do that much for him. Eridanos, who understood and pitied, carried him to the Rhine and bid the current to take his body after gently persuading Lorelei to release him. She'd been shattered.

She never sang again, not until coming to Nashville.

"I've never told anyone else about it."

"It was an accident. You didn't mean to do it." It was a statement, not a question. He'd rolled over to face her. Sometime during the telling, he'd also taken her hand. He wasn't angry or disgusted. He showed her the same concern and empathy she longed to give him.

But Vincent saw her as a human woman, not her true self. He wouldn't think her capable of harm.

If you only knew.

"No, I didn't mean it. But he's still gone."

"I didn't either. Doesn't matter, though. She's dead and I've spent the greater part of eight months wishing I was."

"Do you still?"

He let out a hoarse sound, something between a bark and a cough. It echoed against the bathroom tile, shattering the quiet intimacy. Gods, had she made him choke? The trembling in his body morphed into quaking, and when he turned back over to face her, tears streamed down his face. Rather than wearing the look of anguish and abject defeat, his face had contorted under the strain of breath-stealing, belly-aching laughter.

She stared at him, stunned.

"I'm…sorry…" he said between gulps of laughter and fresh chuckles. "I'm not trying to be an insensitive prick, really. God, you probably think I'm insane, or just an asshole for laughing like this, after you just spilled your guts to me. It's just—"

"Just what?"

"It's just in all these months, no one, I mean not one single person, has ever flat out asked me if I wanted to die. Most people tiptoe around the issue, but to just put it right out there? You're the only one. It's official. You are Attila the Healer!"

"Is that a good thing?"

Vincent's laughter faded. He wiped his eyes and managed to push himself up to a sitting position. Reaching one trembling hand up to cup her cheek, he said, "Yeah, that's a good thing."

She closed her eyes and leaned into his touch, her heart somehow lighter in spite of the pain of reliving her worst memory. Perhaps confession was good for the soul, assuming she had one.

"But I'm truly sorry for what happened to you. For what you lost and for what you've been carrying around in your head and your heart because of it."

His voice and words held no pity, no judgment, no platitudes. He understood. In all the long, lonely centuries since she'd lost her first love, she'd never encountered anyone, mortal or immortal, who understood. She took his hands and opened her eyes, fighting back the tears. "This is all wrong, you know. I'm supposed to be helping you, not burdening you with my sorrows and bullying you into forced confessions."

He squeezed her hands and pulled her back to him when she tried to squirm away. "No need to apologize, Lorelei. If anyone needs a cosmic kick in the ass, it's definitely me."

"Is it enough to make you want to live?"

"It's a start."

"Will you let me help you back to bed now?"

"Okay."

She helped Vincent pull himself up from floor. Putting his arm over her shoulders, she supported him as they walked back into the bedroom, though she insisted that he sit in the corner rocking chair while she changed his sheets. That task completed, she persuaded him to drink some water and then helped him settle into bed.

Though she wanted to do more for him, could do so much more with her healing powers, she honored his wishes and resisted the urge to intervene as he endured the effects of his prolonged withdrawal. She didn't stray far from his side through the long hours of the night, wiping the sweat from his brow and torso, coaxing him to drink more water, and holding his hand as tremors and pain wracked his body and delirium seized his mind. Sometime in the middle of the night, he even allowed her to cradle him in her arms, and sleep finally claimed them both.

Chapter 17

"What the hell is *that*?"

"Good morning to you, too," Lorelei complained, rolling away from Vincent and stretching her aching limbs. When she opened her eyes and squinted as the harsh rays of dawn hit her eyes, she said, "That, Vincent, would be the sun."

"No shit, sugar. I was talking about that God-awful noise coming from downstairs. When did you get up and turn on the radio?"

"I didn't." As her sleep-deprived brain defogged, her ears picked up on the twangy chords of old-timey country music floating up from the kitchen, along with the glorious smells of biscuits, bacon, and best of all, coffee—one of the greatest achievements of mortal kind as far as she was concerned.

"Well, I sure as hell didn't. You expecting company?"

"No," Lorelei replied. She wasn't particularly concerned. They were in one of the many common residences of the local water guardians. She'd simply persuade the intruder to leave, or use more forceful means if necessary. Still, it wouldn't do to expose her mortal to such activities. She'd need to distract him. "Perhaps it's one of the groundskeepers or some other caretaker. I'll go check it out. Why don't you take a shower, if you're feeling up to it?"

After another stretch, Lorelei threw off the covers and hopped out of bed. She walked over to the window, drew back the curtains, and opened it, infusing the room with fresh morning air and sunlight. Closing her eyes, she took a deep breath and allowed the scents of lake and forest to fill and energize her. It didn't have quite the same effect as a good swim, but it would have to do.

A low groan emanated from the bed behind her, jolting her out of her reverie.

"What's wrong? Are you still in pain? What can I do to help you?" she asked, concern and a rush of panic rousing her sleepy body and mind into high alert as she turned to face him.

Having emerged from his morning grogginess, Vincent sat upright in the bed and stared at her. His green-eyed gaze was filled with heat and the same intensity that she'd seen on stage. He swallowed hard, Adam's apple bobbing. His broad, bare chest heaved as his breath quickened. Between his hot gaze, glorious half-naked body, and the memory of caressing that soft skin covering steely muscle, her body responded with a pooling heat low in her belly, dampness between her thighs, and hardening of her nipples.

Her bare nipples.

Looking down, she realized she was standing before him stark naked.

I must have forgotten to conjure clothing last night.

Nudity was of little import in the world of elementals, so it was easy to forget the strange unease most humans had with it. Americans in particular seemed much more reserved than the mortal dwellers of her native continent. She'd always found the convention of modesty quaint and a bit ridiculous. But now, watching Vincent drink in her body with his hungry gaze, seeing his response, *feeling* her own, she understood the appeal. Looking upon a beautiful naked body, normally hidden from view, could be a sensual, erotic experience, laced with decadent novelty and a dash of the forbidden.

The way her mortal man looked at her now made her feel more powerful than the churning of river rapids and more beautiful than a waterfall at sunset.

Her breath hitched when he rose from the tangled mess of sheets, stood, and walked toward her. His lean, muscled body gleamed in the morning sunlight as she raked her gaze over his shoulders and chest, down to the tight, defined muscles of his stomach, and below to the thickening flesh between his legs. He moved closer, close enough for her to reach out and run her hands over his chest.

Gods, she wanted him, too. She wanted him to unleash all of the passion and fire he poured into his music on her, and to unleash the tidal wave building within her on him. They were almost of a height, but she still needed to tilt her head up a bit to meet his gaze when he stood before her. Those green eyes, burning with hunger that matched her own, devoured her once more before he lowered his mouth to hers.

He wasn't gentle, and neither was she. Hot, hard kisses mirrored hot, frenzied hands as they explored one another. She couldn't get enough of him, though desire warred with worry over the too-prominent ribs and jutting hipbones beneath her fingertips.

"You need to eat," she whispered in his ear, between licking and nibbling, and trailing her fingers up and down his torso. "You're far too thin."

"Hmm, not where it counts," he replied, pressing his erection against her.

She braced her hands against his shoulders as he slid down her body, trailing fiery kisses over the fluttering pulse at her throat, her collarbone, and down to her breasts. Keeping his gaze locked on hers the whole time, he flicked his tongue over one aching tip before taking it into his mouth, drawing a low moan of pure need from deep in her throat. He released her nipple and blew on the wet skin, thrilling and frustrating her. She closed her eyes and gave herself over to the pleasure as he alternated between each breast with eager fingers and mouth.

She almost fell apart when his fingers grazed the top of her sex.

Then, all of a sudden, he released her and she barely stopped herself from falling on top of him as he collapsed onto the floor.

"Damn!" He groaned, rolling over on his side and pounding his fist against the hardwood floor.

She bent down over him, worry overriding her lingering arousal. Beads of sweat covered his brow and his skin had grown pale. Cursing herself for failing to notice his distress sooner, for putting her own selfish desires ahead of his health, she tried to turn him back toward her.

"Shh, it's okay," she murmured as she tugged on his shoulder. "It's just too much for your body to handle right now. You need more rest to heal, you're too—"

"Weak?" he growled. Lorelei flinched at the volume and tone of his voice.

"I didn't mean it like that, Vincent, I—"

"Just get off me, okay? I don't need you poking and prodding and treating me like some useless cripple!"

"Let me at least help you back to bed—"

"Just go already!"

He shoved her hands off his body and struggled to get back on his feet. His gaze had gone from fire to ice in mere minutes, and his scowl hit her like a slap on the face. How could he not trust her after all they'd shared last night and almost shared this morning?

It hurt, but she refused to give him the satisfaction of letting it show. Squaring her shoulders and lifting her chin in defiance, she glared right back at him and said, "Fine. Don't blame me if you fall down and injure yourself, and don't even think about calling for me!"

She turned on her heel and stomped out of the room before he could respond, slamming the door behind her.

Once out in the hall, the sounds and smells wafting from below reminded her of what had dragged her out of bed in the first place, before she'd gotten lost in the sea of lust and longing and before Vincent did a one-eighty on her heart. He'd wounded her to the core by turning her away. He didn't trust her. After she'd nursed him, held him, and shared her most painful secret with him, he still didn't trust her. She should have known, should have realized when he didn't return the favor and tell her what happened with his Maggie.

The sting of his dismissal lashed most at her feminine pride. No mortal man had ever turned her away in the heat of passion. Even if he cared little for her feelings, for how much she wished to soothe and heal him, he surely wanted her, didn't he? His heated gaze, his passionate kisses, the fiery caresses over her skin—those were real, weren't they? Or perhaps they were not. Maybe he was just paying her back for yesterday, when she'd gotten him all hot and bothered before throwing his demon, his *weakness*, in his face and leaving him cold and...unsatisfied.

He told you he wasn't a nice guy.

Her mother had warned her often enough that mortal men were treacherous and vindictive. They could satisfy a river woman's carnal needs, but they wouldn't hesitate to use that power against any mortal woman or Nixie if she was foolish enough to place her heart in his keeping. Perhaps she should have listened.

Perhaps it was too late.

Preferring not to dwell on that alarming thought, Lorelei conjured clothing and stomped down the stairs. Not bothering to disguise her powers, she held her hands at the ready, prepared to unleash some pent-up nixie fury on whoever might be waiting for her in the kitchen. She turned the corner, fingers blazing, and belted out the chorus of "You're No Good."

Her target, a gargantuan giant of a man sporting silver hair and a long handlebar mustache, turned away from his pan of frying bacon to face her, apparently unfazed by her call. Shaking his massive head and giving her a sad chuckle, he said, "I guess things ain't looking so great this morning after all, are they darlin'?"

Chapter 18

"God damn it," Vance groaned, leaning his back against the shower wall and sliding down into the tub as the water sluiced over him.

At least he was alone now in his humiliation, though a part of him locked deep inside the pit of his heart ached with regret at sending Lorelei away. Truth was he needed her. He didn't want to, never wanted to need anyone, or be needed by anyone, ever again.

Maybe this was part of the karmic debt he owed, to want and need someone so fiercely, to have her so close, but be unable to have her.

Oh, his spirit had been more than willing, but as loath as he was to admit it, most of his flesh remained weak, except for his aching cock. He'd taken care of that himself upon entering the shower, though his release had proved less than satisfying. Maybe it was for the best. His body would heal if he stayed clean and sober. That was a pretty big "if." Some sleep and a few good meals would probably get him halfway back to human. Of course, it would have to be restful sleep, not the short bursts of slumber he'd experienced last night. He'd been plagued by vivid nightmares—he recalled the awful sensations of suffocation and hands clawing at him, dragging him down into some icy depths, and a dark-haired woman trying to pull him back to the surface.

Seriously messed-up Freudian shit and a symptom of his real problem: his screwed-up head. That's where addiction really sunk her claws in. The soul-sucking depression that followed physical withdrawal lingered much longer and drew far too many back to the bottle. He'd seen it and lived it before, and it swelled within him now, drawing him to her familiar darkness.

No one could save him from it, not even Lorelei, though she seemed determined to try. He could see why, in light of her late-night confession made on the floor of this very bathroom. Caught up in her own quest for atonement, she needed someone to save. *Too bad you picked a lost cause, sugar.* He should tell her. He knew all about lost causes and trying to save them. They only dragged you down with them, and they left you behind to deal with the aftermath.

He didn't want to drag Lorelei down with him. He should just go.

But, fuck it all, he couldn't leave now, not after she'd called him out on running from his problems. She'd still think him a coward as well as an asshole, especially after his epic bedroom fail. He didn't want to dwell on when and how her opinion of him came to matter so much, but it did. No one should have that kind of power over him.

He'd just have to show her he was man enough to take care of himself. He didn't need her. When she realized that, *she'd* leave *him*, and he could get the hell out of here and do whatever he wanted with his wasted life. Or end it, since he was still on the fence about the whole question of life and if it was worth living anymore.

He pushed himself up and willed his legs to support his weight. After he finished washing his hair and body, he dried, dressed, and psyched himself up for the trip downstairs. He needed a distraction from his discomfort, the tangle of regret and sorrow lodged in his brain, and his longing for Lorelei. Once he got something in his stomach, he figured he could head outdoors and find some tasks to keep him occupied, like splitting logs for the fireplace. He'd spent a fair amount of time working on the docks back in Jersey. Something about an honest day's work through manual labor had always been satisfying. You didn't have to think too much. You just kept your hands busy, got the job done, and you could sleep easy knowing you'd earned your rest with sweat and muscle.

He walked downstairs and paused at the bottom step, trying to work out what to say to Lorelei. Her voice, along with another, unfamiliar one, caught him by surprise. Hearing her respond to the deep male voice with her low, sensual alto made his blood boil. One word careened through his brain and threatened to burst forth in a fit of rage.

Mine!

* * * * *

"Morning. Glad you could join us, son. Name's Jack." Catfish Jack extended his hand to Vincent.

Lorelei eyed both men with nervous anticipation. He'd done his best, but Jack didn't exactly blend in the human world as well as she and her Nixie kin did. Perhaps he was out of practice.

"Vincent." To his credit, Vincent accepted Jack's proffered hand and mumbled some sort of greeting through gritted teeth.

"So, Vincent, have a seat and let's see about getting you some vittles."

She almost smiled when he introduced himself as Vincent. Almost. She tried not to notice his slow, lumbering gait as he walked to the table, or the wince he tried to cover as he sat down. Anger warred with concern, but she wasn't about to help him.

His cool, inviting scent, evergreen laced with his own unique musk, didn't help, not when it evoked the fresh memory of her lips and tongue caressing his heated flesh.

Rather than dwell on his enticing scent and wounded sexiness, she busied herself pouring coffee and juice. She placed them on the table, half irritated and half warmed by his muttered thanks. He took a small sip of orange juice and settled his glass back on the table, head lowered and hands slightly shaking.

Anger still rolled off him in waves, but at least he made an effort not to show it or to take it out on Jack. No, she was his target. He didn't even look at her as he filled his plate with the hearty breakfast Jack prepared, and the three of them ate in silence.

He didn't eat much. The vein at his temple pounded, and he wiped the sweat from his brow at least three times. He was still hurting, and making a monumental effort not to show it, which tugged at her heart even more. Why wouldn't he let her help him?

Vincent pushed his chair away from the table and rose slowly, knuckles white from the death grip he maintained on the armrests for support. She moved to reach for him, but Jack stopped her by placing his massive hand on her shoulder.

Appearing not to notice, Vincent cleared his plate and placed it in the sink before turning to announce, "It may get chilly again tonight. I'm going to head out and chop some firewood. Know where I can find an axe?"

"I keep a few out in the shed. Here, you'll need these," Jack replied, reaching into the breast pocket of his flannel shirt and pulling out a key ring. He handed it over to Vincent and then proceeded to dig back into his plate full of pancakes.

Of all foolish things he could do to avoid her, she'd never have thought a man who'd spent half the night sick and shivering in his bed would be stupid enough to go out and risk life and limb pummeling wood with an axe.

And yet, he did just that.

He stumbled out of the door, and made his way to the tool shed. About two minutes later, the crack of splitting wood hit her ears. Worse still, Jack had given him a hearty smile and told him exactly where to find that axe.

She stood and walked toward the door, determined to follow him. Just because he was angry and couldn't stand to be in the same room with her didn't mean the idiot needed to go out and injure himself. For the second time, Jack's hand on her shoulder made her stop.

"He has no business going out there, Jack. He's still sick and exhausted, for Neptune's sake! What is he trying to prove?"

"He's trying to prove he's a man, darlin'."

"Well of *course* he's a man, but what's that—"

"We need to have us a little heart to heart, dear."

Jack heaved a long sigh. Taking her hand, he led her to the couch, sat her down, and settled his massive bulk down on the sofa across from her. The wood and steel frame groaned in protest, but thankfully it was able to support his weight without breaking.

"I know you ain't gonna like this, but you're gonna have to let him go out and do what he needs to do today and stay out of his way, even if he gets hurt in the process."

"Oh, that is just ridiculous! Why does he—"

"How old are you, darlin'?"

Lorelei bristled at his audacity. Maybe she wasn't as old as her ancient companion, but she'd been around the proverbial block a time or two. "By human standards, I am old enough to be counted among the wise. I'll have you know that I've observed and interacted with humans for centuries."

Jack had quirked a brow when she'd mentioned being wise. Typical. She'd been around less than a millennium, but still? She wasn't a child anymore. Instead of commenting on her youth, however, Jack took a different approach. "Uh-huh, you've observed the odd human for a day or two, maybe even a week. And then you moved on to the next man, and then the next, am I right?"

He had her there, but she wasn't willing to admit it. "Well, yes.... I mean, *exactly*. I've observed thousands of them, and not just in the bedchamber I assure you. I've spent time with them in battle, and...and in taverns, and...well you get the idea. I'm not completely new at this."

"Maybe not, but when it comes to spending time with one man, outside of the bedroom or barroom, you ain't got a clue." He must have read the scowl on her face, because he held up a giant palm and said, "Now don't go getting all bent out of shape, little Nixie. Let old Jack help you out here. You been tending to him since you brought him here, right?"

"Yes, of course. I only wish to restore his health and his spirit."

Jack chuckled. "I have a pretty good idea about how you want get his spirits back up, but that's a whole other can o' worms. He's been going through a rough patch, ain't he?"

"Well, yes."

"Sick as a dog, I'd imagine, ain't been on his feet, and you been hovering over him like you're his mama."

She nodded. He'd held up better than she expected for a human, fighting valiantly against his body and his demons. She admired his strength of mind and body and had done all she knew to make that obvious.

"With all of that, I'd imagine his pride is hanging somewhere in the vicinity of his ankles right about now, and it's pissing him off. You running after him's only gonna make it worse, darlin'. He's gonna want to go out there and work out his mad on some logs, demonstrate his might to himself and to you, too, while he's at it."

"Me? He doesn't have a thing to prove to me. He's not even interested in me at all, at least not since this morning." Her skin flushed with heat at the memory of his hands and mouth.

"Sure he does, darlin'. I've seen how he looks at you. Believe me, he'll be ready to demonstrate his might in your general direction soon enough," Jack said, chuckling and waggling his bushy silver brows. "You just got to give him some time and some space."

"But he needs looking after!"

"Don't you worry. I'll take care of that. You go on out and have yourself a swim. Best be ready for some company, too," Jack said, his expression growing harder. "Seems like your mama got wind of your little detour and sent one of your aunts to come check up on you."

"How did she find out? I've been here less than a—" Lorelei stopped short, realization dawning on her. The house began to rumble under the strain of creaking pipes until water burst from the kitchen sink with enough force to blow off the fixture. Judging from the loud cracks and clangs from upstairs, the bathroom sinks had burst as well.

"Easy now, Nixie. Try and rein it in before you blow the durned house up." Jack said. Then he sucked in a deep breath that took the force of her power with it.

"Sorry," she muttered.

"It's okay, darlin'. Lucky for you, I'm a pretty good plumber." A flick of his wrist undid the damage. "What's got you all riled up?"

"A hateful little Fairy with a grudge and a penchant for tattling."

Chapter 19

"I told you to steer clear of Sylphs." Jack heaved a great sigh. The grim set of his human features after hearing about her encounter with Maurelle didn't bode well.

"Yes, you did warn us. Too bad it was *after* Ilsa accidentally called two of them into the water."

"So Maurelle's back in town, is she? I'm surprised. Last I heard she was sniffing around California looking for movie stars she could suck dry. You're lucky her rapscallion of a brother was there. If y'all had kept at it much longer, you'd have lost more than your man."

"And I could still lose him and more if Mother finds out." The first prickles of real panic pricked at Lorelei. "Which aunt did she send?"

"Ondine." After giving her a long look, Jack continued, "That bad, huh?"

"Definitely not good. She doesn't trust humans, men in particular."

"What is it with y'all and mortal men?"

"You've never heard our family history?"

"Some. I know your daddy was a mortal—some kind of nobleman, wasn't he?"

"Yes, as was my grandfather. That's how it all started—with him and my grandmother, Pressyne. Elynas, the great king of Albany came upon her near a fountain and was taken with her at first sight. She was quite beautiful, and all mortals are drawn to our elemental power."

"And she fell hard for this fella, huh?"

"Oh yes. She loved him in return and agreed to become his wife. As a condition of their union, for one is always required when immortals mate with humans, she admonished Elynas that he must never, ever enter her chamber during bath time or when she bore his children. Our communion with water is sacred, and not for the eyes of mortals. Of course Elynas, being male, didn't listen—no offense."

"None taken," Jack said with a shrug. "Go on."

"When she birthed Melusine, my mother, and her sisters, Elynas couldn't resist taking a peek. That ended their marriage and started a generations-long family grudge against mortal men that continued with Mother. When Melusine found out about her father's broken promise, she and her sisters hunted down Elynas and locked him away in a mountain in an act of vengeance."

"Pressyne was none too pleased, I take it."

"No, she wasn't. Though he betrayed her, she still loved him and was furious with her daughters for dishonoring him. In a fit of rage, she transformed my mother and her sisters into Nixies. They were still water nymphs and could still assume human shape for short periods of time, but were henceforth forever tied to the water and compelled to assume the form of mermaid when water bound. That is how our Nixie clan came to be."

"So what happened to your mama?"

"Melusine succumbed to the charms of a Frenchman, Raymond of Poitou—my mortal father. Like Pressyne, she married him under the condition that he keep out of her bathing chamber. And, much like her father,

Raymond let his curiosity get the better of him, sneaking a peek and seeing her fins."

Lorelei shuddered and lowered her head. She took a moment to blink back the unshed tears that threatened to spill before continuing. "Mother tried to learn from her mistake. She forgave him, at least until he called her a serpent in front of his entire court later after a nasty domestic spat. He…he looked at her with such disdain, and us, too, Jack. I don't think Ilsa and the twins remember, thank the gods. They were young…"

"But you do, huh?"

"Yes."

The sofa groaned and dipped when Jack scooted closer. He didn't speak, but a massive palm landed on her back and rubbed small circles. When she opened her eyes, she found an old-fashioned handkerchief resting on her lap.

"Thank you," she muttered, wiping her eyes.

"What happened, darlin'?"

"Naturally, Mother wasn't quite so forgiving after the public insult against her and her children. In her rage, she transformed into a rather large and frightening dragon before flying away and taking us with her. She didn't kill him, but none of us ever saw Father again. He died not long after, or so I'm told. After that, Mother bespelled us with the nixie call to protect us from human men, so we wouldn't suffer as she had."

"Well fire of Hades, why don't y'all just stick with your own kind, then?"

Lorelei shrugged. "Our males, the Nix, are quite rare. You know that as well as I do. There are far fewer of them than Nixies, and they're quite hard to tame. And," she said, offering Jack a sly smile, "there just aren't enough handsome and powerful water guardians to go around."

Jack flashed her a winning smile. "Aw darlin', you're gonna make me blush, and I ain't done that in eons."

Lorelei smiled back. "Anyway, we aren't compatible with sky folk or fire keepers, and earth elementals prefer to stick with their own kind. That leaves humans. We can't live with or without them, and it never ends well. Aunt Ondine nearly lost her immortality when she gave her heart to a mortal man, too."

"Oh great gods, what happened to her?" Jack asked, shaking his head in apparent disbelief.

"They started out well enough, when they were both young and caught up in the bloom of youth's passion. After she bore his child and started to age, he lost interest in her and took a lover. She caught them together, asleep but still intertwined. Legend has it that she cursed him that day, using his vow of fidelity against him. He'd sworn to remain faithful with every waking breath, so she held him to it."

When Jack quirked a bushy brow, Lorelei continued, "He kept his breath so long as he remained awake, but as soon as he fell asleep, she claimed it. Lucky for her, his infidelity gave her an exit clause and she got her immortality back, but she's been bitter ever since. If she finds out about Vincent, if she tells Mother.... Oh Jack, she just can't know about him!"

"Why do I get the feeling this is about a whole lot more than saving this fella's hide or having a little fling with him?" Jack asked, dark gaze boring into hers.

She opened her mouth, determined to reassure her guardian that her interest in Vincent was purely noble, that she wanted to restore his health and send him back into the human world in a better state than she'd found him. That was true, but even she couldn't deny the truth of Jack's words. There was a whole lot more to her fascination with the handsome, stubborn, talented, tortured, and infuriating mortal man. She wasn't only interested in healing him, hearing him play, or sharing his bed for a night or two.

She wanted to *know* him.

She longed for more fireside serenades and the freedom to sing along. She wanted him to tell her of his life's sorrows and trust her with his pain. She also wanted his joys and triumphs, would tolerate his volatile temper and his highs and lows if it gave her the chance to see just one more smile of pure happiness cross his lips.

Lorelei wanted him. She feared she'd already lost her heart to this man, and they'd both suffer for it.

"Aw great gods, you're fallin' for him, aren't you?"

"I'm trying really hard not to," she replied in a small voice. "And it doesn't matter, anyway. I still have to let him go soon."

Jack's gaze softened a bit. Heaving a deep sigh, he said, "You'd best be heading back to the river to meet your aunt, darlin'. Don't worry about your man. I'll look after him."

"Thank you, Jack."

"Don't thank me yet, gal. You still need to work out how to keep your aunt away from here and what you're gonna do when the time comes to send your human back. He won't like it any more than you will."

"Of course he'll like it. He's been trying to get away from me since I brought him here."

Jack shook his mighty head, turned away from her and started walking toward the door. He paused on his way out and said, "No, he won't darlin', cause the damned fool's fallin' for you, too."

Chapter 20

"I'm so very glad you talked me into this, my dear," Ondine said, fiddling with the massage settings on the pedicure chair. "I haven't had a foot massage in ages. Of course, I haven't worn feet for more than a few hours at a time in decades, either, though that is neither here nor there."

Fortunately, the young woman busy at Ondine's feet didn't speak old German. Would her aunt never learn to be more discreet about their nature among mortals?

Probably not. Then again, worst-case scenario, she could always pass the stately water sprite off as an eccentric older woman.

"I'm glad you're enjoying it," Lorelei replied from her own pedicure chair.

The pedicure suggestion was yet another ruse to keep Ondine occupied so she wouldn't press Lorelei about her decision to remain in Tennessee, or worse, insist on visiting the cabin. After more than two hours of shopping, lunch, and another hour of pounding the pavement in Green Hills, Lorelei's aching feet welcomed the soothing water and skilled fingers of her aesthetician.

At least entertaining Ondine had taken her mind off Jack's rather startling revelation. Not that it was true, of course. Vincent didn't love her. First of all, he hadn't known her long enough, his short mortal lifespan notwithstanding. Second, he was too busy sorting through his excess baggage to bother with healthy emotions. Third, after she'd stomped all over his male ego this morning, she doubted he even felt any physical attraction to her anymore.

Oh, Neptune, if it could only be true, though…

She snapped out of her thoughts and focused on the task at hand. Ondine had done remarkably well, considering she'd rarely set foot in the human realm since the Middle Ages—except for shopping and man-hunting trips, of course. With a little guidance from Lorelei, she'd taken on the appearance of a very attractive older human woman. The "older" part still stuck in her craw, but it couldn't be helped. Her mortal aging could not be reversed upon her return to the realm of elementals. To Lorelei, however, she carried an air of wisdom and beauty tempered by maturity, and she'd been turning mortal heads since emerging from the water, both old and young. With glistening silver hair, a trim and slender physique, and winning smile, her visible age only added to her allure.

"Of course I am enjoying myself, especially in the company of my favorite niece. But, as lovely as it has been surveying the latest in mortal fashion, cuisine, and creature comforts, I am still duty bound to inquire about your change in vacation plans."

Here we go. "I just like it here. I mean, I *really* like it here. The music, the scenery—"

"The men?"

She did her best to brush off the insinuation. "You'll have to ask Ilsa about that. She's the one who can't seem to keep her legs together when she wears them."

"I did speak with Ilsa, dear, not to mention your younger sisters. You know you've put your mother in quite a state, calling Gwen and Gisele away. She's worrying herself sick."

Oh, this was exasperating! "Mother worries herself sick whether we're at her side or not, Auntie. It's suffocating, and we're far too old and experienced for her to fret over us like fresh fry. I can't believe she had you cut your tour of Asia short on account of us. I'm sure Ilsa, Gwen, and Gisele are getting along just fine. Otherwise you would have alerted me. That should prove to you and to Mother that we are capable of looking out for ourselves."

"Hmm, yes," Ondine muttered. She'd become engrossed in choosing between sparkling pink and candy apple red polish for her newly buffed toes. "Actually, I was quite happy to come to America at your mother's request. I'd grown weary of the dragon festivities. Mortals don't believe in us anymore, you know. Why, during our last personal appearance, several young engineering students actually climbed on my back, looking for my on switch! Something about advanced animatronics. At any rate, we wouldn't have to worry about you little Nixies so much if you were all *together*."

"I told you, I just loved it here so much I wanted to stay for a bit longer. I'm perfectly safe, I assure you. Catfish Jack, guardian of the Cumberland, is looking after me personally."

"I'll be the judge of that, my dear."

Having selected her color, Ondine settled back into the chair and sighed as the mechanical hands dug deep into her shoulders.

Time to take another approach. Softening her tone to something resembling reverence, she said, "There's really no need to go to such trouble, Auntie."

"Nonsense, my dear. I simply must meet this fish!"

"What?"

"He became quite the legend in our circles after your great-grandfather traveled to the New World. And besides, protocol dictates that I seek an audience with him so that I may pay my respects and offer tribute."

"But Auntie—"

"No buts. The matter is settled. Now please sit still, Lorelei. If you keep fidgeting like that you'll ruin your nails. Honestly, dear, I don't recall ever seeing you so jumpy. I thought vacations were supposed to be relaxing."

Lorelei sat back and tried to relax, failed, and settled on twiddling her thumbs. She'd hoped to persuade Ondine to follow Ilsa and her other sisters north with the Mississippi. Since she couldn't, she needed to come up with a way to explain Vincent, or to warn Jack they were coming so he could keep Vincent out of sight.

"Well, Jack is a bit busy at the moment, Auntie," Lorelei began, trying her best to sound casual. "He has a…a tenant."

"Tenant?"

"Yes, a mortal tenant to, you know, to help him out and…keep up with the lake house and property while he's away. Like, um, like Lars!"

She crossed her restless fingers, hoping that her spontaneous flash of inspiration would work as a suitable cover story. While Ondine still carried a grudge against her late husband, she was no more immune to the charms of mortal men and the needs they served than any other water nymph. She kept several around to serve as groundskeepers for her many residences and to "service" her needs. Former male model and reputed modern-day Adonis Lars Männlich was her current favorite.

"And he's…*busy* with this tenant?"

"Oh, not like that," Lorelei said with a chuckle. "He's showing him what sort of work needs to be done around the property. Like chopping firewood and keeping up with the landscape work."

"Catfish Jack? Performing manual labor? My, my, our New World cousins are rather down-to-earth, aren't they?"

And the Old World gentry are rather uppity. "Oh, he's quite strapping, Auntie. And he's a wonderful cook."

Ondine's eyes widened and, even more surprising, she blushed. "Well, he sounds like quite a catch, indeed. Do you know if he's attached to any nymph in particular?"

"He hasn't mentioned anything to me," Lorelei replied, grinning as another flash of inspiration hit. "But I can certainly find out, discreetly of course. Why don't you let me lay a little groundwork today? I could arrange for you to drop by tomorrow evening to discuss your tribute over dinner, and I'll even keep the mortal tenant occupied so you two can have the cabin all to yourselves."

Pleaseworkpleaseworkpleasework...

"Well, I suppose I could postpone my visit until tomorrow, if it isn't too much trouble for you, dear," Ondine replied, fluffing her hair and then smoothing her hands over her skirt.

"It's no trouble at all."

"Very well. I shall be staying at the Opryland Hotel. It's just off the Cumberland, and they even built a river inside the hotel. Can you imagine? It's as if it was *made* for a water nymph."

* * * * *

Though his back and shoulders ached, his legs still shook a bit, and his head hadn't stopped pounding, Vance smiled in triumph when he realized that the sweat pouring from his bare torso had come from nothing more than a big dose of honest-to-God work. He let a healthy sense of satisfaction wash over him after he added the last log to the large stack of firewood he'd chopped. He could build a big-ass fire tonight, roast some marshmallows, even make some s'mores.

Maybe Lorelei would enjoy some chocolate.

The smile faded. What in the hell was he doing, planning a date night in with the woman he'd failed in the bedroom this morning and then yelled at like it was her fault he was such a mess? The woman who was, for all intents and purposes, his rehab counselor, though he hadn't asked her for help. Hell, he didn't care what she thought anyway, did he?

Of course you do, asshole. That's why you're out here playing Davey Fucking Crockett.

What a startling realization *that* was, but it was true. She mattered. When he'd walked into the kitchen and found her wrapped around that giant hulk of a man, he'd almost lost his shit. His alpha instincts had kicked into high gear then, and he'd made certain to swing the axe extra hard when Lorelei walked outside and announced she'd be out for the afternoon. He'd squared his shoulders, stood tall and willed his damned legs to hold him steady so she'd see that he didn't need a nursemaid. Vance Idol ruled the stage with his guitar and the cabin with his axe and biceps. No, he didn't need anything.

He didn't need anything except her approval, and maybe her.

Oh, man, what the hell is going on in my head?

"Why don't you take a load off, son? Have some lunch."

He looked over his shoulder and saw Jack the Giant walking toward the patio table, holding a tray overflowing with sandwiches. He was about to tell the man to leave him alone, but the beast in his belly let him know it wanted food ASAP with a hearty rumble. Plus, given his size and imposing demeanor, telling the man no might very well get his ass kicked. Setting the axe aside and wiping his brow with his bare arm, Vance nodded and walked over to the table. He groaned as his ass hit the seat and his body experienced the soothing cool of the shade.

He grabbed one of the glasses full of iced tea and downed half of the contents in one gulp. Then he helped himself to a sandwich and tore into it, table manners be damned. He was starved, and he took comfort in the feeling that he might be able to keep this meal down. After his second bite, he frowned, settled the remaining sandwich on the napkin he'd spread out before him on the table, and raised his eyes to meet the towering man's unblinking gaze.

Man, I'm such an ill-mannered bastard. "Thank you for this, Jack. I should've said it sooner, but I'm not really good at the whole manners and gratitude thing. Haven't been for a while. Hell, I'm not good for much these days, truth be told."

Jack didn't say anything for a moment, busy settling himself into a chair that was about three sizes too small. Still, he managed to do it with surprising grace. Then he said, "You're welcome, son. Maybe that whole manners and gratitude thing is something you ought to work on."

"I'll add that to my list for once I'm done with the staying clean and sober thing. Maybe find a twelve-step program for recovering assholes. So, um, how do you know Lorelei?"

A deep chuckle erupted from Jack. "I'm an old friend of the family, and she's like a daughter to me. You better do right by her. You feeling me, son?"

"Yes sir."

"That's good. Now then, there's a few things you ought to know about Lorelei. She ain't like other gals you might have known. She's—"

"She's something else, for sure. Coddling me one minute until I think I might suffocate and then handing my sorry ass to me the next. She doesn't mince words, and I haven't run her off with my bullshit yet. Don't know why. Probably because she's stubborn as hell and just trying to get under my skin because she knows it drives me crazy."

After a pause, Vance muttered, "Um, sorry. Didn't mean to interrupt."

"She's all those things and more, but you gotta deal with a few other things if you want to keep her."

"Who says I want to keep her?"

"You don't have to, son. When you've been around as long as me, you get a pretty good sense about these things."

Vance didn't confirm or deny Jack's assessment. He just said, "So what's the problem, other than all my baggage?"

"Hers, or rather, her family's. Her Ma and Pa split under some bad circumstances, and her Ma's kept her on a tight leash for her whole, long life up until now."

Vance snorted. "Can't be that long. She's what? Twenty-four, twenty-five?"

"Older than you might think, but that's another problem I ain't gonna explain. Once she decides to share it, and you decide you can handle it, you'll need some advice on how to manage things. We'll talk if and when that happens."

Stopping himself short of blurting out some other smartass remark, he considered the implications. Lorelei had baggage, too? Funny, it hadn't occurred to him until she'd told him about her first love, but he'd assumed that was it. She carried herself with the confidence and poise of a much older woman, at least older than she appeared. If she was over thirty then she should be sharing her secrets with the beauty product industry, because she could make a killing.

That notwithstanding, he'd been a supersized douchebag, neglecting to ask about her life. No, he'd been too busy burdening her with his. Of course, the last time someone had shared her pain with him, he'd bailed when the going got too tough. Self-preservation aside, he could have tried harder to help Maggie. He could have been stronger. He could have done a whole lot more.

But it was too late, now.

"Aw, hell, Jack. I'm no good at this. I can't even take care of my own baggage, let alone hers. I—"

Jack cut him off with a hard look and a low, menacing voice. "Then you'd better get good at it, son. You'd better stop whining, wallowing and get busy locating your balls and manning up. Ain't none of us good at dealing with most females until we try, and try harder, and work on being the kind of men they ought to have. *She's* been working hard for you and making her own mistakes along the way."

"Yeah, and I made her feel like shit for it."

"So apologize. Ain't that a part of the whole road to recovery gig?"

"Yeah, but—"

"Then I suggest you eat up, grab a shower, and get busy figuring out how you're gonna make things up to her. She'll be back just before dinner, I expect."

He nodded, for lack of anything else to do. Then, looking out at the area around the lake, he got an idea. He'd seen a trailhead near the woods and suspected it ran along the lake. Maybe, if there was a clearing not too far down the trail....

"I think I know just what to do, but—" He swallowed a lump in his throat and a whole lot of discomfort before continuing. "Um, I'm going to need your help."

Jack's massive face split into a smile. "All you had to do was ask."

Chapter 21

Vance got out of the shower and went through his plans again. His limbs twitched and a fine sheen of sweat covered his brow, but not because he needed a drink. No, this was a simple case of pre-date jitters. Maybe he still thought she'd turn him down, or maybe he still felt a little unworthy—okay, a lot unworthy—and scared, or maybe because the thought of apologies just made his ass twitch, but he was jittery as hell.

Still, he was one hundred percent committed.

Speaking of commitments and apologies, he really needed his phone. Remembering Lorelei's admonition that he'd never find it, however, he'd probably need to come up with another solution. Walking down the stairs, he searched out Jack and found him in the living room, camped out on the couch in front of the television.

His jaw dropped.

"Man, what the *hell* are you watching?"

"*Hillbilly Handfishing*. Bunch of city slickers out noodling in the river. Good stuff, though they ain't seen nothing if they think *that's* a big catfish. Care to join me while you wait for your lady?"

"Actually, I was hoping to use the phone." When Jack's expression hardened, he quickly added, "I got a few folks who are probably pretty worried about me and I'd like to get in touch. Part of that whole recovering asshole program, you know."

Jack reached into his shirt pocket and handed Vance a mobile phone. "Go on."

"Thanks."

He walked outside and dialed before he could lose his nerve. After three rings, he almost gave up. She picked up on the fourth ring, though, and his chest grew warm and tight all at once when he heard her voice.

"Hello?"

"Hey, Ma. It's me. It's Vincent."

He'd expected her to gasp, or maybe start crying, or cursing. Hell, he could deal with anything except silence on the line. Had she hung up?

"Um, look, I know I haven't called in a while. I don't call enough. I don't do a lot of things enough, but I wanted to call you and, um, tell you that I'm sorry for, you know, everything."

He ran a hand through his hair and started pacing. What he wouldn't give for a cigarette. The awkward silence killing him, he opened his mouth again and hoped like hell that a decent apology would fall out. "I'm sorry for being such a pain-in-the-ass son and for worrying you and for—ah, hell. I'm no good at this. But, um, Ma, I love you and I'm getting help right now and I'm gonna get better and be better, you know? I'm gonna be a better son and a better man, and I…just wanted you to know that."

Still nothing. He stopped pacing and leaned back against the wall, tempted to bang the back of his head against it. Maybe it was too late, but he hoped she'd heard him. He hoped maybe, someday soon, she'd welcome him back and give him the chance to prove he wasn't bullshitting her.

"Yeah, so anyway, that's all I wanted to say. You take good care of yourself, Ma. I'm going to take better care of me. I'll call again soon, okay?"

"Vinnie?"

"Yeah, Ma?"

"Don't go yet. I...I'm so glad to hear your voice."

He gulped and had to blink hard a few times before he found his voice. "It's good to hear yours, too, Ma."

* * * * *

"Jack? Vincent? Anyone home?"

Lorelei sat her shopping bags on the ground in the foyer and walked to the living room. She didn't see either of her men in the lower part of the cabin. Cursing, she headed for the door to the patio. Jack had promised her he'd look after Vincent, but some fit of testosterone-fueled camaraderie probably made him decide that letting Vincent work himself into illness or serious injury was acceptable so long as it made him feel manly.

Males!

She froze with her hand on the doorknob, caught up in the sight just beyond the glass door. Vincent stood with a phone in his hand, talking and…smiling. He was sinfully handsome when caught up in singing, or even as a scowling and brooding man, but to see him smile with such ease and with such a look of peace? The sight left her breathless.

Then her chest constricted and her breath left her out of panic. *He's on the phone. Where did he get a phone? Oh no! He's calling someone to come and get him. He's leaving me.*

"You'd best head upstairs and conjure yourself something nice but comfy to wear, darlin'," Jack called out. "He'll probably want to get going as soon as he gets off the phone."

She couldn't stop the tears that welled up in her eyes. She didn't want to let him go, though he looked much healthier and content than when she'd found him. But it wasn't enough yet. He needed to stay a little longer, until he'd fully healed, until she was convinced he'd be okay. She could maybe let him go, then.

She hoped.

She spun around and threw herself against Jack's broad chest.

"Hey now, what's all this about? You don't want to go getting all worked up before your night out."

"What? I'm not going out. I won't let him leave without saying goodbye, Jack."

"Whoa, there, little Nixie," Jack said, pulling back until she raised her head and met his gaze. "He ain't leaving you right now."

"But, he's on the phone, and you said—"

"If you spent more time listening and less time jumping to conclusions, you'd have heard the first part about putting on some comfy clothes, as in he's planning to take you out on a little walk in the woods this evening."

The first stirrings of hope filled Lorelei's heart, though she could scarcely believe that Vincent wanted to take her out. She turned back around and looked at him through the glass door. He was dressed in a casual blue T-shirt and jeans, and he'd put on a pair of hiking boots. When he turned toward the door, he caught her eye and offered her a small, tentative smile. He also held up his right index finger, letting her know he was almost done speaking to whoever was on the phone.

"Who did he call?"

"His family, I expect. He did ask me if he could text one of his bandmates and someone named Katie, too."

She turned back to Jack and stared at him, raising her brows and waiting for more in the way of an explanation.

"Word of advice, darlin'. Don't push him too much tonight. Let him take the lead and give him a chance to get things off his chest in his own time and in his own way, okay?"

"What did you say to him this afternoon?"

"We had us a nice man-to-man talk. That's all I'm saying. Now, it's time for you to skedaddle up to your room and get ready for your own heart-to-heart."

At a loss for anything else to say, she climbed the stairs and walked to her bedroom. Upon entering, she noticed the bed had been made and the contents of the room ordered. Someone had cleaned.

Someone had also left a shallow glass bowl on her nightstand, filled with water and a single, gorgeous water lily floating in its center. She inhaled, astonished to catch the amazing fresh scent of lake water. Next to it was a note. She unfolded the paper with trembling fingers and read the meandering script.

Dear Lorelei,

There's a trailhead not far from the cabin. Jack tells me it runs along the lake and opens up to a little meadow after about a half a mile. He says it looks like heaven at sunset. I'd like to go there tonight, and I'd like you to come with me.

I owe you a guitar lesson. I owe you my life, too.

I'd like to thank you for it.

Come with me, please.

Vincent

She closed her eyes and breathed in the scents of lily and lake water. He couldn't have known how much they'd mean to her, their *power*. Taking it as a sign from the fates, she slipped out of her sundress, dipped her fingers into the lake water in the bowl, and anointed her body with the elixir that had traveled from glaciers and through the oceans and rivers, through the sky and then to the lake as rain.

It fortified her and called to her elemental nature, imbued her with strength and courage. She didn't know how long she'd have this amazing mortal man, for another week or for this one night, but she would respond to the offering he'd made and gift him with her own. Water and life, fortifying and healing—they would share this and more.

She conjured more suitable clothing for a walk in the forest and readied herself to answer to his call.

Chapter 22

Vance hung up after speaking with his manager. The band still hadn't made it to the studio to lay down tracks, but the guys had been rehearsing. Surprising, since he'd been out of commission for longer than he'd thought. Like close to a week. Didn't seem like it, but maybe that was just a side effect of getting his head back on straight. Before he worked up the nerve to ask, Eddie told him that they hadn't called B.J. yet. Eddie also said he was proud of Vance for manning up and getting help, managing to sound more concerned for Vance's well-being than his own paycheck.

He wished he'd been able to get a hold of Sticks, but he didn't pick up. Vance left him a voicemail letting him know he was okay and he'd call soon. No magic wave of relief washed through him after his first attempts at reaching out and making amends. If anything, he was more strung out on the emotional stuff than he'd been on the booze and pills. Still, he forced himself to focus on the present and the task at hand.

He owed Lorelei, and it was time to start paying.

When he turned to walk back inside the house, he was surprised to find her waiting for him just outside the door. Jack must have briefed her, since she wore a casual white tank top, jeans, and hiking boots. She'd braided her hair again, and he found himself mesmerized by the rogue raven strands that managed to escape and fell in wisps that framed her beautiful face.

She'd tucked the water lily he'd left in her room behind her right ear.

Standing before him, she almost looked like an ordinary, albeit gorgeous, young woman ready to accept his invitation for a meal and some soul sharing, and that was all he'd intended. He could control his masculine instincts, even with a beautiful woman. He'd had plenty of practice. It wasn't the way she looked that threw him off and made him question the wisdom of this outing. It was something else.

If asked, he would have been hard pressed to pinpoint what is was about her in that moment that made his heart beat faster and his breath hitch, but he *felt* something more surrounding her, about her. Something deep and primal, fundamental as air—*no, water*—made the hair on the back of his neck stand up straight and take notice.

And not just his hair.

It drew him in and made him want much more than conversation. *Time to clamp down on those urges.* After making an all-day effort transitioning from asshole to recovering asshole mode, he didn't want to make tonight about a quick screw in the woods. He didn't want her to get it in her head that he was out to prove something after this morning. And he damned sure didn't want to embarrass himself again. Tonight wasn't about rushing. It was about proving he was the kind of man she ought to have, like Jack said, or at least showing her he was making an effort.

Mr. Happy seemed hell-bent on making that harder for him. Literally.

Suck it up and get going.

"Hey," he said, finally locating his voice. "You ready?"

"Yes."

"Great. If you grab that basket, I'll get the rest of our stuff and we'll head out." He pointed to the picnic basket sitting on the outside table.

Picking up his guitar case and grabbing another bag, he and Lorelei set out for the trailhead. Though the days were getting warmer as spring gave way to summer, the air had cooled by late afternoon and the light breeze kept them comfortable. Taking even more comfort in their companionable silence, he willed his body to calm as they made their way through the sea of oak, hickory, and dogwood that parted at the entrance to a small meadow.

Perhaps it was their silence, or the fact that twilight was approaching, but there seemed to be quite a bit of wildlife hanging around the area this evening. If he didn't know better, he would have sworn a pair of blue herons swooped down and smiled at Lorelei. And what had gotten into the tree frogs? He'd never heard such a chorus of croaks. Not since the night before, when he'd had that strange dream about Lorelei emerging from a night swim in the lake.

Something flashed in his peripheral vision, interrupting his thoughts.

"What the—"

The biggest crow he'd ever seen shot out of the tree line and into the late afternoon sky, cawing like its tail feathers were on fire. Had it been hit by lightning? Wait, was it the same bird who'd visited his windowsill the night before? He spun around and caught sight of Lorelei. The look on her face shocked the hell out of him.

Between the hard set of her jaw, furrowed brow, and thin line of her lips, she seethed with rage. Every muscle in her body seemed tense, and predatory energy rolled off her in waves. God, her eyes…were they glowing?

"You okay, Lorelei?"

The fury seemed to bleed out of her gaze as it met his, though she remained tense. She looked back toward the tree line, muttering something under her breath in a language he didn't understand or recognize. As soon as she finished speaking, a fog rolled in from the lake and surrounded the meadow, swathing them in a warm, soothing mist. Vance opened his mouth, ready to launch into the mother of all what-the-hell spiels, when a bit of moist air hit his lungs.

Man, that is some sweet air.

What was he going to say?

"I'm fine," Lorelei said, her voice as placid as her expression. "Shall we?"

He shook his head and resumed walking. Reminding himself to thank Jack for mowing a substantial patch of grass and the path to it, he led her to the middle of the field and set about spreading a blanket. He relieved her of the basket and laid out their meal, which they shared in companionable silence.

"Wow, I didn't realize how hungry I was," she said, then lowered her gaze and added, "I didn't mean to make such a pig out of myself."

"Oh, no, it's not that. I just zoned out there for a minute."

Ah hell, he'd been staring at her again. Cursing himself, his mind scrambled for something else he could use as a distraction. "Would you like me to play a little for you while you finish up? I'd, um, I'd like to tell you a little bit more about Maggie…"

Her eyes widened and she nodded as she swallowed a mouthful of fruit.

Fighting a case of the jitters, he brought out his guitar and balanced it on his right knee, shifting his body and straightening his back so he could settle into a more comfortable position. He'd planned to play for her, but hadn't had a song in mind until they'd made it to the meadow. After a few warm-up chords, he settled into "Fields of Gold," adding his voice after a minute or two. The way she responded to the music didn't help with suppressing his arousal. He had to shift his hips more than a few times to get comfortable.

Watching the rise and fall of her chest and the way her delicate nipples strained against the white shirt made him remember their sweet, salty taste, the way those peaks had tightened in response to his cooling breath. Her face held a blissful, almost ethereal rapture, those lovely arched brows furrowed and eyes closed as she lost herself in the music, and he couldn't resist losing a little more of himself to her.

Just for a moment. I'll give in for just a moment.

"Maggie and I worked pretty close after she got out of rehab the first time, when we pulled her off the street and got her into the band. She wrote the lyrics and I worked on getting the right music. Josh worked with us sometimes, but he stopped hanging around as much when he realized Mags was into me."

He chanced taking a glance at Lorelei. She'd scooted closer, moving behind him. He could feel the warmth from her body, and sighed when she placed a tentative hand on his shoulder. It gave him the courage to go on.

"We hooked up and things went great for a while. Making music, making love, getting a taste of success at our gigs, it was everything I'd ever hoped for and everything I never knew I wanted. But then I found her rig, and I couldn't ignore all of the other signs that she was using again."

He remembered all of those signs he'd missed—the jitters, the weight loss, and the hollow look in her eyes. He'd always been a straight arrow before he met Maggie, never drinking to excess and never even smoking weed, though he'd been offered that and more after gigs. Though pissed as hell at her for dropping off the wagon, he loved her by then and thought that his love would be enough to save her. He thought if he tried to understand her darkness, to experience it with her, he could pull her back.

"What happened, Vincent?"

"I made a mistake and it cost us both."

To her credit, she allowed him to take his time and regroup, his fingers absently strumming the guitar as he prepared to speak.

"She went back to the needle and I started hitting the bottle. It was a piss poor way to deal, I know, but at the time it was the only way I could cope. Maybe...I wouldn't shoot up with her, I knew no good could come from that, but when I'd been drinking... I guess I thought if I could join her in some way, go with her into the dark and try to pull her out...I was stupid."

"You were human."

"Right. Well, as you can probably guess, I got in way over my head. I couldn't sleep, didn't eat, and I sure as hell couldn't think straight. I wasn't much good to myself, let alone Mags. All I could think about was my next drink. Then there were the pills. When I couldn't play anymore, I knew I had to stop."

He closed his eyes and took a deep, shaky breath. As if of their own volition, his fingers tightened around the guitar's neck and he began to play the opening chords of "This Is Home," the last song Maggie wrote before she died, as the pain of those memories washed over him. The music helped, as did the warm weight of her palm on his shoulder.

"I got myself to treatment and got Maggie back in rehab, too, after we broke up. I loved her, but I knew we'd end up dragging each other back down if we kept it up. When we got out, she moved on to Josh."

"That must have hurt."

"He was my right-hand man and best friend, so yeah, it hurt like hell. He'd always wanted her. She must have seen him as some kind of goddamned knight in shining armor after she got out. Maybe if they'd just told me..."

He had to stop. Everyone said confession was good for the soul, but fear gripped him at the prospect of owning his part in the ugliness that followed. He had to face it, though, even if it meant Lorelei would turn her back on him. He'd tell her the truth.

"You found them? Together?"

That she guessed the first part made it easier.

"Yeah, I did, and I went ballistic. I should have just punched Josh and let him punch me back, but I took it out on Mags. The things I called her, Lorelei, the things I said—I knew every dark corner of her heart and I used it all against her. Hell, I might as well have ripped it right out of her chest."

"You were hurting. You had the right to be angry."

"I didn't have the right to say all of those things. I didn't have the right to push her over the edge so that she'd—"

He stopped playing. The final sour note echoed through the clearing, nearly destroying the peace and beauty of the place. But then again, he excelled at destruction. He swallowed hard, his vision blurring, and he had to look down to finish. "She overdosed later that night. I drove her to it. I killed her."

He'd thought it plenty of times. Those words had been the looping soundtrack in his head ever since the news of her death hit. Josh sure as hell blamed him, just like he blamed himself. But he'd never spoken the words aloud until now.

She removed her hand from his shoulder. He waited for her to remove her body from his and leave him in his cold hell with only the memories of his past wrongs for company. God, it hurt like hell, but he deserved it, and he'd accept it.

He didn't hear her footsteps retreating, though. Instead, she shuffled back in front of him and lifted the guitar from his hands. Not sure what to make of the unexpected gesture, he kept his head lowered and his eyes closed.

"Did you forgive Maggie?"

"Yeah," he whispered. "Josh, too."

"You haven't forgiven yourself, though."

He sat still, not daring to move, to lift his gaze, or even breathe.

"You need to forgive yourself, Vincent. What you've been doing, slowly killing yourself, isn't going to bring her back or honor her memory. Living a full life as a whole man will. Forgiving yourself will, too."

"I can't."

"You can. It's okay," Lorelei said, reaching out and cupping his face in her palms. He let her lift his head, but didn't dare open his eyes.

"Look at me."

"Don't do this to me, Lorelei."

"I said look at me."

Her harsh, commanding tone, clanging out in such stark contrast to her gentleness a split second earlier, forced him to open his eyes on shocked reflex. Releasing a gasp, he sensed that strange, intangible power surging just beneath the surface of the woman sitting in front of him. It hit him with the force of a tidal wave, and for a moment he wasn't certain if he would drown in it or if it would carry him home.

"You need to forgive yourself."

"You can't make me. This force of will you're throwing down, or whatever it is that's going on here, it can't save me."

She released his face, only to grab his shoulders and force him onto his back. She lunged and then was on top of him, pinning his wrists to the ground and bending her body over his with a strength he'd never have guessed she possessed. Leaning down, she pressed her lips against his in a gentle whisper, though her grip on his wrists tightened.

Pulling back, she waited until he opened his eyes before she spoke. "No, I can't make you, Vincent. But I can give you permission, if that's what you need. I can give you that and so much more if you'll let me."

Chapter 23

Jesus, what the hell is happening here?

His chest tightened right along with the tightening in his groin. Like the first time she'd sat astride him, her confidence and commanding nature *really* turned him on, just as the power of her acceptance made him think that maybe, just maybe, he could really forgive himself and become the man he'd once been. He'd already taken the first steps. Maybe she was right. Maybe he could make the rest of the journey, or at least make a start, if he would but grant himself permission.

Strange as it was, flat on his back and at her mercy, she'd somehow given him his power back.

She kept a firm hold on him but didn't move. He'd been lost in his thoughts for a good little bit, but she hadn't bent to kiss him again. Given her position, he figured she couldn't have missed the hardness that had sprung up between his legs or the heat of his gaze. He wanted her, and she had to know it. During their brief association, he'd never known her to be coy or shy. She didn't play games. So what was she waiting for?

"Are you waiting for my permission, Lorelei?"

"Yes."

"Then consider this my gold-embossed invitation," he said, raising his head slightly to bridge the distance between them. He found her lips, and gave himself over to a heady combination of lust and adoration, the stuff of life.

And for the first time in a long while, he didn't bother to question whether or not he deserved it.

After taking some time to savor her, his kisses grew more urgent and he lifted his hips, seeking the friction he desperately needed. Her low moans and undulating hips were all the encouragement he required. Though he struggled to free his wrists, she refused to let go and surprised him yet again with her strength.

"I want my hands back." He managed to get the words out between groans of appreciation and want.

"Not yet."

He started to struggle again, but the kisses she planted along his jawline, neck, and over his earlobe stilled him along with her murmured assurances. "Let me take care of you first, Vincent. Trust me."

He smiled against her mouth and said, "I hope this isn't about what happened this morning. I'm feeling a helluva lot better now."

She froze and a flash of uncertainty clouded her gaze. He quickly followed with, "That was a joke, by the way, and an apology. I'm, you know, working on being the bigger man, here."

Then she threw back her head and laughed. The throaty sound of pure joy escaped from her lips and made her body shake, sending a wave of comfort and delight through him. He couldn't help but join her.

After she recovered, she leaned over, arched her brow, and ground her body against him. "Hmm, I think you've got the whole 'bigger man' thing figured out. Now, may I continue?"

When he nodded his agreement, she eased her grip and ran her hands down his bare arms with light fingertips and continued down and over his shoulders, across his collarbone, and over his chest, her mouth following her fingers. The vixen looked up and flashed him a sexy grin full of mischief. She then leaned down and scraped her teeth over one of his aching nipples through his shirt, biting down gently when he groaned and arched his body in response.

"That good, is it?"

"Take. My. Shirt. Off. Now."

"Hmm, yes sir."

She reached down and tugged at the hem of the tee, pulling it over his torso and up above his chest before taking a moment to run her fingers and tongue over his bared flesh. "You can move your arms now to help me get this off, but then I want them back down at your side."

He muttered a "yes" and helped her take off his shirt. Flashing a wicked grin of his own, he sat up, tugged her white tank up above her breasts, and lunged, taking one coral tip into this mouth before she could stop him.

"Hey!" Lorelei gasped, sounding anything but unhappy. "I thought I told you to keep your hands at your side."

"They are. You didn't say anything about my mouth." He swirled his tongue around her nipple, flicking it lightly before sucking it back in. After giving her other breast equal treatment, he sat back and grinned.

"Are you finished, Vincent?"

"Not by a long shot. I'm just waiting for you to make your next move. And Lorelei?"

"Yes?"

"Have I mentioned how much I love it when you call me Vincent?"

She smiled at him then, a warm, wide, sexy smile. Pushing him back down, she unbuttoned his jeans and allowed him to help her pull them off, along with his boots, socks, and underwear. She stood and began to undress, allowing his greedy gaze to drink in every inch of naked flesh she exposed. Her back to the setting sun, he got a little lost in the sea of curves framed by the golden halo of light. The effect shadowed her body and gave that air of mystery surrounding her a raw edge. One word kept springing into his mind.

Goddess.

When she dropped to her knees, spread his legs, and cradled herself between his thighs, he swore he'd died and gone to heaven. All thoughts ceased when she parted her lips and flicked her tongue around his head, teasing him while she held his gaze. Then she took his length into the heat of her mouth and he had to close his eyes to conjure more control. Holding on to the blanket, his hands twisting the fabric, he savored her incredible mouth, her tight lips and swirling tongue driving him to the brink of madness. A growl erupted from deep within his chest and he sat up, pulling her with him so he could claim her mouth with his.

He took his turn exploring the contours of her body with his hands and tongue, loving the way she leaned into his touch and the gasps and moans of pleasure she made in response. Now that his brain had defogged a bit, he began cataloging those responses to his touch, making certain to return to the places that made her sigh and groan in pleasure again and again—those pert, gorgeous nipples that beckoned his mouth, the sweet spot at the nape of her neck that made her shiver and moan, her inner thigh. When he stroked the silky slickness between her thighs, they both groaned.

Oh God, so wet, she's so wet for me.

Ego buoyed, he couldn't resist entering her with one finger, and then another, and massaging the bundle of nerves at the top of her sex with his palm. He had her mewling and writhing against his fingers, and he held the small of her back and pressed her against him tighter, encouraging her to ride his hand harder and faster.

"That's it," he whispered. "Keep going. Let me see you come for me. It won't be the last time tonight. I promise."

Three more thrusts and she fell apart against this hand, her inner walls convulsing as she cried out and muttered words in a language he didn't understand. Though she'd released, he noticed the strained look on her face as she recovered, like she was holding something back.

"Don't hold back, baby. You can cry out all you want," he whispered, withdrawing his fingers and pulling her against him for a kiss. "Trust me, it's music to my ears."

He swore he saw a flash of utter despair cross her fine features and wanted to soothe her, reassure her, comfort her about whatever caused that unexpected reaction, but his efforts were lost when she pushed him back down, covered him with her body and guided him inside of her after rolling on the condom that seemed to materialize out of nowhere. Christ, but she was so warm and wet and achingly tight, and the pleasure of it drove him out of his mind.

Then she began to ride him, slow at first, and then picking up the tempo as need fluttered through her body, need he could feel in her tightening all around him. He matched her pace with his thrusts, determined to make her come again and to come hard. He didn't want her to hold back anything from him, and he wanted to give her everything he had, too.

"Look at me, Lorelei," he said, his voice a harsh rasp. The pressure kept building and she was right there with him. God, but he needed this connection with her. "Don't hide from me."

Her pace became erratic. "I'm sorry…I can't…don't want—"

"Please," he bit out through gritted teeth. "Look at me. Come with me!"

She opened her eyes wide and clamped down on him as her orgasm roared through her. It milked him until he quickly followed, thrusting through it and holding her gaze the whole time.

When he returned to his senses, he noticed she'd bitten into her lower lip hard enough to draw blood. Male satisfaction warred with concern, and concern won. He pulled her close to him, wiping the blood away with his tongue and gasping. She trembled in his arms, but her quaking didn't feel like fear. It roared over him like a tsunami of raw power.

"Lorelei, what's happening? Are you—"

He froze as a single note burst forth from her throat. She sang it out in a voice of unparalleled beauty the likes of which he'd never heard before, except once, in his dreams. It called to something deep within him and filled him with a long-sought peace that soothed every ache his soul had borne.

"That's so beautiful," he whispered, before darkness swallowed him.

Chapter 24

Lorelei stopped and heaved great gulps of air. Between the mother of all rock-your-world orgasms and the impromptu aria, she needed to breathe. She needed to laugh and cry and shout with triumph and the sheer joy of loving Vincent Violetti.

Oh Great Neptune, I just sang!

She looked down and panicked. Vincent stared up at her, his face awash with awe and bliss. Placing a trembling hand on his face, she rubbed her thumb back and forth across his cheek. *Please be okay, please be okay, please be okay….*

"Vincent," she whispered. He didn't respond.

Her heart raced and her breath came in short gasps that burned her chest. She clapped her hands in front of his face, willing him to snap out of the spell. Tears spilled from her eyes and fell onto his beautiful, placid face.

"No, no, no," she moaned. She couldn't lose him, not this way. Not like before.

Leaning down, she placed her head on his chest and heard the slow, steady cadence of his heartbeat. She felt the rise and fall of his chest and breathed in the musky scents of sex and man, all signs of life. But where was *he*? Had her call taken his soul after she'd taken his body?

She'd given herself over to slow, shuddering sobs when strong arms enfolded her and a warm hand traced patterns over her bare back.

"Shh," he whispered. "It's all right, beauty. I'm here. I've got you."

If this is a dream, please dear gods don't let me wake up.

She struggled to speak, but all she could manage was a strangled, choked sob. He held on tighter and began to rock her in his embrace, whispering the words of a love song in her ear and soothing her. She didn't understand, couldn't fathom how he'd survived her call. Though shorter than the call that landed him in the Cumberland, this burst of song had been infused with intense power borne of his water offering and the power of their union.

"You're okay," she murmured, running her hands over his arms and shoulders.

His deep, rumbling chuckle filled her ears and heart. "Better than okay, especially after that. You?"

"I am now."

"Jesus, you have the most beautiful voice. I've never heard anything like it."

No, and you never will again. Ever.

"Lorelei, you sure you're all right? I didn't hurt you, did I?"

She almost choked at the absurdity. After unleashing her call, again, he was worried that he'd hurt her? Gods, she'd been as caught up in the rapture of the man as she'd been in the rapture of his music the night she'd nearly drowned him. But he recovered this time. He shouldn't have, but he'd listened to her nixie song and lived.

"Talk to me, baby," he said, cradling her face in his palms and searching her eyes, concern painted over his expression. "Tell me what's wrong."

Oh, could she do nothing right? First she almost killed him and when he survived, she caused him more worry. In a few short moments, she managed to erase the look of peace and contentment and replace it with guilt and distress. *Some healer I turned out to be.*

"I'm okay," she said, trying to sound convincing. "Just overwhelmed in a very, very good way."

He smiled then, an astonishing smile full of affection and aching hope. "Come on, beauty. Let's get up. I promised you a lesson, and there's nothing I'd love more than to dress you in my guitar and nothing else."

Still shaken, she complied with his request, mostly to avoid explaining her breakdown. She missed the heat of his body and the connection as soon as they separated.

Perhaps later. Please let there be more.

She sat up on the blanket and he slid behind her, sending delicious shivers over her skin when his naked body came back in contact with hers. After he situated the guitar between her crossed legs until it rested on her right knee, he guided her left hand to the neck and her right to the body. His gentle fingertips guided hers as they caressed the strings.

"Good," he murmured as he coached her through a few simple notes. "Keep going. You're doing great. You ever played before?"

"Not this particular instrument, but I am…familiar with many."

"Hmm, you're a natural."

He managed to teach her the basics in an hour, and had her strumming three-chord blues soon after. While she appreciated his praise, her skill had less to do with being a quick study than it had to do with her elemental nature. The flip side of the nixie curse was their love of music and their natural talent for making it. Not to be outdone, he took his turn dazzling her with everything from old school Robert Johnson riffs to Elvis and the Beatles.

The most remarkable part of the evening, aside from their lovemaking of course, was his ongoing immunity to her call when he coaxed her to stop biting her lip and to sing with him. She resisted at first, and then compromised by gently humming. After he prodded her some more, she sang three lines and held her breath while watching him for any signs of distress.

And for a miracle, they didn't come.

The only reaction she inspired in him after half a song was having him set the guitar aside, grab her body, and pin her beneath him for another round of intense, mind-blowing sex. It was more than she'd ever dreamed possible for herself and she relished every caress, every kiss, every groan and muttered curse that let her know the man she'd helped restore was as lost in her as she was in him.

By the time they'd had their fill of one another, darkness had descended, so they walked back toward the lake house. Halfway there, she sent out a silent request to keep the mosquitoes at bay. Though winged creatures fell under the dominion of the Sylphs, the small, midge-like flies relied on water to complete their lifecycles and therefore responded to her kind. While they walked and she waited, a disturbing thought occurred to her.

What if they can't hear me anymore?

If the legends were true, falling in love with a mortal and having that mortal love her back would have rendered her mortal. Then again, she hadn't lost her powers with Gairovald. Did that mean he didn't love her? Or was the legend a lie, perhaps invented by her elders as another way to keep her kind from mixing with humans?

There was one easy way to find out.

"Go on ahead, Vincent. I'll catch up," she yelled over her shoulder as she turned and ran toward the lake.

"Lorelei, wait! Where are you going?" he yelled, his voice fading.

"Trust me!"

Cutting through the brush, she made it to the water's edge, stopping to catch her breath, and to muster her courage. She listened to the night sounds of nature all around her, half wondering and half praying that she hadn't lost her connection. With a deep breath and a leap of faith, she summoned her power and jumped into the water, hoping her fins would follow.

Chapter 25

The familiar surge of energy surrounded her once she breeched the surface. Bones shifting, skin sliding to make way for scales, gill slits emerging from her neck in a soft tickle, she dove into the water as woman and emerged as mermaid. Relieved, but not quite satisfied, she willed her body to assume the form of a large trout as a test of her power. When that worked, she morphed into a minnow, then into a spotted turtle, and just to be certain, she transformed herself into a bright Japanese koi.

"Could you *please* just pick one form already and stick with it? My head is spinning."

She shifted back into her nixie form as she shot out of the water and unleashed a burst of elemental energy in the direction of the deep voice.

"Hey, that stings! Do all of your kind shoot first and ask questions later?"

"Bruce, I'm really not in the mood for this right now," she grumbled upon recognizing the voice. "I've already zapped your harpy of a sister tonight to stop her spying. Don't think I won't do the same to you." She reined in her power and settled her fins back into the water, hoping against hope that the annoying Sylph would leave her alone with her confusion and misery.

No such luck.

Bruce materialized in a cloud of white smoke worthy of the most flamboyant of human magicians, his glowing skin reflected in the rippling surface of the lake as he hovered. In spite of his tousled hair, disheveled clothing, and scowl, he looked magnificent surrounded by an aura of raw power. He stretched and cracked his neck and shoulders, managing to look elegant while doing it. When he turned his attention to her, the smirk he sported almost made Lorelei zap him again.

"Show off," she grumbled.

He shrugged. "It's easier for Slyphs to materialize through air. It's our element. I'm sure you'll get the hang of it in time. I could give you some private lessons."

"Cut it out, Bruce. I already told you I'm not in the mood for this."

"Well, well, well," he said after taking a deep breath, concentrating as it filled his nose and lungs. He licked his lips and closed his eyes as though savoring a rare vintage. "You've had an interesting evening, I see, or rather taste. Not that it's improved your flavor or disposition. Why is that, goldfish? Did the human fail to live up to your expectations?"

Flabbergasted and beyond angry, she stammered, "Wait a minute—how did you—were you *watching* us, too?"

He rolled his golden eyes but kept that infuriating smirk in place. "No, I wasn't watching, dear. Actually, I was rather busy myself, entertaining a couple of delicious and insatiable Dryads, who incidentally give new meaning to the mortal phrase 'throwing wood.' Ergo, I didn't see a thing."

"Too much sharing, Bruce—"

"I did, however, get an earful. You're quite the screamer when in the throes of passion, aren't you?"

Refusing to take the bait, she shifted the conversation to more urgent matters. "If you heard us, then you must have heard me sing."

He'd opened his mouth, no doubt ready to throw out another salacious remark, but stopped short. Cocking his head to the side in what she assumed was his thinking pose, he said, "Come to think of it, yes, I did hear singing. That was you?"

"Yes."

"Oh dear," he said, stooping down and placing a hand on her shoulder. The sudden shift in his playful mood, along with the unexpected concern, took some of the bite out of her anger. "Is he still breathing?"

"Yes, thank the gods. But he shouldn't be. There was a lot more power behind my call this time, after we, um, well, you know..."

And the smirk was right back on his face again, along with a bit of wide-eyed wonder. He released her shoulder, then conjured a small cloud and bid it hover over the surface of the water. Sitting down on his makeshift cushion, he said, "In that case, I take back what I said about your mortal's performance. Does that always happen when you come? Gods, you Nixies must burn through lovers, or remain inordinately frustrated. Of course, when Slyphs come, we—"

"No, Bruce, that doesn't always happen when we mate with mortals. But there is something about this mortal that makes me want to sing all the time, and I thought I might have killed him, or damaged him beyond repair…"

To his credit, Bruce gave her a blessed few moments of silence to regain her composure, turning his attention to the night sky while she wiped the tears from her eyes. Without looking at her, he spoke. "So tell me, goldfish—now that you've managed to…acquire your heart's desire, and keep him alive in the process, why so glum? Shouldn't you be seeking him out again so you two can make beautiful music together?"

She laughed. Gods damn the arrogant Sky Guardian, but she couldn't help it. He did have a way of putting things into perspective. And, loath as she was to admit it, the guy made her feel better, too. At least, he did when he wasn't being such a cad. "You know, Bruce, I think I'm starting to get you."

"That's what the Dryads said, just before they got me a second time."

"Oh, you are insufferable!"

"But you like me. You know you do."

"Anyway, to answer your question, the reason I'm here in the water instead of with Vincent is to test my power. I was afraid that if I'd lost my call, I might have lost my other elemental gifts."

Bruce snorted. "Oh, *that* old legend. Believe me, dear, if falling in love with a mortal really robbed us of our powers, I wouldn't be standing here right now—"

He stopped short and averted his gaze. She was taken aback by his clenched jaw and tense shoulders, but she recognized the pain behind them.

She reached her hand toward his shoulder, but he leapt from his cloud and moved away before she could reach him. Clearing his throat, he said, "Well, um, all of your powers seem to be in good working order, it appears."

"I still have two I need to test."

Before he could even blink, she unleashed three soft notes. They had the desired effect. Bruce froze and she summoned her nixie power to hold him suspended above the water. Placing her hands on his massive shoulders, she willed her healing powers to infuse him with comfort, hoping the power was still in her possession.

His jaw unclenched and the crease between his furrowed brows smoothed as he relaxed. The tension in his muscles eased just before she released him. When the fog lifted from his gaze, his eyes widened and he stumbled backward with a mighty splash.

Oops, apparently she'd forgotten to will the cloud cushion back underneath him.

He emerged from the water looking equal parts put out and amused. "Well played, goldfish. Well played. Your call still works, as does your…"

He trailed off, cheeks turning pink as he busied himself by shaking the excess water from his wings. Though sorely tempted, she didn't tease him, nor did she press for details about what she assumed was his own personal tragedy with a mortal lover. That she'd eased him with her healing energy was enough, and since he'd been instrumental in proving that her elemental powers and call remained intact, she figured they were square.

"I should probably head back now, before Vincent gets worried," she said. "Thank you for keeping me company."

"You're welcome, goldfish. I wish you luck with the mortal, though I suggest keeping your bedroom window closed tonight, since not all of us are immune to your call."

"I don't know for certain that he's fully immune."

"He survived tonight."

"It may not be permanent."

"Stop being so negative. Perhaps it was the magic of true love's first kiss."

"We'd already kissed."

"True love's first shag?"

"Goodnight, Bruce," she said, turning away and gearing her fins up for a brisk swim back to shore. If she stayed any longer, she might give in to temptation and dunk him again.

"Positivity and life," he yelled as she dove. "Try it, Nixie, you might actually like it."

Chapter 26

Vance stopped outside of the patio door and waited for Lorelei, concern pricking at the cocoon of warmth and satisfaction he still carried from their time together, not to mention the profound sense of relief he experienced after his confession. On the one hand, she'd accepted him, baggage and all. Instead of turning away and leaving him to his demons, she'd enfolded him in her arms and demanded that he let go of the guilt and pain over Maggie.

But then she'd run off.

He got the impression she was deeply worried about something, but he couldn't understand what. Of course, Jack mentioned that she had some baggage of her own, baggage of the family variety. Maybe that was bothering her. She could have laid it all on him, trusted him with her pain as he had trusted her with his. Didn't she know that?

Other questions burned through his brain, too, now that the euphoria of sex had dampened enough to allow thought. What had happened back at the lake when she sang? Her voice was amazing, hypnotic even, and the effects were strangely familiar. She must have had some sense of its power as well, since she'd clamped down and refused to sing again until he'd coaxed it out of her.

Then there was the whole issue of her appearance in his dreams. He could let that slide were it not for the strange energy emanating from her general direction all afternoon. And then there was his ongoing struggle to reconcile the blood he'd found on the edge of the bathroom counter earlier that morning. He'd also discovered bloody towels shoved into the back of the closet in his room; all of that, but not obvious wounds anywhere on his body. He'd hit his head the night before. Hard. Even in his whacked-out state, he'd felt the impact and expected blood and a good-sized goose egg on his noggin.

He shook his head, unclenched his fists, and decided to hell with it. She was his, whether she knew it or not, and he needed to go find her.

He glanced toward the lake and had to do a double take. *What the hell?*

"Boy, looks like you been caught hook, line, and sinker."

Spinning back around, he came face to face with Jack. The big guy had a pipe in his mouth and a shit-eating grin on his face as he looked from Vance to the water and back again. Vance sensed an energy emanating from him as well, like Lorelei's but with a different…flavor.

"Yeah, um, Jack?"

"Yeah?"

"Something really weird's going on here, but I can't…I mean, it seems nuts, but…did you just see what I think saw out there in the water?"

"What'd you think you saw?"

"Fins, man. Really, really big fins, as in bigger than any fish I've ever seen, stocked lake or not. Look, I'm not the superstitious type, but do you suppose we have some kind of Loch Ness-type creature sneaking around out there? Because if something that big is hanging around, I don't like the idea of Lorelei taking midnight dips in the water."

Jack clapped him on the back and said, "I wouldn't worry none. This ain't exactly Nessie's stomping grounds.

Come on in by the fire. I imagine your little lady'll be back in directly."

* * * * *

Lorelei crept back to the shore and hid behind some nearby bushes while she conjured clothing. Now that Vincent was lucid, she couldn't count on explaining away her naked nighttime swims as a side effect or hallucination. Of course, that left one bigger problem.

How could she possibly explain that swimming was mandatory for her, or, if she kept it a secret, how could she manage to take care of her water needs on the sly for the rest of their time together?

And how long would they have, anyway? Though she couldn't explain the loss of her call's effect on Vincent, she obviously still retained her elemental nature, and he was only human. That left them with a very big problem. He'd age while she remained ever youthful, and then someday he'd die.

She didn't think she could bear it.

Could she become human? If she could, did she even want to? If it meant staying with Vincent and sharing his life, she suspected she could and would. But is that what he wanted? And even if he did now, what about the future, when she got older? Would he turn his back on her and leave her to suffer like Ondine? Gods, Nixie women didn't have the best track record with love.

"So, you gonna tell him?"

Jack's voice took her by surprise. She didn't see him on the nearby shoreline or in the adjacent woods, which left only one other plausible place.

"What are you doing out here?"

"Same as you," Jack replied, his great catfish head rising out of the water. "Recharging my battery, so to speak. 'Course, you've been out here a bit longer. Something on your mind?"

She took a deep breath and blew it out, suddenly exhausted in spite of her swim and the renewal of her elemental energy. Closing her eyes and bracing for a lecture, or worse, she said, "I sang again, Jack."

No harsh words came, nor did any comfort. She'd expected some sort of reaction, but then again, given his first question, he must have seen for himself that Vincent was okay and suffered no ill effects from her call. Perhaps he was as confused as she was. When she opened her eyes, prepared to face the proverbial music, he stood before her again in his large, human form.

And he was smiling.

The ear-to-ear grin, coupled with a glint of knowing mischief in his gaze, gave her pause. "What aren't you telling me, Jack?"

"Nice flower you got there, Nixie," he said, reaching out to stroke the water lily she'd placed back behind her ear. "Gift from your fella?"

"Yes. He left it in my room, floating in water from the lake." She couldn't help the shiver running up her spine, or the gooseflesh that erupted over her skin as she remembered running the water he'd gifted to her over her flesh. It had been almost as sensual as his touch.

"Hmm, seems like an offering of sorts. A mortal offering of thanks to an elemental guardian, made up of the very elements she represents and protects...powerful magic in that, I reckon, especially if a mortal offers himself along with the tribute."

More shivers raced up her spine and her heart pounded in her chest as a new and long-buried emotion swelled within her. Could it be true? For the first time in centuries, she dared to hope.

"Oh Jack, you knew, didn't you? You knew if he made an offering he'd be safe with me," she whispered.

"I had an inkling it might. Sometimes the simplest magic works best. Don't mean it's a cure, but it might stick if he pledges himself to you."

"What should I do now?"

"I think you should tell him, darlin'. He already suspects something, and keeping secrets ain't gonna win you any points with the man."

"Oh, Jack, I don't know. What if it freaks him out? Scratch that—what do I do *when* it freaks him out? Humans don't believe in us anymore, or much of anything else as far as I can tell."

"I ain't gonna lie to you. He might not be able to handle it. But if you want to stay with him, you'll have to fess up so he knows what he's getting himself into. And if you decide to leave him, he deserves to know why."

"Do you know if I can become a human woman?"

Jack cocked his great head to the side. After a moment, he blew out a gurgling sigh and said, "I don't know, darlin'. That'd take a fair amount of magic. You'd probably have to ask your great-granddaddy. And then there's always your mama."

"Don't remind me."

She thought for a moment. Vincent had trusted her with so much, and she didn't want to violate that trust by keeping her true self from him any longer. Plus she owed him the truth about how he came to be in her care. After all, he wouldn't owe her his life had she not almost taken it in the first place. But admitting that she'd almost killed him might drive him away, even if her fins didn't.

But, he'd shared his truth with her. She knew she had to share hers with him.

"Okay, I'm going to tell him tomorrow night. Let me have one more night with him in case he runs away. Oh, and by the way, I need another pretty huge favor from you."

"Why ain't I surprised, darlin'? You still ain't paid me the tribute y'all owe for crossing my waters," he grumbled, but he also gave her a wink. "What's the favor?"

"Well, how would you feel about going on a date with my Auntie Ondine?"

Chapter 27

"You okay, sugar?"

"Sure. I'm great. Why do you ask?"

"You should cut the bullshit, Lorelei. It's not your style. Tell me what's on your mind." He hated to kill the mood, since they were having a really nice, really normal, low-key evening out. He'd asked her if she wanted to walk down to the bar at the local marina for some food and music. Sometime during their third tango between the sheets last night, he'd gotten the itch to see those long legs move across a dance floor with him.

The marina bar and restaurant was bigger than some of the hole-in-the-wall joints he'd played in the past, but not by much. It looked as though someone had stacked a few ramshackle kid clubhouses side by side over some wooden dock planks and called it an eatery. For what it lacked in size and amenities, it more than compensated for with some out-of-this-world steaks and a killer view of the lake at sunset. Most of the boat owners had docked their expensive toys and abandoned the marina for other watering holes, so he and Lorelei pretty much had the run of the place.

They'd enjoyed dinner and drinks, though naturally he'd opted for soda instead of alcohol and earned a smile full of pride and affection from his lady. Still, between her fidgeting and lowered gaze, he knew something was up. Whatever it was, it made his heart race and the hairs on the back of neck stand on end.

Maybe now that she'd had time to think about what he'd told her the day before, about Maggie, maybe she was having second thoughts. Not that he blamed her. His baggage wasn't pretty, and even he knew it would be a hell of a lot for anyone to take on. But she had seemed so sincere in her acceptance and desire. He hoped she'd be willing to give him a chance. Though he tried to stay calm and wait for her to open up, he couldn't help but worry that she was preparing herself to tell him goodbye.

It would kill him if she did.

She looked up at him, her blue eyes blazing, and said, "We need to talk."

Ah, hell. Here it comes.

Vance Idol had never begged for anything in his life, not even when he'd just been Vincent Violetti. Now he was prepared to say absolutely anything to keep Lorelei from walking out on him.

"Look, I know what you're going to say, but before you do, let me tell you this. I know I've got a ways to go, but I'm committed to seeing this thing through. I can be a better man. I want to be a better man, Lorelei. For you."

He hated the desperation in his voice, but he couldn't help it. He was a man in love. He hated the glassiness in her eyes and the way her shoulders slumped even more. He didn't want to guilt her into staying, but he couldn't stand to let her go, either. Not without a fight.

"I, look, I know we haven't known each other that long, and maybe you're worried about that whole counselor-patient line we crossed, but if you could just trust me enough to give this thing we've got between us a chance, to give me a chance—"

"Vincent, I'm not really a counselor," she blurted out.

"Lorelei, please—"

"Wait a minute," she said, looking like a light bulb suddenly went off in her head. "You think I'm...you think I'm leaving you? You think I don't want you?"

He cleared his throat and said, "Well, the thought had crossed my mind."

"Oh, Vincent! It's not that at all. I just...."

He breathed a huge sigh of relief, but decided to press on. Her confession gave him pause, though it wasn't all that surprising in retrospect. Still, whatever she was, therapist or healer or even some New Age guru, she'd managed to reach into the very core of his heart and soul to find something of the man he used to be—the man he wanted to be again, because of her. And he wanted her to tell him all of her troubles and let him share the load, to show that he could give as well as take.

"Just what, Lorelei?"

"I have to tell you some things that you might not like. Some things about me."

He didn't know what shocked him more, the notion that he could not like anything about her, or the quiver in her voice. He wondered if he should let her know that he and Jack had talked a little about her family, assuming that's what was bothering her. A man-hating mother he could handle. Hell, he could just turn on the rock star charm.

Of course, Mama might not find the details of his past problems all that charming, especially considering how he was still struggling with them, but he'd own up to it and work to earn her family's trust.

He reached across the table and took her hand, rubbing his thumb over her knuckles. "Nothing you say will change how I feel about you."

"How can you be so sure? You don't even know what it is yet."

He frowned, but didn't let go of her hand. "Well, why don't you just tell me now and we'll start dealing with it."

She looked back at him and her expression stabbed him through the heart. Sorrow, longing, and something akin to pleading painted her lovely features. He wanted to pull her into his arms, kiss and hold her and erase the uncertainty he read in her gaze.

"I'm done running, Lorelei, and I won't run from you, no matter what you tell me. You've seen the worst of me, and you're still here. You've brought out the best in me, too. I'm asking you to trust me enough to do the same for you."

She drew in a gasping breath and exhaled with a shudder. Nodding, she said, "I'll tell you everything tonight when we get back the lake house, I promise. But right now, I want to spend time just being with you. Please."

"I have an idea," Vance said. "Hold that thought."

Strolling over to the classic jukebox in the corner, he fiddled with the machine until it allowed him to select a song. He made it back to the table by the time the first haunting notes of "Sleep Walk" floated out around them. The steel guitar chords thundered almost as loud as his heart.

He held out a hand to Lorelei and asked, "May I have this dance?"

Her blue eyes widened and she smiled. When she gave him her hand, some of the tension bled out of him and he was glad for it. He led her to the small dance floor next to the open windows that faced the water. Someone had turned on the string of white Christmas lights adorning the rail of the dock.

They were almost as bright as the light in her eyes.

He pulled her close as they slowly swayed to the bittersweet tune. Feeling her warmth, the slow cadence of her heart beating in time with his, surrounded by the cool air and lapping waves in the background, he experienced something he hadn't in a long, long time.

He was at peace.

Pressing soft kisses along her temple, over her forehead, in her hair, he took a leap of faith and whispered, "I love you."

A minute stretched out into eternity as his heart started racing. God, he didn't want to push her, didn't want to force a confession of love out of her by pressuring her, or worse. He couldn't abide her pity. He came close to pulling away.

No, I promised I wouldn't run. I'm not that man anymore.

Instead, he forced his breathing to slow and bid his body relax. When she leaned into him and rested her head on his shoulder, he sighed and let a wave of relief wash over him. At least he hadn't scared her off. She moved her hands to his shoulders as she pulled back, her head lowered, not meeting his eyes.

Jesus, here it comes.

She looked up into his eyes. Hers were full of tears. Slowly, she slid her hands up to cup his face and said, "I love you, too, Vincent Violetti."

* * * * *

As she leaned in to kiss him, Lorelei wondered if this was how the sky people felt when they spoke of soaring.

No, it couldn't be. Nothing compares to this.

This man loved her, and she loved him back. That was a miracle. He'd heard her song and survived. That was a miracle. No other obstacles they faced would prove insurmountable.

When she pulled away from the kiss, she smiled at him and then steeled herself to face their next obstacle. "I'm ready to talk now, to tell you those things about me that you might not like."

"I'm listening."

She glanced around the restaurant to make sure they had enough privacy for the conversation they needed to have, and for Vincent's likely reaction. Just as she turned back to face him, she sensed a change in the atmosphere around them, an energy surge that could only come from an elemental. Worse, it was an emotionally charged elemental, too, if the drop in air pressure, temperature, and choppy waves breaking in the roiling lake around them were any indication.

Oh no!

She pulled away from Vincent and rushed to the window so she could look out over the expanse of water. Seized by panic, her first thought was getting her mortal out of there. They had no car, so she'd have to convince him to take off on foot.

Spinning around, she took three quick steps and grabbed Vincent's hand, pulling him with her toward the door.

"Lorelei, what the—"

"We have to go. Right now!"

"But I haven't paid—"

She conjured some money and plopped it on the hostess stand on the way out. She registered his hesitation. He stiffened when she conjured the money, though she continued to pull him. She imagined his eyebrows were probably stuck somewhere in the vicinity of his hairline, but explanations would have to wait.

After they'd made it out of the restaurant and stood dockside, Vincent tugged hard on her hand and brought them to a stop.

"We have to go," she urged. The hairs on her arm were standing straight up. Something *major* was about to happen.

He crossed his arms in front of his chest, nostrils flaring. "Not until you tell me what's going on. You're freaking my shit out right now, you know that right?"

"I'm sorry, I—"

"Gal, we're in trouble," said a familiar disembodied voice.

Lorelei spun around as Jack appeared. Vincent was about to get even more freaked out. Then again, she was having a hard time holding it together herself.

Vincent paled and his eyes widened when Ondine materialized beside Jack in a shimmering series of waves that coalesced into her human form. Well, almost human—her eyes flashed silver and her skin rippled with scales that hovered just beneath the surface. She was either agitated or influenced by the water energy surging around them. Lorelei's own flesh itched to morph into her true form.

"Where the hell did you two come from?" Vincent asked, taking a step back and nearly tumbling over the side of the dock.

"Son, I ain't got time to explain," Jack said in a lazy drawl that belied the urgency of his request, "but y'all need to either high-tail it outta here or get ready to face the wrath of Lorelei's Ma."

Mother? Here?

"I didn't tell her, my darling," Ondine said. Her face was tight and she seemed almost… apologetic.

"Where do we go?" Lorelei asked.

Jack looked back and forth between her and Vincent. "It'd be faster if y'all hit the water. We can stall her for a little while." He shrugged. "Maybe even talk her down."

Fresh panic coursed through Lorelei. "But I haven't told him yet. How's this going to work?" she asked, nodding toward Vincent.

Jack took Vincent by the shoulders and gave him a serious stare down. "Vincent, you're just gonna have to trust our gal here to see you safely home."

Vincent's eyes went wide with panic. "Can you just please tell me what's going on? What are we running from?"

"You ain't running, son. You're swimming."

Lorelei took Jack's cue, grabbed hold of Vincent and said, "I love you. And I'm sorry."

"Sorry for—"

She leapt and pulled him with her. Once airborne, she willed her fins to replace legs and summoned a protective bubble of air around Vincent's body.

Then together they plunged into the depths of the lake's dark water.

Chapter 28

Jesus, he was trapped in his own nightmare.

Only this time he was awake.

This time it was Lorelei dragging him down into the cold water. He struggled to free himself from her grip so he could get back to the surface. He had to get back to the surface or he'd drown. Heaving a deep breath, Vance tried to pull away.

Wait, I'm breathing?

Impossible, and yet he sucked another great gulp of air into his lungs, let it go, and gulped down another. Water swirled all around him, yet he remained dry, enveloped in some sort of air pocket. He couldn't see for shit, but Lorelei's hand gripped his and led him through the water at the speed of a torpedo. How was she holding on? How was he breathing? How was *she* breathing?

After their descent ended, their movements shifted to some sort of undulation. He hadn't felt the sensation since the last time he'd been fishing. So long as the boat's motor had propelled them forward, everything was cool. When they'd stopped, however, and the boat was rocked up and down by choppy waves, he'd turned into the human chum factory. Damn, but his buddies rode him hard about the four buckets of puke he'd hurled over the side. As Lorelei pulled them through the dark waters, that same sensation threatened to overtake him.

"Lorelei," he said, fighting to keep the bile from rising in his throat, "I think I'm gonna be sick."

"Hang on, we're almost there."

A weird echo followed her voice. The words sounded garbled, and he had the strangest feeling that they'd come through water. Not just through the water separating them, but that she'd spoken directly into the water.

"Do you have an air bubble around you? How did I get one? What the hell is going on? Who are we—"

"No time! Just close your eyes and hang on!"

He closed his eyes and focused on breathing, trying to keep the contents of his stomach down. He barely managed to keep from flipping the hell out. He also did something he hadn't done since his days as a choirboy.

He prayed.

After an eternity, she brought him back to the surface. He spotted the lake house in the distance, illuminated by the outdoor landscape lighting. He sucked in great gulps of fresh evening air and hoped it would clear his head enough to deal with whatever had just happened.

"Can you swim the rest of the way to the shore?" she asked.

"What? Why? Jesus, Lorelei, what's going on?"

"*Vincent*, can you swim?"

"Not until you tell me what the hell is going on!"

"My mother is here and she's angry," she said, eyes darting about as if looking for danger. "If she finds you, she'll kill you. You need to get out of here."

He heard the words. His brain tried to process them, but they just didn't make any sense. He was in serious danger of coming unhinged and he needed her to be his anchor. More than that, he needed to be her anchor.

"I'm not going anywhere. Not without you." He grabbed her waist and pulled her flush against his body before realizing that something was off. Instead of gripping wet fabric covering feminine skin, he felt something else.

Oh God, those feel like…

He yanked his hands off her, gasping in shock. She withdrew from him, shoulders sagging and arms folding to wrap around her body. Though she averted her eyes, it wasn't quick enough to hide the flash of raw pain and vulnerability they held.

"I'm so sorry…I wanted to tell you," she said. A moment later her upper body disappeared beneath the surface and was replaced by an iridescent silver tail.

Oh, God, this cannot be real.

It was his last conscious thought before darkness swallowed him whole.

* * * * *

This time it was the force of her spell that stole his from consciousness rather than the nixie call.

Lorelei fought back tears of sorrow and rage as she pulled Vincent back to shore. How could she let this happen? She fought the urge to scream her anguish to the universe. After all these centuries, she'd finally dared to hope again. She'd dared to love and now another mortal man would pay the price, leaving her behind with her misery.

No. I won't let this happen. I won't let her take him!

She settled him on the shore and conjured a blanket out of reeds. Wrapping it around his body, she whispered a prayer to the river gods, imploring them to keep him safe. After planting a tender kiss on his lips, she returned to the water, donned her fins, and prepared to face her mother.

Melusine arrived in water dragon form, huge and powerful as bat-like wings carried her over the water. The twin ends of her split, serpentine tail, adorned with red and green scales, dragged along the surface of the lake and her raven hair whipped in the wind surrounding her. Fearsome and beautiful, she called out for her daughter, her voice smoke and flame.

"I am here, Mother," Lorelei answered, rising from the water until she could meet the powerful Water Fae eye to eye, something she'd never dared before.

"What have you done, my child?" Her voice trickled over Lorelei like summer rain, deceptively gentle while building momentum to a storm surge. "Did I not admonish you and your sisters to avoid mortal men? I would protect you from their treachery. You are my eldest and wisest, Lorelei, and I am most displeased with you."

She bowed low, hoping to appeal to Melusine's mercy in spite of her continued defiance. "I do not wish to displease you, Mother, but I must follow my own path. I am more than the monster you made me. I wish to be a healer. I—"

The air pressure dropped and great twin whirlpools formed around her. Melusine's wrath. Never had she felt so small and insignificant, but she stood her ground. She wouldn't allow her mother to harm Vincent.

"You dare defy my commandments, daughter? Take care, my Nixie. My love for you runs deeper than all the oceans, yet so does my rage borne of your disobedience. Where is the human?"

"You shall not have him."

"No, I shall not. *You* will call him now and end his suffering. And then you will come with me."

"That wasn't part of our bargain. The human is mine!"

Lorelei whirled around, her own rage building as she came face to face with the treacherous Sylph. Maurelle had assumed a similarly fearsome form. She had wings of a great dragonfly and a wasp-like lower body ending in a deadly barb of a sting. Her black, soulless eyes shifted from Lorelei over to the shoreline, no doubt searching for Vincent.

Chapter 29

A chilly breeze tickled Vance's face and hair, bringing him back to consciousness. Damn, what kind of messed-up nightmare was that? He'd assumed he was done with hallucinations, but maybe not.

"Lorelei?" he called out, his voice a rough rasp.

"Not quite," a deep, male voice answered. "But I'm here to help."

His eyes flew open and he tried to sit up, but couldn't manage. Something bound his limbs and torso, and struggling only made whatever it was tighten until he feared it would strangle the life out of him. Looking down the length of his body, he could scarcely believe what he saw. A tangle of reeds had woven around him, undulating as if some sort of collective consciousness controlled them and bid them to hold him immobile.

"What the *hell*?"

"Stop complaining," the voice said. "At least you didn't get zapped or dunked. Your lady is a bit of a spitfire, isn't she? Going by the action out on the lake, she must get it from her mother's side of the family."

A huge, winged man landed beside him on the shore. Vance yelled, "What *are* you? Jesus Christ, what the hell is going on here?"

With a mane of white hair, leather pants, and hooked nose, the big bastard looked like the unholy offspring of Bret Michaels, C.C. DeVille, and the angel of death. Vance's litany of curses died almost as soon as they left his throat, as if it had been sucked out from his lungs along with the rest of his breath.

The big guy leaned down and grabbed him by the chin, forcing Vance to meet his gaze. "Look, bro, I understand you've just had the shock of your life, but I'm gonna have to ask you to calm down and keep quiet. We don't have much time."

"Now then," he said, stooping down lower and putting his face right in Vance's. Jesus, were those his real eyes? "If I give you back your voice, do you promise not to scream like a little girl anymore? Nod your head for me."

It took Vance a few tries to find the right muscles, but he nodded, fighting waves of panic at not being able to breathe. The invisible grip on his throat loosened, and he sucked in great gulps of air. Between coughs and wheezes, he whispered, "What the hell are you supposed to be?"

"The bluebird of fucking happiness," Birdman quipped.

"Right. And here I had you pegged as my fairy godmother, but whatever. Where's Lorelei?"

The big bastard laughed so hard he rocked back on his heels and fell on his ass. "I've changed my mind. You're anything but dull. No wonder she likes you. So, you've a mind to save your fair river lady?"

"You're goddamned right I do!"

And he did. Whoever or whatever she was, he loved her. He'd be damned if he'd ever run out on someone he loved again. Not when she was in trouble.

Birdman nodded. "First things first. Let's get you free."

He hovered over Vance and sucked in a deep breath. Then another, and another. To Vance's amazement, the reeds that held him became brittle and dry, their writhing movements creating fractures along their tortuous links. Birdman grabbed him by the shoulders, yanked him out of the brittle mess, and set him on his feet, which somehow supported his weight.

"How did you do that?"

"Let me give you the CNN version—we're elemental guardians. I'm Bruce, by the way, and I'm a wind guy. Your woman is a water gal. So if you want to save her, you need to offer her tribute in the form of water to fortify and strengthen her for battle."

"I have no idea what that means, but if it'll save her, I'm on board. Lead the way."

"Okay," Bruce said, shaking his head as if amused. "Hold on and try not to scream again."

Vance braced himself and muttered, "Fine, but for the record, I did *not* scream."

He almost did, though, as soon as they were airborne, and promised himself he'd punch the guy if and when he ever made it back to the ground.

* * * * *

Lorelei lunged at Maurelle, belting out a series of lethal notes into her oversized ear. She hoped no innocent bystanders would be caught in her musical crossfire. Alas, instead of rendering her immobile, all the nixie call appeared to do was piss the Sylph off. She grabbed Lorelei around the neck and flung her back toward the water.

"Oh, didn't your mother tell you?" The Sylph's mouth split into a hateful grin. "She granted me immunity in exchange for divulging your whereabouts and activities with the mortal."

The water around her churned. Lorelei dove back down into the depths, barely evading Maurelle's barb. Gods, this was bad. How could she protect Vincent from her mother *and* that blasted Fairy?

She had to take out Maurelle first.

Fortunately, Melusine was currently distracted by something flying near the shoreline. No, not something—someone.

Thanks be to all the gods of wind and water for Bruce.

Gulping down great mouthfuls of water, she burst from the lake and somersaulted over Maurelle, pelting her wings with bursts of elemental energy. "He's not yours, Fairy. You will not take him."

The serrated edge of Maurelle's stinger grazed her back just before she breeched the lake's surface. Lorelei winced as she dove deep, building up supernatural speed for a second assault.

She shot out of the water and latched onto the stinging barb, coiling her tailfins around it, and pulling with all of her might in an attempt to dislodge its deadly point. Maurelle roared and bucked, flying higher into the sky. Lorelei fought to hang on.

Then the Sylph's form expanded.

Lorelei's grip slid and her body fell lower, dangerously close to the poisonous barb's tip. A thousand pinpricks of pain already radiated from the gash between her shoulder blades, draining her powers as they moved away from her elemental source of strength. A few inches more and she'd be lost.

The Sylph continued to grow as they ascended, her power increasing in her elemental cloud-filled sky domain.

Clouds!

Drawing on her last reserves of power, she willed the moisture from the surrounding clouds and shifted from her nixie form as she released her hold on the Sylph.

"Where did you go, water bitch?" Maurelle shouted, her voice warped and filled with rage. "Come out and fight, you little coward."

"I'm still here," she said, her buzzing voice echoing through the clouds. "And it's time you learned that bigger isn't always better, *Fairy*."

She poured out her fury until it coalesced into a swarm of mosquitoes that landed directly on Maurelle's oversized body, stabbing her with trillions of tiny, stinging mouths. The Sylph screamed, writhing in pain as Lorelei drained the elemental energy from her. Shrinking and strength waning, Maurelle plummeted out of the sky and down to the lake below.

* * * * *

"What is that thing?" Vance shouted into the wind, "And what is it doing to Lorelei?"

"That would be my sister," Bruce yelled back, swooping down closer to the water with Vance in tow. Luckily, he was holding up better flying than he had swimming. "And don't worry. Your girl is more than a match for her. It's mommy dearest we need to worry about. Now grab that water!"

Vance took the urn that materialized in his hands and dipped it into the lake, filling it to the brim with water as Bruce had instructed. It seemed insane, but then again, so did being surrounded by a mermaid, a dragon, and a giant wasp woman, not to mention being flown over a friggin' lake by a man sporting wings.

He didn't have much time to dwell on his circumstances, however, once the dragon caught sight of them. He began speeding over the lake's surface with the smooth glide of a hovercraft. Bruce pulled them up so fast Vance was afraid they'd stall, but at least his aerobatics got them away from the beast.

And then everything went silent.

True to his word, Bruce used his powers to generate a vacuum in and around their ears, blocking the sound of dragon's voice, which could apparently kill him. After a second circuit around the lake, Vance spotted Lorelei emerging from the water. Keeping one hand on the urn of water, he used his other hand to reach up and tug on Bruce's arms.

Oh hell, those aren't arms.

The talons gripping his shoulders dug in, pain bringing Vance's focus back to the task at hand. He extended his arm and pointed toward Lorelei just as Bruce banked hard and carried them in her direction. Channeling all of his love and devotion, he silently pledged tribute to her. Then, passing overhead, he tipped the urn and poured its contents out over Lorelei.

* * * * *

Water rained down upon her from above, its power washing over her as Bruce carried Vincent back into the sky and away from danger.

Her mortal had anointed her with water. And whatever he'd infused his tribute with, it packed one hell of a punch.

A tsunami erupted within her the likes of which she'd never experienced. She barely registered the crack of bones and splitting of skin as fury unleashed a burst of water power that catapulted a giant wave over Maurelle in her diminutive pixie form, plunging her back down to the depths of the lake below.

Lorelei turned her attention back to her mother, speaking in a warped voice she barely recognized as her own. "I will never again call a mortal man, Mother."

Melusine's eyes glowed as she focused her angry gaze back on Lorelei. She ducked to escape the angry blast of fire her mother spat in her direction. Mustering her courage and conviction, she burst forth from the water and grabbed Melusine from behind to stop her scorched earth campaign.

"You dare defy me?" Melusine roared, "You choose a human over your mother?"

"My father was human. The mortal man you once loved is part of me, as is my lover. I ache with you in your sorrow, but yes, I choose him. Let him go! Let me go!"

Despite her struggles, Melusine seemed unable to free herself from Lorelei's grip. Lorelei wondered how was she able to hold such a powerful elemental force immobile. It had never happened before.

A glance down at their intertwined bodies gave her the answer.

Her fins were gone, replaced by a pair of muscular serpentine tails. Each was more than twice the girth of her human form and coiled around her mother's torso and neck. And her hands! Great Neptune, her enormous hands were covered in the same iridescent scales, fingers hooked and ending in a series of razor-sharp talons that tore into the Melusine's flesh. She didn't have to glance back to know that dragon's wings had sprouted from her aching back.

"Oh, dear gods, no," she moaned.

Melusine managed a choking laugh in spite of Lorelei's strangle hold around her throat. "You are your mother's daughter, indeed, Lorelei. You choose him, but would he choose you in this form? Or would he abandon you as did your father and grandfather before him?"

Melusine's words cut her to the core. No, Vincent would never accept her in this monstrous form, not after he'd recoiled from her mermaid shape. The look she'd seen on his face would haunt her through the rest of her endless existence. Her chest tightened in a vice grip of pain and sorrow that threatened to drown her with its intensity.

"No," she said, tightening her hold on her mother, pitting her iron will against the crushing tide of sadness and guilt. "He may not choose me, but I still have the power to choose another fate. I don't have to succumb to bitterness and hatred. I don't have to become a monster like you."

A deep voice thundered across the lake. "Stop!"

Mother and daughter ceased their wrestling match as a great wave crashed over them and extinguished Melusine's fire. Melusine whipped up another series of waterspouts, one of which caught Lorelei and hurled her fins first into the swirling vortex.

"You'd best settle down, Melusine. You're in *my* territory now, without permission and without the offer of tribute." Jack's deep, gurgling voice boomed out from the depths. He emerged from the river as merman, rising to a terrifying height as his white beard and hair swirled around him. Great gods, was this his true form? He was as fearsome as Eridanos, perhaps even more so.

"I came for my daughter and the cursed mortal who means to take her from me," Melusine said, her angry voice laced with fear. "You knew of this, Maanameg, and yet you did not intervene. Nor did you, my sister, though you know as well as I the dangers of mortal men."

"I knew not until this evening, Melusine. Still, given the chance, I would not have interfered. Our children must make their own choices and live with the consequences," Ondine replied as she emerged from the water, assuming the same dragonesque form as Melusine. Power radiated from her to match that of her sister's. Power that Lorelei now held in her form.

Thank the gods. With both of them on our side, perhaps Vincent will be spared.

Lorelei plummeted back to the river as the waterspouts vanished. The remaining waves let her know that the gathered river folk still harbored great anger and tension. Steeling herself, she shifted back into her nixie form and swam out to meet Jack and Ondine, prepared to bargain with them to keep Vincent safe from her mother. Her freedom would be too much to hope for, so she settled on protecting her lover. Risking a glance back to the shore, she saw him standing next to Bruce, wondering how much he'd seen and heard.

The look on his proud, beautiful face told her he'd witnessed it all.

She only hoped that he'd understand, and, perhaps someday, forgive her.

*****

"What the hell is happening?" Vance growled. More giant, fearsome creatures had emerged from the lake and were too close to his woman for comfort. Instinct propelled him toward the water so he could protect her.

A strong hand on his shoulder held him back.

"Get your fucking hands off me, asshole," Vance warned.

Bruce spun him around, grabbed him by the shirt and lifted him off the ground. Face to face, close enough to read anger and fear roiling in Bruce's hard gaze. "Watch the attitude. Believe me, this is not a situation you want to mess with, human."

The way he said "human" struck Vance like a sucker punch. Human. Weak. Not like the strong, god-like birdman holding him back, keeping him from fighting for Lorelei.

He'd left Maggie to fight her demons alone. Mortal or not, he wouldn't desert Lorelei.

Using Bruce's overconfidence to his advantage, Vance slammed his forehead down against the asshole's hooked nose with all the force he could muster. It worked. The guy dropped him like a sack of potatoes and fell on his ass, moaning in pain.

Wasting no time, he turned and ran toward the water, gaze fixed on Lorelei as she floated between the three giant monsters. He'd waded in up to his ankles when a movement nearby caught his attention. It was the wasp woman, only smaller, and somehow familiar…

It's that bitch junkie from my last gig.

The woman emerged from the lake, small wings shaking off the water as she rose. He risked a glance back in Lorelei's direction. They were all so caught up in their supernatural pissing contest that they hadn't spotted the evil thing.

The evil thing in question fixed its gaze on Lorelei.

"Hey," he called out. "Remember me?"

She turned to fix her dark gaze on him, and her malevolent expression morphed into hunger. Hunger and lust swirled around her in gusts, the air so thick with her desperation he could taste it. Vance choked against the familiar, acrid flavor of a junkie's need.

"Oh yeah, you remember," he said, deepening his voice and pulling out the best rock star bravado. He had her attention and he needed to keep it. He'd seen what she tried to do to Lorelei. He'd be damned if he lost his woman to this sick bitch.

"You came back to me, baby," she said. Her voice wasn't the seductive drawl he remembered. It was a small voice, filled with terrible longing. She swooped down and landed in the water next to him, staggering toward him with outstretched arms. "I knew you'd come to me. You're mine. I knew from the moment I saw you."

Images flashed through his mind, memories that chilled him to the core and pierced his heart like a thousand knives. He was sitting in a dark hotel room, shaking so hard he could barely force the bottle to his lips. Anger, pain, self-loathing so thick he almost suffocated. And she was there, smiling, feeding on those terrible feelings and relishing the euphoria.

He was her drug.

No, she didn't crave *him*. It was the darkness he carried inside that fed her. Anger boiled through his veins. She wanted to use him, like countless others, and she enjoyed the destruction and suffering she left in her wake.

"That's right, baby," she said, her voice stronger, expression triumphant. "Give me what I want."

Forcing his thoughts away from the darkness, he focused on the one thing he knew could bring him light. Lorelei. Maurelle recoiled, horror painted across her features as she stumbled back. Her body writhed and a small scream escaped her throat. "No, you're mine. You were supposed to be mine!"

"Sorry, bitch. You'll have to find another meal ticket."

She sank back down into the water. Vance turned his attention back to the action across the lake, so focused on getting to Lorelei that the blow caught him off guard.

"You may scream like a girl, but you head butt like a mountain goat." Birdman's voice cut through the fog.

"And you whine like a bitch, so I guess we're even," Vance muttered. Stars danced before his eyes as he fought to remain conscious. The asshole must've knocked him pretty hard.

"Not quite, though I apologize for this one. Can't have you going off half-cocked again."

Another blow, and it was lights out for Vance Idol.

Chapter 30

Something wet hit his face, dragging him out of slumber.

"Lorelei?"

His back cracked in protest as he rolled over on the hard, rock-lined lakeshore, but those aches were nothing compared to the pain slicing through his head. After a few moments, he opened his eyes and looked out over the water. All was calm, save for the light rainfall whispering over the land, the lake, and his skin. Aside from a few plaintive frog croaks and birdcalls, no other sound pierced the steady cadence of falling rain.

Gone. She was just…gone.

Scanning the lakeshore, he found himself utterly alone. No sign of birdman Bruce, or Jack, or any other nightmarish beasts of myth and legend to be found.

No Lorelei.

Though every muscle in his body screamed in protest, he hauled himself off the ground and stumbled back toward the lake house. Everything was in order outside, from the bistro table and tool shed, to the neatly stacked pile of firewood he'd split in his fit of anger. Wind whistled through hanging chimes as the storm picked up steam, pelting him as he made his way to the back door.

Lucky for him it was unlocked.

"Lorelei!"

His desperate cry echoed through the silent home. No one answered. He went through the motions, searching every room in the house and calling her name until his throat went raw, but he knew. She'd appeared out of thin air, and she disappeared into it as well.

No, she'd come and gone from the water.

Seeing it all was one thing, but believing it?

Holy hell, she's a mermaid!

Jesus, the scary ass creature who apparently birthed Lorelei said that the woman he loved, if she really was a woman, had almost killed him with her voice. Then she tried to do the same. But Lorelei had stopped her by turning into a similar nightmare creature. And she'd saved him.

But where was she? Was she safe? Was she alive?

Had she left him?

Oh, God, what if she did? Just like Maggie, she could've escaped to peaceful parts unknown while he was left behind with only himself. And wasn't he just fan-friggin-tastic company? Leaving him alone was the worst thing she could have done. He wasn't ready and he knew it, but what the hell was he supposed to do now?

He paced around, restless, twitchy, wanting nothing more than an escape from the mountain of misery waiting for him. Running a hand through his hair and nearly ripping a hunk out from his scalp, he wanted to scream and tear the place apart. He could still see her in the kitchen through the lens of memory, working hard to nourish his body. Stomping into the living area, he couldn't escape the memory of them sitting together in front of the fireplace—the place where he'd sung to her and bared his soul.

No way in hell was he going back to the bedroom.

Instead, he walked toward the front door and stopped when he spotted his bag and guitar case. Someone had left them there, waiting for him. He focused on the bag, knowing an escape from all of his pain rested in a pocket just inside of it. Addicts never forgot where they left their stashes.

He'd never in his life been so tempted.

Vance lurched toward the bag and stumbled as he fell to the ground. Digging with rabid determination, he ripped the bag and yanked out his bottle of Jack and bag of pills, holding them with trembling hands. He had enough to take a nice, long ride to oblivion.

It could even be a one-way ticket.

It would be so easy.

He took his stash to the kitchen, dumped the pills out onto the counter, and stared at them as they rolled to a stop near the sink. He was right back where he'd been at his gig. He looked up from the sink and, instead of facing himself in a mirror he looked out the window onto the lake.

Fuck. This.

Before he lost his nerve, he grabbed the pills and bottle, ran out the back door, and raced toward the water. He almost stumbled off the dock when he reached the end. Falling back on his ass was all that stopped him from taking a dip. Hell, he could've knocked his head, fallen in, and drowned. That was another way out.

No.

He stood up and launched his poisons as far out into the lake as he could throw them. Then he fell to his knees and roared out all of his hurt and rage, letting it echo across the water and the woods beyond. Rage won, but this rage tasted different than his normal brew. For the first time in a long, long while, he was pissed off enough to live.

"I'm done with this! You hear me? I'm done!"

No one answered, of course. He was still alone. But he knew what he needed to do. Walking back to the house, he went inside and searched the place until he found pen and paper.

An hour and a half later, he pulled his guitar from its case, sat on the couch next to the lyrics he'd scribbled and started to play.

Chapter 31

Vance stood outside of Playground Studio, the weight of his guitar case and nerves bearing down on him. He'd asked Eddie to let the guys know he was on his way over so it wouldn't be a huge shock. He had no idea what to expect from them, or if he should expect anything at all. It had been a month since he'd spoken to any of them, though it felt like an eternity.

A month since he'd left the lake house determined to get his shit together and get his life back in spite of the ragged, gaping hole in his heart.

After finalizing the legal stuff, he didn't have any sway over the band anymore. There was no love lost between him and Josh, of course. Sticks would have his back, which would leave Mark to cast the deciding vote if it came down to kicking him out. He hated to put Mark in that position.

So I won't.

Hell, it wasn't that he wanted out. He'd been around enough to know this was it. Not only would he never get another shot at the big time, he'd never find another band like this group of guys. He wanted to fight for it, aggression surging through him. If it didn't go well, he'd be in deep shit. He'd really need to call his AA sponsor.

He went ahead and sent a text to Jason Storm, hard-assed Iraq war veteran who'd rubbed him the wrong way at first. But since they'd hooked up after his first meeting three weeks ago, he hadn't slipped. Anytime he called, day or night, Jay had his back and talked him down. He'd come to rely the guy to keep his act together. Between his sponsor and marathon songwriting sessions he'd been working since he'd left the lake house, he'd managed to stay clean and sober. Regular meals and visits to a local gym rounded out his new routine, putting him back on his way to a healthy weight and better physical condition.

Too bad none of it helped his heartache.

Two minutes later, he received a reply inviting him to meet for coffee and a nice, long talk after he got out of the studio, good news or bad.

Feeling a little stronger, Vance walked inside and made his way to Studio A.

"Hey, my man! What's happening?" Mark clapped him on the shoulder and then pulled him into a rough guy hug after Vance put the guitar case down.

"Good to see you, Mark."

"Hey, brother. You doing okay?"

Vance let Mark go and stood in front of Sticks. "Yeah, I'm tight. I, um, want to thank you for, you know, the swift kick in the ass. Man, did I need it."

Sticks grabbed him and held tight enough that Vance feared he'd lose it entirely. He also had the strangest feeling that, if he did, Sticks would keep hold of him through the storm and wouldn't ever give him shit about it. Man, he'd missed the guy.

When he let go, they both had to rub their eyes a little. Coughing, Sticks said, "We're taking a little break. Josh is out in the lounge. Why don't you go see him while we grab some grub and bring it back? What do you think, Mark, about thirty minutes?"

"Sounds about right. You cool, Vance?"

"Yeah, I'm cool. Listen, if I'm outta here when you guys get back, don't worry. I'll call."

Mark opened his mouth to protest, but Sticks put a hand on the man's shoulder to stop him. Yeah, Sticks was good like that. Nodding his goodbye, Vance turned and walked toward the lounge. He found Josh sitting on a cream-colored sofa, his head leaned back on the cushion and his eyes shut. Vance took a deep breath and prepared to face the man who'd once been his best friend.

After clearing his throat, he said, " 'S up, Josh?"

Josh heaved a sigh. "Didn't figure we'd ever hear from you again, unless it was a call from the morgue."

"I might be offended if you weren't right," Vance replied.

Josh opened his eyes and gave Vance a long, level look. It pricked at his control, but he held himself in check. If the guy felt like ripping him a new one, he'd let him. Hell, he deserved it. Plus he was obliged to take it as a part of the whole making amends thing, as his sponsor reminded him before he got back in touch with the band.

"So what now?"

"You tell me, Josh. It's your band." *Just like you always wanted.*

"No, it's not. It's you they need. Always has been."

Vance didn't miss his use of "they" versus "we." Was the idiot planning to bail?

"Look, you and me have a whole lot of history and unfinished business, but the band needs you, too."

Josh continued to give him the stone face treatment and Vance had to fight a fresh wave of pissed off. The program goals didn't include anything about punching the lights out of one's inner circle, but he thought he'd suggest adding that step. After all, he hadn't been the only one at fault.

Ah, hell, let's just get all this shit out on the table.

"I'm sorry for everything I put you and the band through. I'm sorry for holding the songs over your head, and I'm sure as hell sorry about Maggie."

He had to stop for a moment and cough a few times. Saying Maggie's name still did that to him, and probably always would. "What went down with the three of us was messed up and I take the blame for—"

"Jesus, just stop, man. I can't do this right now," Josh said, voice shaking. He leaned his head back against the couch, closed his eyes again, and scrubbed his face hard.

"Gotta get it out, bro, before I lose my nerve."

"Is this a part of your personal ticket out of hell? It's a great speech and I hope it eases your conscience, man, but it ain't helping me."

Vance bit back a nasty reply. Jesus, at one time he'd have died for the guy, and he still bled for him every time he thought about what happened with Mags, which was why Josh could get under his skin with such ease. Yeah, Josh knew just how to hurt him.

Didn't mean he had to hurt the guy back, though.

He took a deep breath and ran a hand roughly through his hair. Then he took a leap of faith. "I'm sorry about that, too. You may not believe this, but I've missed you as much as I miss her."

"Seriously?"

"Yeah, man, as much as it hurt then and as much as it hurts my pride to admit it now, it's the truth. You were my best friend. I lost you, too. I know part of it was my own doing, and that's been killing me."

"So it's my fault you fell off the wagon?"

"No, that's not what I'm saying," he bit out. Then he clamped his mouth shut. Damn, he'd hoped…at least he'd tried. He took a deep breath and let everything go. "Look, this was a bad idea. I said my piece. You can take it or leave it. I'm sorry, Josh. And I'm outta here. Good luck with the deal. I hope B.J. works out for you guys."

He turned around, fighting not to put his fist through the wall on his way out the door. *Can't win 'em all, man. Some folks on your list will let you make amends, some won't. You just gotta roll with it and you gotta head out and meet Jay. Do not pass go, do not collect two hundred dollars, do not go downtown and score more uppers and booze. You're done with that shit, that's your new mantra.*

"It wasn't just you, you know? I kicked her out that night, too."

"What?" Vance spun around, not believing his ears.

Josh leaned forward and put his head in his hands, forefingers massaging the bridge of his nose. He looked older. Vance figured late nights rehearsing, playing, and recording caused the dark circles under his eyes, but, man, he just looked worn down. Vance recognized the look. He'd seen it enough times staring back at him from the mirror.

"I didn't mean to sleep with her that night. She just kind of showed up. Said she needed a friend and she couldn't get a hold of her sponsor. I couldn't turn her out. I mean, she had this look in her eye like she was ready to call it quits, you know?"

"Yeah, I do," Vance whispered. He didn't want to hear it, couldn't stand it, but he made himself listen to Josh.

"We spent most of the night just talking about stuff. Well, she talked. She talked about Katie and her folks, smiling a lot. Then she talked about her uncle and all that stuff he did to her when her folks weren't watching, and…hell, we both cried."

"Jesus, Josh—"

"Got to get this out, bro, before I lose *my* nerve."

Vance nodded. It was all he could do. The fight had left him. Now he had a whole lot of empty and nothing good was coming out of this conversation to fill it.

"We talked about you, too, but I won't tell you everything about that. That's between her and me. What I can tell you is that we got caught up in a moment. We both needed each other and we both gave in. I wish to God you hadn't walked in when you did, and I would take that back if I could. And I'd take back what I said to her after, too."

Some of Vance's shock must have shown, since Josh said, "Come on, you don't think I heard what you said? Don't blame you, by the way. If I had been in your shoes, I would've done the same thing, except I would've beaten the shit out of me for good measure."

"Damn, Josh."

"Yeah, real friggin' mess, huh? See, here's the thing. I was mad at her because I knew I was losing you."

"What?"

"Maggie and her baggage cost me my best friend, and I gave her hell for it after you left. So you can stop blaming yourself for driving her back to the needle. Part of that was me, part of it was you, but most of it was her. She was too lost, Vinnie. No one could've saved her, except her, and she knew it. She made her choice."

The confession and swirl of emotions washed over Vance until he thought he'd drown. He should feel better now, knowing that Josh had a hand in driving Maggie over the edge, shouldn't he? But it only made him feel worse. His eyes stung and his chest got too tight to breathe.

"I got to go, man," Vance said, his voice a raw scrape.

"You running out on us?"

"I don't know. All I know is I got to meet up with my sponsor right now before I do something really stupid."

"Vinnie?"

"Yeah?"

"Let me drive you."

"I don't know, man—"

"I won't talk anymore, and you don't have to either. I just…I want to get you where you need to be. We'll worry about the rest later."

Vance nodded.

True to his word, Josh didn't say a word during the ride. Vance figured he was lost in his own dark thoughts.

Oddly enough, Vance wished there was something he could say to make the guy feel better, to make things right between them. Perhaps there would be time for that later. All he knew was how grateful he was for the ride.

When Josh pulled to the curb and put the car in park, Vance sat still for a moment. Then, he turned, looked at Josh, and said, "Thank you."

Josh sighed. His eyes were rimmed with red when he turned to answer. "I'm glad you're okay."

"I'm not there yet, but I'm on the road. You?"

"Yeah, I'm on my own road, too. So, what do we do now?"

"We take it one day at a time, brother. One sweet day at a time."

As he eased out of the passenger seat, Vance said, "Hold on. There's something I want to show you."

He pulled his guitar case from the back seat and put it down on the sidewalk to open it. He pulled out a stack of papers, which he handed over to Josh. Josh accepted, flipping through them and nodding, brow furrowed.

"Think you can do anything with them?"

"Yeah," he muttered, "Yeah, I think I can."

Yeah, I can see you arranging and revising my chords in your head.

"So," Josh began, "you want me to pick you up after you talk with your sponsor? Or, um, you can come by tomorrow, you know. We'll be back in Studio A laying down tracks. You up for singing?"

"Sure, um, I guess I could come by tomorrow."

"Yeah, that'd be good. We'll see how it goes, and then maybe we could jam a little with your new stuff after, if you're up for it."

"Okay. Drive safe, man. I'll see you tomorrow."

"Stay tight, brother."

Vance stood in paralyzing numbness as Josh drove off, fighting the gnawing ache that tore through his chest. While he hadn't expected the reunion with his bandmates to be all warm and fuzzy, tearing open the old Maggie wound so close to the fresh one left by Lorelei was almost too much to bear. He took two steps toward the coffee shop and looked through the wall of windows inside.

Jay wasn't there yet.

In less than two minutes, he could walk downtown and find a dealer.

God, he was so tempted.

A piercing shriek sounded above him just as he was about to turn around and go for that little walk.

"What the hell?" A soft breeze swirled around him, and he looked up in time to spot the biggest hawk he'd ever laid eyes on perched on a nearby streetlight. It didn't take off when he walked over to get a better look. It just stared down at him, its sharp gaze fixed and unblinking.

Out of nowhere, the wind picked up and grew unseasonably colder, turning Vance's bare arms into a mess of gooseflesh and chilling him to the bone.

"You gonna stand out here all night freezing your nuts off, or would you like to get a cup of Joe?"

He spun on his heel and came face to face with his sponsor.

"Um, yeah, man, let's get inside. What the hell's up with the deep freeze out here? It's mid-June, for Christ's sake."

Jay shrugged, or at least made an effort. The guy had his arms wrapped around his torso and was shivering like a wet dog. "That's Tennessee for you," he replied. "Don't like the weather? Stick around an hour—it'll change."

"Right."

"So why are you standing out here anyway?" Jay said, stomping his feet a couple of times, probably trying to warm up.

"Waiting for you," he said through chattering teeth. "And checking out the freaky urban wildlife."

Vance turned back around, ready to point out the big bird of prey, only the damned thing wasn't there anymore.

Chapter 32

Two hours, three cups of coffee, and a whole lot of talking later, Vance was a little less raw. He told his sponsor what had gone down with the band and about the bombshell Josh dropped on him. Too bad he couldn't share the other half of his heartache and head fuck, but if he started telling tales about mermaids and flying men, he'd never convince Jay he hadn't fallen off the wagon again.

"Shit," Jay said, leaning back and stroking the five o'clock shadow along his jaw. "That's pretty messed up, man. Are you sure about getting back with the band? Could be one hell of a trigger."

"I thought about walking away. I can't tell you how many times in the past month, but…"

"But what?"

He took a deep breath and closed his eyes. "After I hit rock bottom, I met someone who became…close to me, through my songs. She's the one who got me straightened out and brought me back to the music, and it saved my life, man. I mean, if I hadn't had my guitar with me the night before I showed up at my first meeting, when I was seriously thinking about drowning myself in Jack Daniel's, I wouldn't be here."

To his credit, Jay didn't interrupt when he needed a minute to just breathe and gather his thoughts.

"She told me I needed to live a whole life, that I could honor Maggie's memory by doing that. And, well, the only way I can do that is by making music. Me and the guys, we make great music. It's all I've got left."

"So I take it the someone who got you back on track is out of the picture?"

"Yeah," he replied, running a rough hand through his hair. "But I owe it to her to keep clean and keep playing."

He braced himself for an argument. The rock-and-roll lifestyle really wasn't conducive to recovery. Even if the guys let him back in the band and watched out for him, they couldn't have his back twenty-four/seven. He was over twenty-one and there was a liquor store on every corner in every town no matter where they'd be touring. There would always be a dealer just around the corner, or a groupie with a stash, and it would only take one slip on his part, just one lapse in judgment. Then again, there would be liquor stores and dealers around the corner no matter what he did from here on out. And alcoholics came from all walks of life and all professions, didn't they?

One thing was certain—without the music, he didn't have any reason to stay sober or keep breathing. Not without Lorelei.

Vance leveled his gaze on Jay and said, "My mind's made up, bro. I've got to do this, and not just for her. Making music is what I do, and it's what I'm going to keep doing. For me."

Jay stared back at him, unflinching. Great. Now wasn't the time to lose his sponsor.

"Come on," Jay said, yanking him out of his musings.

"Where?"

Jay checked his watch. "Meeting's in half an hour. I'll go get the car."

"So that's it? You aren't going to brow beat me about getting back in the band?"

"No, but I'll be riding you every day to keep you from screwing up. You will drag your sorry ass to a meeting after every session. I don't care how late and I don't care how tired you are. No excuses. They piss me off."

Vance had to smile as Jay stood up and loomed over him. Damn, the guy could give R. Lee Ermey as Gunnery Sergeant Hartman a run for his money with the hard-ass drill instructor routine. He wiped that smile off his face pretty quick, though, remembering there was no such thing as an ex-Marine. Jay had told him more than once that he'd love nothing more than to wipe the floor with him and his rock star attitude. Given Jay's six-foot-four frame full of muscle trained for combat, he had no doubt his sponsor could back up that threat.

"You picking up what I'm putting down, pretty boy?"

"Yeah, man, I hear you."

"And you're going to call and check in with me. I don't hear from you, I'll hunt your ass down, and if I have to do that? You'd better pray the paramedics get to you first."

"Anything else?"

"Yeah, one more thing. I want tickets to your first big show."

Okay, that was unexpected. He waited for the punch line, but Jay just loomed over him, arms crossed over his chest and one brow arched beneath his buzz cut while he waited for an answer.

Wait, is he serious?

"You just going to sit there with your mouth hanging open, or you going to answer me?" Jay asked.

"Um, yeah, I can get you tickets," Vance replied, still at a bit of a loss.

"That would be 'yes sir,' asshole. Now get up so we can get going."

The hard-ass didn't crack a smile, but he did give Vance a hearty slap on the back after he got up out of the chair. Well wasn't this day just full of surprises?

"I have to say, man, I never would've figured you for a rock fan."

"What, you thought I was into techno or some shit?"

He grinned and replied, "Nah, I was thinking more along the lines of Eurodance."

That remark earned him a not-so-soft punch in the arm. "Okay smartass, just promise me you and your boys ain't one of those dumb-fucking hair bands or crazy bite-the-heads-off-bats metal acts and we're cool."

"Man, you need to get out of the '80s."

Vance chuckled as his unlikely pal headed off down the street to pick up the car. Breathing in the now warm evening air, a strange feeling tugged at his gut. It made the fine hairs at the nape of his neck stand at attention and sent an uneasy jolt through his spine. Panic threatened, but this didn't feel anything like the cravings he'd experienced. No, this was something else.

Someone was watching him.

He did a slow three-sixty, scanning the area around the downtown coffee shop. Tourists milled about on the busy sidewalks, paying him no mind. He half expected Jay's horn to blare from up the street with the universal car call of "get your ass in gear," but the man and his Mustang were nowhere in sight. No one watched him from inside the coffee house, either.

The wind picked up again, and Vance looked up into the evening sky in time to spot the dark shape before it disappeared into the clouds.

He caught sight of a dusky feather the size of his palm in his peripheral vision, latching onto it before the breeze could carry it away. There was a small slip of paper wrapped around the large quill. Unwinding it, he read the neatly typed message that looked like something you'd find in a fortune cookie.

Let your love flow like a mountain stream

Vance snorted, then muttered, "The Bellamy Brothers? That's the best you could do, Birdman?"

He flipped the paper over, thinking maybe the oversized airhead had left him something less vague and more useful, like winning lotto numbers and a cure for his heartache.

To his surprise, it was even better.

"Hey, guitar guy? You coming?"

"Yeah, man," Vance yelled back, gaze still fixed on the night sky. After a moment, he shook his head and walked toward his ride, throwing a little wave over his shoulder as he went and hoping the big guy would catch it.

Chapter 33

Their first recording session went as well as could be expected. It took a while to get back in the groove, but they managed to get a few decent tracks the first day and wrapped up the album after a couple of weeks. Eddie was busy working to get distribution and told the guys to take a little breather before digging into the new material and getting geared up to tour. They could still keep playing local gigs to generate buzz.

The hours were grueling and kept Vance busy, but not busy enough, in spite of Bruce's admonition to hold tight and wait for their meeting. At least the guy gave him a sign from time to time, like raptor sightings, or wind, or that swarm of fireflies that showed up outside of his apartment two nights back. Vance kept his end of the bargain by staying sober and working on keeping himself together. Whether he spotted him or not, he knew the birdman was watching.

Mark and Sticks were tight with Vance again. He and Josh were working on it. They'd joked about hauling their asses to a family counselor, but settled on a weekly boys' night out for pizza and pool. For the most part, they'd kept their issue out of the studio, so that was progress.

Josh insisted on driving Vance to most of his AA meetings and check-ins with his sponsor. Vance never turned him down. He figured Josh needed to make amends, too.

"So, you want me to pick you up later?" Josh asked after he pulled up to the curb.

"Nah, I'm good. I'll have Jay drop me back at my car when we're done."

"You meeting us later for pool?"

He ran a hand through his hair and then reached into his pocket, his fingers caressing the note Bruce had dropped out of the sky. The thing was wrinkled and worn from the number of times he'd read and rubbed it. It had become his talisman over the past few weeks.

He'd clung to it and the hope it offered

"Um, I think I have to bail this time. There's someone I need to see."

Josh's furrowed brow and steel gaze spoke volumes, so Vance quickly added, "It's not a dealer. It's a friend—someone who helped me out of a jam once. I'm hoping he can help me out of another."

Some of the tension bled out of Josh's expression. Heaving a sigh, he said, "Is he going to help you get your girl back?"

"What? How did you—"

"Come on, Vinnie. I've known you a long time, and I've been up to my ears in your new songs for the past month. You've never been the type to pound out ballads just so you could get laid. You put it all out there when you write songs, whatever you're feeling. So I'm guessing there was someone after Maggie," he said, shaking a finger while thinking out loud. "Someone recent and someone who had a hand in keeping your ass clean and sober."

"Am I that obvious?"

"Put it this way, with a mug like yours? I wouldn't put any serious green on Texas Hold'em if I were you.

You've been sporting that special I-got-my-heart-ripped-right-the-fuck-out look since you came back from rehab."

Vance just stared at his buddy, dumbfounded.

"Look, I'm not gonna get up in your biz, but just…"

"What?"

"Be careful. If it doesn't work out, promise me you won't go out and do something stupid, okay?"

Damn. He hoped like hell things would work out, but if they didn't? Could he keep a promise like that? "I've made it this far, man. I got no plans to go back where I was or to check out anytime soon. That's the best I can do."

Josh nodded, and then held out his hand. When their palms met in a firm shake, Josh said, "Call me if you need anything."

"Will do, bro."

* * * * *

After the meeting and dinner with his sponsor, Vance made his way down to Riverfront Park. Bruce's choice for a meeting place had surprised him. He figured the birdman would've gone for low profile. Not that it mattered. He'd meet the guy in the middle of Bridgestone Arena, stark naked, if it gave him a shot at seeing Lorelei again.

He had the oddest sense of *déjà vu* as he got closer to the river.

Shaking it off, Vance made his way down concrete stairs and walked across the grassy knoll. To his surprise, the area was pretty well deserted aside from one homeless guy snoozing in the shade and a couple of pigeons that waddling around, most likely trolling for food. He pulled out a couple of twenties from his wallet and slipped them into the worn backpack sitting beside the sleeping man, whose only response was a loud snore. Then he parked his ass on the lawn and waited.

He closed his eyes and took a few deep breaths, savoring the fresh air that filled his lungs and the sounds of water lapping and wind rustling through the nearby trees. He ran his fingers through the grass, blades gently tickling his skin while the late afternoon sunlight bathed him with its soothing warmth. Surrounded by the elements, Vance reveled in the simple pleasure of just…being. No matter how much his heart ached, or how tough or shitty things got, he made it a point to take time out every day to savor sobriety and the wonder of living without the pain of withdrawal and physical cravings. It made his ongoing struggle with the psychological stuff much easier to bear.

And it was a hell of a lot better than wallowing.

A warbling sound nearby made him open his eyes. Those pigeons had wandered closer to where he sat on the grass. He thought about shooing them away, but then reached for his backpack, unzipping it and rooting around in his snack stash.

"Let's see…. Pickings are slim, but I've got a couple of protein bars. You like chocolate or peanut butter?"

The smaller of the two birds flapped its wings and turned its beak away, as if to snub his offering.

"Hey, beggars can't be choosers. What about you?" he asked the larger pigeon. It hopped over and cocked its head at him in that inquisitive way birds had. A cool breeze swept in and tickled his skin as the bird hopped close enough to inspect his food.

The wind picked up, swirling around with greater force and sending a shiver down his spine—but not from the cold. The air around them churned and coalesced into something akin to a miniature tornado. It hit him with such force that he closed his eyes even as a scream threatened to tear from his throat.

Only, there was no air in his throat or lungs to power the scream.

After some time, the roaring wind stilled and was replaced by a familiar voice. "You still scream like a little girl, and I wouldn't wipe my ass with this sorry excuse for food."

Chapter 34

He opened his eyes in time to catch a glimpse of Bruce morphing from a pigeon to the more familiar birdman form. Between inhaling great gulps of air, Vance noticed that the asshole had at least made an attempt to pass for a normal guy. A long trench coat covered the wings, though the uneven, lumpy pattern created by the fabric covering them made him look like an oversized hunchback. A matching Fedora completed the Bruce-in-disguise look, which might have been funny if not for the swirl of power emanating from him.

"You could've just walked here, you know." Vance's voice was little more than a hoarse whisper. Still, he managed to get to his feet on his own without accepting Bruce's proffered hand. Score one for dignity. "And I do not scream like a little girl."

"Only because I took your voice," he quipped, smirking.

"Fuck you. By the way, how's the nose?"

"Better than your noggin, I'm sure. Now, let's get down to business before we disturb the locals."

Vance glanced back over at the homeless guy who somehow managed to snooze through the melee. He walked over to him and slipped the protein bars into his backpack next to the cash he'd put there earlier. He was about to give Bruce more grief about his overly dramatic entrance when he spotted the small figure hunched over next to the stairs, her emaciated body shivering in spite of the summer heat left in the wake of the wind's disappearance. Clumps of matted black hair peeked out between slim fingers wrapped around her head.

He stumbled back as if doused with icy water, then spun around, anger rising in him like a tidal wave. He marched up and got right in Bruce's face. "What is *she* doing here?"

He half expected Bruce to punch him, or maybe just unleash some more wind power and knock him over for copping an attitude. The guy didn't flinch, though, or even blink. Instead, a mixture of sorrow and weariness flashed in his gaze before he masked it with his normal expression.

"Maurelle is here to apologize."

The statement left him speechless. When he found his voice, he said, "I find that hard to believe."

Bruce heaved a sigh and gestured to the ground, which had somehow sprouted a blanket and two cushions. Vance parked it across from Bruce and waited while the birdman appeared to study him. The scrutiny was a little disconcerting, but it didn't come across as a threat. "You look well, mortal."

"Yeah, good meals and clean living will do that. Your sister doesn't look so hot. What gives?"

"Her confrontation with Lorelei weakened her, and she's also suffering from something akin to withdrawal."

Now that was unexpected. "Your kind can get hooked on drugs, too?"

Bruce offered a small, sad smile. "Her drug of choice is a little different, but I imagine the effects are comparable. Our kind, the Sylphs, normally feed on positive life energy, and we feed the natural world with positivity using our elemental powers. Maurelle is addicted to human suffering. That is why she was drawn to you."

He expelled a breath he hadn't realized he was holding. "So she what? Sucks the misery out of people and then…kills them?"

Bruce nodded, lips tight and brows furrowed in obvious strain.

"Jesus."

"It is something we try to discourage."

"Maybe you should try harder," Vance muttered. Then something else occurred to him, something that pricked at his gut like a thousand tiny knives. "She's done this before, hasn't she?"

Bruce didn't respond for a long, long time, which was probably answer enough. After all, if everything he'd read on the Internet about Mermaids, Sirens, Sylphs, and all the gods and goddesses from various pantheons was true, then interfering in the lives of one or hundreds of mere mortals would mean little to these creatures. Maurelle had probably sucked the lives and souls out of countless humans.

Talk about an abuse of power.

"Why'd you let her get away with it?" he asked, snarling as he stood and towered over the creature in front of him. Vance did nothing to conceal his anger, arguably foolish, but at the moment he just didn't really give a damn.

"I did all I could," Bruce replied. The big bastard even sounded sincere. "She was one of our grandfather's favorites, and I'm afraid he was rather…indulgent. He turned a blind eye for decades. I, on the other hand, no longer could."

"Well fan-friggin-tastic for you, asshole."

That last statement must have finally gotten to the birdman, since Vance found himself flat on his back on account of the force of a cold blast of air. The chill persisted even after the wind died down, and all Vance could do was shiver and hope that Bruce would spare his balls from frostbite, even if he didn't spare his nose.

"I like you, mortal, but even my patience has its limits. Suffice to say, I had a hand in saving you from my sister's cruelty. And she will be punished." The way Bruce uttered the last sentence sent a chill down Vance's spine that had nothing to do with the temperature.

And then as fast as it had gripped him, the chill dissipated.

After he recovered, Vance sat up and returned to his cushion facing Bruce while Maurelle continued to shudder and whimper next to the stairs. The homeless guy had slept through the whole thing. Lucky him.

"So what do you want from me?"

"For you to accept Maurelle's apology."

"Why should I? Come to think of it, why does it even matter to you? I'm sure she doesn't give a damn."

Bruce sat very still, his eagle-eyed gaze flashing with some emotion Vance couldn't quite identify. "She needs to make amends, Vincent. It is part of her punishment."

Though he shouldn't care, and he wasn't certain he wanted to know, he still had to ask. "What's the rest of it?"

Much to his surprise, Bruce answered. "She will be stripped of her elemental powers for fifty years, during which time she will remain locked in a human form. She'll still work for our kind, but as a mortal—she will support herself or she will know hunger, she will know mortal frailty and suffering at the hands of others, and she will age."

"Doesn't sound like such a big deal to me," Vance muttered. Perhaps it was a tad defensive, but being a mere mortal himself, who could blame him?

Bruce smiled and said, "It is for one as powerful as my kind. And it should be quite a learning experience for her. If walking a mile in her victim's shoes doesn't breed empathy in her, then nothing will."

"And supposing it doesn't?"

Darkness filled Bruce's gaze. "Then we will try more…extreme measures."

Vance nodded, fighting against the lump of dread lodged in his throat. When the big guy smiled and joked, it was easy to forget what he was. The look and that last statement was a pretty grim reminder.

Still, something that had been niggling at the back of his mind came to the forefront. Given the guy's mood, it was probably a really bad idea to ask, but maybe he could use it to his advantage.

"You say you want me to accept your sister's apology."

Bruce nodded, face neutral.

"Because she needs to make amends."

Bruce nodded again, though the sudden swirl of wind around them belied his calm.

"And if I refuse?"

"I wish you wouldn't."

"Why?"

The wind picked up and thunder rumbled somewhere across the river. Those yellow eyes narrowed, brows furrowing to a deep crease above his hooked nose as he glowered. Looked as though Vance had finally gotten under the guy's skin.

Squaring his shoulders, he mustered all of the hot-blooded Italian male bravado he had and glared right back at Bruce. It wasn't hard. Finding out he'd been a pawn in a supernatural freak's sick game had already lit a fire in his belly. But being asked to forgive the monster who'd almost destroyed him?

"Here's what I think, Birdman," Vance bit out through gritted teeth. "I think there must be more to making amends for you and Maurelle than some moral obligation, otherwise you wouldn't be so insistent. Knowing you, you'd probably beat it out of me, or worse, but you haven't. So I figure this is a strictly voluntary deal on my part. A favor."

Bruce cocked an eyebrow, but didn't deny it.

"So if you want me to grant my forgiveness, then I'm going to want something in return. I want to see Lorelei, and I want you to take me to her.

Chapter 35

Vance waited, astonished by Bruce's hesitation. How could this come as a surprise? Hell, the only reason he'd agreed to meet the birdman was so he could find his woman…mermaid…whatever she was. It didn't matter. She was his.

"Don't tell me you weren't expecting this, Birdman. Figured you'd be cheering me on. Unless, of course, helping out at the lake and that little love note you left me a few weeks back was your way of asking me out?" He added the last part as a joke. Then again, Bruce was a little on the metro side.

"Sorry, you're not my type, mortal."

"Then were you playing Cupid?"

Bruce rolled his eyes. "Do I look like fucking Cupid to you?"

Vance cocked his head to the side and studied the guy. "I don't know…throw on a diaper, grab a bow and arrow, you could probably pull it off."

Instead of taking the bait, Bruce leveled him with a hard gaze and asked, "Do you know what she is?"

Vance nodded. "I saw the fins, remember?"

Bruce sighed and rubbed his head like it was hurting. "Do you know how you came to be in her care?"

Well that one stumped him. Come to think of it, he'd never asked. Sure, he'd thrown out the theory that Sticks had slipped him a mickey or something the night he'd walked out on the band, but honestly? He couldn't remember what happened that night. Instead, the memory of Lorelei morphing into a giant woman-dragon hybrid flashed in his mind. Cold fear crept up his spine. He opened his mouth, intent on speaking, but his voice had deserted him. He couldn't blame Bruce this time, either.

Fortunately, or maybe not, Bruce cut him some slack. "She didn't do it on purpose. The nixie call, siren song, call it what you will, but she has no control over it. It's a curse. She didn't know you were around when she started singing that night."

"What happened?" His voice held an awful calm that belied a despair surging within him.

"You answered her call and fell into the river. She pulled you out."

"So if she knew this might happen, that this call or song or whatever it is can kill someone, why was she singing?"

He didn't want to believe it, but he'd done his own investigating online, read the myths. Betrayed maiden, Siren, her legend was a part of Rhine lore and it wasn't pretty. She called sailors to their deaths, or so the stories went. Did she do it for sport? Was she like Maurelle?

No, he knew his lady and couldn't believe she'd harm anyone or anything deliberately.

The wind picked up again, which probably meant birdman was getting pissed off. Too bad. How could these creatures be so careless with their powers? Vance ran a rough hand through his hair as he got tangled in the memories of Lorelei the healer and tried to reconcile them with Lorelei the monster. Had she rescued him out of guilt? Pity?

Bruce's voice jolted him back to the present. "You love your music, right?"

"Yeah, but what the hell does that have to—"

"Take that love and multiply it by a thousand, then another thousand for good measure. Her kind live for song, it's as essential to them as the water they rule. Now imagine knowing that if you sing, which you must, that you have the power to destroy those around you—to suck the will and life out of them. That is what your lady has endured for centuries."

He flashed back to that awful first night, when he was almost crushed in the iron grip of withdrawal. Lorelei told him of her first love and how she'd lost him to some accident too terrible to name. She'd blamed herself. Hell, she was right, it would seem.

And she'd almost done the same thing to him.

Vance coughed a few times, his throat suddenly tight. "Is that why she left? She was afraid of…hurting me?"

Bruce nodded. "She also believed that you would find her frightening or repulsive once you'd witnessed her transformation."

Vance stood still, numb from the afternoon's revelations. He was still pissed off at the birdman, his sister, and the supernatural elemental universe with which he'd recently become acquainted, but he was also pissed off with himself. Lorelei had left him because she though he wouldn't accept her, that he'd be too afraid of her.

And who did he have to blame for that?

He'd recoiled from her as soon as his hands touched her fins, and he could only imagine the look she'd seen on his face while she was battling her mother.

"I don't care," Vance said.

"Excuse me?"

"I don't care what she is or what she did to bring us together. I know she saved me. She saved me from drinking myself to death, she saved me from your sister, and she saved me from her monster of a mother. I know I heard her sing at the lake house and survived. I know I love her. I'd like to tell her that in person."

"She's immortal."

"Doesn't matter."

"You aren't."

Vance shrugged. "Whatever life I've got left, I'll give to her."

Bruce studied him, his eagle-eyed gaze boring with such intensity that Vance wondered if the birdman was trying to hypnotize him. Then Bruce inhaled deeply. After two more gulps of air, a shudder ran through his big body. Vance wasn't sure if it was pleasure or pain.

He wasn't sure he wanted to know.

The big guy grinned. Okay, guess it was pleasure. Why did the notion make him so uncomfortable?

"Hope suits you, mortal. It has a much better flavor than anger or despair."

Okay, he wasn't touching that one. "So if I let your sister make amends, will you take me to Lorelei?"

"It's against the rules."

"You don't look like the kind of guy who follows the rules."

Bruce grinned. "Good point, mortal. I cannot directly interfere, but I can tell you that you might consider returning to the lake house. It belongs to the local water elementals."

"Will they take me to Lorelei?"

"Maybe. You are quite persuasive, for a human."

"That's all you're going to give me? I thought you immortal types were supposed to be more helpful."

"Where did you get that idea?"

"*The Odyssey*."

"*Argonautica* would serve you better. After all, Orpheus trumped the Sirens with his lyre. Maybe you could do the same with your guitar. Music speaks to the water folk."

"That the best you can do?"

"Afraid so, mortal. Take it or leave it."

Vance thought for a moment. He'd hoped it would be easier. Then again, nothing worth doing was ever easy. He stuck out his right hand and Bruce accepted. With a resigned sigh, he followed birdman over to the whimpering puddle that was Maurelle so he could fulfill his end of the bargain.

* * * * *

No lights were on and the door to the lake house was locked, so he made his way out back and stared out over the water. It was as far as he'd go. The meadow held too many memories that might take him back to a bad place. He knew better than to risk his sobriety so soon after getting it back.

Pulling out his guitar, he took a deep breath and started singing Little Texas. Honestly, he'd never been a big fan of country, but "What Might Have Been" seemed to fit the occasion. He hoped the music would call her, if she was still around, if she hadn't gone back to her native Rhine. Still, maybe one of the other water folk would hear and relay his message. It was a long shot. Bruce had warned him that it might work or might not. Regardless, he'd needed to come back here to face himself and his memories.

Nothing was happening.

His voice quavered as hope turned to grief, his song of longing transformed into a bittersweet goodbye. He needed to send his gratitude out to Lorelei and hoped that wherever she was, she'd feel it. Even though he'd lost her, she'd given him his life back. As hard as it got, he swore he wouldn't waste such a precious gift.

And, like a complete pussy, he cried when he reached the end.

Good thing no one's here to see it.

"Son, that was some mighty fine singing. Did Nashville finally get in your blood?"

Or not.

"Hey, Jack. How've you been?" Vance asked, not turning around.

"Can't complain. You?"

"I'm fine."

"Liar."

Vance turned around then, itching for a fight, but the giant man just looked sad. His broad shoulders slumped and he shuffled more than walked along the lawn leading to the lakefront. Once he got closer, Vance noted pain and regret in his dark, fathomless eyes. *Guess I'm not the only one suffering.*

"Takes one to know one, my friend," Vance said, turning back to look out over the water. "What brings you here, Jack?"

"Same thing as you, I imagine. Can't decide whether I want to scream or wallow. That's what females do to you, right?"

"Right. How is she? I mean, her mother didn't—"

"No, Melusine didn't hurt her. Not the way you mean. She's doing about as well as you, I expect. Hurt, sorry, wishing she was here with you right now. Worried sick, too."

He could only imagine all the things she'd be worried about. God, she probably thought he'd gone right back to the bottle and wound up dead. He couldn't stomach the idea of hurting her that way.

"Can you tell her I'm…okay? I got back with the band and I got myself a sponsor, so I'm not planning on checking out anytime soon. Can you tell her that? Because, you know, I don't want her to worry."

"Yeah, I guess I could…"

"But?"

"But I'll likely run into Ondine, and I ain't sure I'm ready to deal with that yet."

Vance reached up and grabbed Jack's massive shoulder, turning him around and waiting until he had eye contact before he spoke.

"Well I guess you'd better get ready to deal with it, my friend. You'd better stop whining, wallowing and get busy locating your balls and manning up. Good advice, right?"

"You gonna use my own words against me?"

"You want her?"

"Yeah, son. Gods help me, but I do."

"Then I suggest we get busy figuring out how we're going to go get our women. You can get us there, right?"

"I reckon I can, but you might not enjoy the ride."

"I don't care if you have to drag me through hot coals, just get me to Lorelei so I can get her back."

Jack's face split into a huge grin. "If we leave now, we should be able to cut her off at the pass in Memphis. Don't say I didn't warn you, Jonah."

"What?"

Vance didn't even have the chance to scream before the giant mouth enveloped him and dragged him into its belly, along with his guitar.

Chapter 36

Lorelei followed behind her sisters, swimming down the Mississippi toward Memphis. Going with the current was much easier than the trip up from the Gulf and required little effort, which was great. She hadn't been herself since leaving Nashville. Ondine had been kind enough to escort her as far as Michigan, where she'd met up with Ilsa and the girls for a tour of Detroit. It didn't improve her spirits, in spite of Motown magic. The city seemed gripped by desolation and desperation.

Kind of like her.

Now, speeding back toward the Gulf, Lorelei ached with the call of Music City and the man she'd left there. It was probably for the best that the Mississippi didn't connect to the Cumberland, otherwise she would have been unable to resist. She could materialize there, perhaps, given the powers her battle for Vincent had awakened, powers he had awakened with his tribute. If that failed, she could go back the long way. If she'd wanted to go back.

She'd have to navigate a series of small connecting streams and underground channels. It had been difficult enough when they'd first traveled there, back when Lorelei's heart had been lighter. She didn't think she could manage now, with her sorrow choking the life out of her.

But she really, really wanted to.

Which was, of course, a really bad idea. As promised, Bruce had been keeping tabs on her mortal. He sent word that Vincent had rejoined his bandmates and was receiving treatment for his addiction. Better still, he was making music again. He was healing, and that was what she'd wanted for him all along.

As much as she wanted to see him again, she didn't want to cause him more pain and jeopardize his recovery.

Ilsa must have sensed her turmoil, since she led them to the shore for a break.

Gwen and Gisele excused themselves, muttering something about visiting some of their reclusive cousins in a nearby branch of water. Lorelei hauled herself up on shore, not bothering to lose her fins. She rolled over onto her belly and placed her head on the warm earth beneath her. She felt Ilsa's hand on her shoulder and it filled her with a sudden surge of gratitude for her sister's presence, support, and love.

"Do you want to go back and find him?"

"What for? I'm sure seeing Mother and I in full-on dragon mode, not to mention this," she said, glaring down at her fins in disgust, "scared him enough for ten lifetimes. I hope…."

"You hope he'll be okay. That he won't turn back to drinking and that he'll stay on track, right?"

"Yes, that's what I wish for him more than anything else."

"And from what you told me, he is on track. So you could go back, you know."

Sure, she supposed she could. After Jack coerced an apology out of Melusine, he demanded she provide him restitution for her egregious breech of etiquette on top of the tribute she owed him. Lorelei's freedom paid her mother's debt, but Melusine cut her off for spite. No longer welcome in her beloved Rhine, she wasn't sure where she would make her home now.

Ilsa and their younger sisters offered solidarity, vowing never to return to the Rhine for the duration of Lorelei's exile, but she couldn't bear to deny her sisters their home. And one of them would rule in Melusine's place someday. Not Lorelei, not after what happened. No, Ilsa was next in line now. She would no doubt feel obliged to go back. Besides, Melusine had only promised Lorelei her freedom, not freedom for the others.

Ondine, her unlikely ally and new favorite aunt, promised to champion their cause upon her return.

She had the feeling that Ondine didn't want to leave, either. She wasn't sure what had happened between her auntie and Jack, but Ondine's affection for the river guardian was apparent. If she had to guess, she figured Ondine and Jack couldn't work out who was going to be in charge and who would forsake territory to join the other. The older generation rarely mated at all, and even more rarely mated one another for those reasons.

Pity. They both deserve happiness.

"Lorelei? Would you like to go back?"

"Doesn't matter."

"The hell it doesn't! You love him. Stop being noble. You suck at it."

"You're really starting to piss me off, sister."

"Well, the feeling is mutual. Look at what you've done, Lorelei—"

She barked out a hollow laugh. "Yes, let's look at what I've done. I almost killed the man I love, once by calling him and later by unleashing the wrath of Melusine. I lost my family ties and my home in the process. I—"

"No, Lorelei. You *saved* the man you love from himself. You healed him and gave him his life back. You *fought* our mother's curse and won your freedom. As for losing the human, I don't think you lost him. I think you gave up fighting. That pisses *me* off, my sister."

Lorelei sat up straight, prepared to give Ilsa a tongue-lashing and, perhaps, a black eye. But, she was right, and Lorelei couldn't deny it. She'd given up. It made sense, given all of the obstacles in her way. Then again, she'd accused Vincent of running from his troubles not so long ago. How was this any different?

"So," Ilsa said as her lips curled into a knowing smile, "Are you ready to go and get him back?"

"Yes," Lorelei replied, her face splitting into a huge smile, the kind borne of love, gratitude, and foolish hope, even as the tears fell.

"Right. Let's grab the girls and get swimming before you change your mind."

"Don't worry. I'm committed now."

"That's good to hear, little gal."

Lorelei and Ilsa turned back to the river in time to watch Jack's great head emerge. Her heart soared. As much as she'd missed Vincent she also missed the great fish who'd become the father she'd never had but always longed for. With Jack's help, they could make it back to Music City even faster.

But…he didn't look so good.

Ilsa reached him first and wrapped as much of herself as she could around his body. "Jack! How wonderful to see you again!"

"Good to see you, too, Miss Ilsa," he replied.

He closed his eyes and winced. The rumble that emerged from his stomach almost shook Ilsa off. Wrapping herself around him, from the other side, Lorelei rubbed his belly and tried to soothe him. He sighed, shook a bit, and then heaved the mother of all belches.

"Pardon me, ladies. I've been holding that one in a while."

"You look unwell, dear friend. Did the trip disagree with you?"

"You could say that, darlin'. Y'all mind helping me closer to the shore. Think I'm gonna be sick."

The Nixies heaved Jack into the shallows, and then used their powers to lift his head and belly onto the shore, leaving his tail in the water. True to his word, the big fish began to cough and heave until he lost the contents of his stomach in a great spasm. Lorelei had a second to wonder what he'd eaten before a guitar emerged, followed shortly thereafter by Vincent Violetti.

*****

When he stopped shaking long enough to speak, Vance said, "Jack, as a personal favor, I'm going have to ask you to never, ever do that again."

Jack croaked back at him. "Don't plan on it. Humans never did agree with me, and no offense, but you taste awful."

Vance chuckled, almost sorry for him. Jack did look a little green, which was about as attractive on a fish as it would've been on a man. It took a bit of effort, but he managed to sit up and wipe some of the nasty goo off his face and hair, trying his best not to get too queasy. When he looked to his left, he saw her.

Jack groaned and muttered, "I reckon I'll be on my way now. If y'all need anything, just—" He paused and burped again, his great body shuddering. "Just send out a call."

"What about me?"

Vance almost jumped out of his skin when he caught sight of the other mermaid, but then he recognized her as the blonde who'd been with Lorelei at his show.

Good God, how many of them are there?

The blonde looked back and forth between Jack and Lorelei.

"You can keep *me* company," said a familiar voice, followed by the appearance of Bruce in the flesh, and feathers. He smiled and winked at the blonde in the water then held out his hand. "Besides, you still owe me a little tribute for that call you unleashed on me."

"And how would you have me make amends?" the blonde quipped, her lips curling into a slow, sultry smile.

"Three guesses, you naughty little Nixie," he replied.

The blonde took his hand and allowed him to pull her out of the water in a blur of motion that made Vance dizzy. Birdman carried her off into the night sky. Jack muttered something about young folks these days. Then he wriggled and managed to push his bulk back into the water before swimming off with speed and agility that seemed impossible. Vance shook his head, wondering if he'd ever grow accustomed to these magical creatures.

Speaking of magical creatures…

Vance turned his attention back to Lorelei.

Jesus, she really is…oh, man.

She was sprawled out on the shore, raven hair falling over her shoulders and almost concealing her bare breasts. The top half of her looked just as he remembered, but as his eyes ran down to her belly and waist, he braced himself for the reality. A seam of thick, shimmering scales rested right where the curve of her hips flared. Smaller scales covered her lower body below and tapered off to a pair of long fins. They reminded him of the elegant fins of a goldfish, or one of those Japanese koi. He thought he'd have to brace himself to keep from being all kinds of creeped out, but she was just too beautiful for words. His lady was truly as beautiful in this form as she'd ever been as a human woman.

When his gaze swept back up from her tail, her arms were crossed and her head was lowered. She shifted her tail, bringing the shimmering mass behind her. God, she was hiding. He'd made her so uncomfortable with his gawking that she was closing up on him.

Damn, stop staring and go *to her.*

"Lorelei?"

He scooted closer to her, taking it slow so as not to spook her and brushing his hands over his shirt as he went.

It didn't help. He was still covered with all kinds of nastiness from Jack's belly. She glanced up at him and flicked her hand in his direction. A second later, he was clean and dry.

Swallowing his shock, he muttered, "Thanks."

"You're welcome."

"Lorelei?"

"Yes?"

"Let me see you, beauty."

He waited as patiently as he could, fingers itching to touch her and arms aching to hold her. She didn't budge at first, and he willed himself to stay put and let her come to him. She met his gaze first, her beautiful blue eyes full of longing and a flicker of hope. He smiled at her, trying to put her at ease. After what seemed a lifetime, her arms unfolded and the tension melted from her body. Her shoulders relaxed and her breath became slow and steady. Vance inched closer.

He couldn't help staring at her tail. Fear had already morphed into fascination, but he asked permission first. "May I?"

After a moment of hesitation, she uncurled her body and brought the delicate fins back in front of her. He touched the larger scales at her hip first, earning a gasp. He hadn't figured such tough outer skin would be so sensitive. Or perhaps he'd hurt her. Glancing back up at her face, he breathed a sigh of relief. He knew that look. She wasn't hurt or scared. The expression she wore was filled with longing and, though she tried to hide it, desire.

The scales weren't slimy or sharp, like he'd expected. They interlocked with tight junctions and felt smooth like the skin of a snake. He moved his hand lower over her hip, loving the texture of the smaller scales sliding underneath his fingertips. When she breathed a low, throaty moan, he knew she loved it as well.

With a wicked grin, he slid his hand a little to the left and lower, wondering if he could drive her mad with pleasure by touching her like this, in her current form. Jesus he was nervous as a teenager, but who could blame him?

He'd thought about…exploring her mermaid form and wondered how he'd feel about it, and how she might react. She gasped and grabbed his hand, pressing it harder against her and leaning close to find his lips. Jesus, even in this form she turned him on like crazy.

"I love the way you feel, Lorelei," he said, and meant it.

"I'm glad. I didn't know if…."

"Lorelei, I love *you*. All of you, legs or fins."

She kissed him again, brushing her lips gently over his. Then she took his hand and moved it from her body.

"There's more you should know."

"You mean the whole Siren thing? I read up on it. Doesn't matter to me. Besides, I've heard you sing at least twice and lived to tell about it, so I'm guessing I'm immune now."

"Yes, I believe you are," she said, sounding hopeful as well as contrite. "When you offered me water as tribute, along with your devotion, it seems to have broken the spell, but…"

"But what?"

She sighed and looked away, eyes filled with unshed tears.

Don't cry, baby. Please, don't cry.

"Vincent, you might not be immune to others of my kind. If we stay together, we cannot avoid them. Not all of them are like me. Many of them are indifferent to mortals, or simply cruel, like my mother."

"We'll cross that bridge when we come to it."

She shook her head and held up her hand to silence him. "I need you to understand the dangers. Do you remember what happened back at the lake? You've seen how fearsome and frightening my kind can be in the throes of our full elemental power." Then, in a small voice, she said, "You've seen how frightening I can be."

"Doesn't matter."

"How can you say that?"

Now it was his turn to hold up a hand to silence her. "Lorelei, you've seen me at my worst, too. Back when I was curled up on the bathroom floor going through hell with cravings and withdrawal." He paused long enough to swallow the lump of shame constricting his throat. "I was a wreck, and I said and did a lot of ugly things. You saw me through it. You didn't run out on me."

"Of course not. I love you," she whispered.

"Then you know exactly how I feel. I told you, I'm through running."

"I'm immortal."

"Don't care."

"I'm always going to be tied to water. I can't keep legs full time."

"We'll live by a lake, or a river."

"Vincent, I—"

"Will you stop arguing and just go with it, woman? Is it always going to be like this with you?"

"Probably," she said. Then she laughed. He loved the sound of it, as lyrical as her voice. He'd never tire of making her laugh. After she calmed, she nodded and gave him her full attention.

"I know what you are. More importantly, I know *who* you are. The only thing I worry about in this scenario is me. I'm a work in progress and I've still got a ways to go. I won't lie. I still want to drink sometimes. Hell, I'm not even supposed to think about any kind of relationship until I've been on the wagon for at least year. But thanks to you, I have a whole lot of good reasons to stay sober."

"That's wonderful, Vincent, but you have to stay strong and live for yourself. Maybe I showed you the door, but you made the choice to open it and walk through. I'm so proud of you."

"So will you come back with me? I mean, can you, after everything with your mother?"

"I'm free of her, and I can't go back home. If you'll have me, I'd love to make my home with you."

"You are my home, Lorelei, for now and for always. I love you."

"Vincent Violetti, I love you, too."

Chapter 37

He came back for me! He came back.

Overwhelmed by Vincent's acceptance, she needed to show him how much his love meant to her. Though her sisters had enjoyed the beds of mortal men during the course of their journey, Lorelei had declined the many invitations she'd received. Vincent owned her heart. She couldn't bring herself to share her body with anyone else, no matter her nixie appetites.

Being denied so long, though, and having Vincent so near, finally hers, her ravenous hunger warred with the desire to go slow and savor the moment. Judging from his hooded lids, heaving chest, and shifting hips, Vincent felt much the same. Still, there was only way to be sure.

"Hey! I'm going to need my pants back…eventually."

"Don't worry, I'll conjure some more from you…eventually. Now come here." She shifted into her legged form and embraced her mortal man.

She guided his hand back to that sweet spot on her lower abdomen, shivering in pleasure as his eager fingertips stroked and pressed her flesh in place of scales. He lowered his head and looked into her eyes, as if asking permission.

Great gods, not only was he not repulsed, he seemed to find her even more appealing. She nodded, and he leaned in and pressed soft kisses against her sensitive skin, adding his tongue when she moaned her appreciation. His erotic exploration was incredibly intimate. Never in her long existence had any of her other lovers touched her knowing of her other form, her true form. The honesty of the moment moved her as much as his gentle caresses. Soon, he had her undulating beneath him, panting and moaning for more.

"I want to make you come this way," he whispered. "Will you let me do that for you, beauty?"

"Yes, please! Just keep going…only faster…oh, gods!"

Vincent complied, using her sighs of pleasure as his guide, keeping his eyes locked on hers. Unable to resist, Lorelei brought her hands to her breasts, caressing her nipples as Vincent drove her closer to the edge. He hummed his appreciation, clearly enjoying the view.

And then, it happened.

"Wow," Vincent muttered as she floated back down from her release. "Just…wow."

All of a sudden self-conscious, Lorelei lowered her head, wrapped her arms around herself, and pulled back a little, uncomfortable with the scrutiny. Perhaps he regretted what he'd done. After all, even in this form she was different from the women he was used to, and humans tended to be uncomfortable with those who were different.

Two firm but gentle fingers lifted her chin. She closed her eyes, unable to meet his gaze, afraid of what she might see in it.

His low, sensual voice washed over her like a soothing current. "Hey, where are you going, beauty? Don't hide from me."

She opened her eyes, mustered her courage, and confessed her greatest fear. "I'm sorry, I just didn't know if you'd be okay with this," she said, gesturing to her lower body and allowing a flash of her scales to emerge.

"Oh, God, Lorelei, come here," Vincent said, pulling her into his arms. As he stroked her hair and soothed her, he whispered, "I'm amazed at how beautiful you are—like this, like that, or any way because all of it is you, and I just wish you could see yourself through my eyes so you'd know."

Warmth spread through her chest and she held him tighter. That this beautiful, incredible mortal man had come back to her, accepted her, and loved her was overwhelming. Not only did he accept her in her true form, he apparently relished it. Gods, what had she ever done to deserve such a man?

It didn't matter. He was hers. And she vowed to show him just how much his gifts of love and acceptance meant to her.

She pushed him down onto the ground, flat on his back, and slid her body over his, savoring the feel of hard muscles and harder arousal over her scales. She slid down lower she rested between his thighs and captured his arousal in her palm. Slowly, lovingly, she stroked him, bringing him to the brink of madness and then pulling back.

"Christ, Lorelei," he said, panting, "you're driving me out of my mind."

"Do you want me to stop?" she asked, knowing full well his answer but wanting him to beg her.

"Never, beauty, never, but I would love you to take me in your mouth. Will you? Please, baby?"

With a profound sense of feminine satisfaction, she took his tip between her lips and teased him, rewarding each growl and muttered curse by taking him deeper. He was so thick and heavy, growing even larger in response to the pleasure she gave him. She tortured him with her lips, teeth, and tongue until his body trembled and then slowed, only to bring him back to the edge again and again. His excitement was contagious, and her legs shook when she moved to sit astride him, a fine sheen of sweat covered the rest of her body.

"Oh, yes, Lorelei! Put me inside you."

Gods, she was so ready for him. Straddling his body, she positioned him at her entrance and sank down, both of them shuddering in ecstasy as their bodies united, mirroring the union of their hearts and souls. She willed herself to remain still, wanting to savor the moment for as long as possible. Leaning down, she pressed a series of worshipful kisses over his lips, whispering words of devotion in her first language.

"I'm not sure what you're saying, but it sounds sexy."

She laughed low and husky. "It is, my love. Trust me."

He pulled her to him then flipped them over with a wicked grin. He began to move, slow pace close to torture for both of them. Savoring his every groan, breath, and heated gaze, she loved him on shore, with one foot in his world and one in hers. How fitting that they should join on the banks of the mighty river from which she would now draw her strength.

They came together, not in frenzy, but in a quiet moment of passion. As she rested in his arms, she tried to stay in the moment, but questions about their future crept into her thoughts, threatening to rob her of the peace they'd found. In spite of his assurances, which she was certain he believed, Vincent couldn't possibly fathom the challenges they would face. She'd spoken at length with Ondine about her first marriage. It had been difficult enough for her with a normal aging process. What would she do as Vincent aged? She would continue to love him, of course, but given his capacity for self-loathing, how would he handle it?

How would she handle his death?

"You think too much. You know that, right?" he said, pulling her closer into his warm embrace.

"Can't help it," she replied, her voice breaking as tears spilled from her eyes. "I don't want to lose you, and I will someday."

"Oh, my beauty. My dear, sweet beauty." He held onto her with strong arms, kissing her hair and offering what comfort he could. It wasn't enough. It would never be enough.

* * * * *

He wished he could ease her, but he remained at a complete loss with this issue. Sure, he'd thought about it. How would he feel as he aged and she remained youthful and beautiful? In truth, that didn't bother him so much, since lots of aging rockers adorned themselves with young, gorgeous women. The idea of her worrying after him as he grew old and his body fell apart, the idea that she'd have to care for him should he become incapacitated, pricked at his sense of dignity. He didn't want to burden her with that, nor did he wish to leave her behind to mourn for him.

He'd speak to Jack about the latter. Surely he'd help see her through the process when the time came. If need be, maybe Jack could fetch her sisters to help. Still, he wished he could do more to protect her.

It didn't change anything for him, though. He'd take whatever time they had together and be grateful.

"And that, human, is why I will help you."

Vance and Lorelei untangled their limbs and jumped up, startled by the deep voice emanating from the direction of the water. A towering figure emerged from the depths, his head adorned with the horns of a bull, massive chest reminiscent of Jack in human form, his lower body that of a serpentine fish. Fear flashed through Vance, as well as the instinct to place himself between Lorelei and the potential threat, but she rushed into the water, transforming her legs back into fins as she went, and threw herself into the creature's arms.

His mermaid and the towering god—for Vance surmised that he, like Jack and Lorelei, was some sort of water deity—spoke in the same language she had used with him as they'd made love. He wished he knew what they were saying, though he figured he and Lorelei became the topic of discussion once they finished their initial greeting.

"Fear not, Vincent. We've come to help."

Ondine suddenly appeared at his side.

Jesus, can't they just walk or swim up like normal people, or at least give some warning? He hated these sudden appearances, but figured he'd have to get used to them.

He didn't think he'd ever get used to conversing with them naked, though. He covered his cock and balls with his hands and lowered his gaze. Figuring he'd turned about five shades of red as heat crept up his face and neck, he muttered, "Sorry, I'm, ah, a little self-conscious here."

"I don't mind," Ondine purred, low and husky. "But if you insist…"

All of a sudden, Vance found himself clad in a pair of tight jeans. "Thanks. So, who's your friend?"

"He is Lorelei's great-grandfather, the river god Eridanos, revered among the Potomoi. He has come to meet you, and to grant Lorelei the means to live with you in peace and happiness."

"Wow. He can do that?"

She quirked a brow at him, regal face painted with haughty amusement. "He's a god, dear, he can do most anything. Now then, are you prepared to offer tribute?"

"Excuse me?"

"You must demonstrate your worth if you wish to claim the hand of a Naiade. What are you prepared to offer?"

His chest tightened in panic. What the hell could he offer a god? Man, this added a whole new dimension to meeting the family. Besides, he knew he wasn't worthy of her. He vowed, however, to spend the rest of his life working to become the man she deserved.

"May I make a suggestion?" She'd placed a light hand on his shoulder, pulling him out of his musings and back to the task at hand.

"Hell yeah, um, I mean, I would love any advice you'd care to throw my way, ma'am."

Ondine smiled and then he found himself holding his guitar. Once he recovered from yet another bit of abracadabra, he let go of the breath he hadn't realized he'd been holding, along with the tension in his shoulders. Somehow, having the instrument in his hands eased his body and mind. He'd always found comfort and confidence in music.

"I can sing as tribute?"

"Of course," Ondine replied. "Make certain it is one of your own songs. Now, if you'll excuse me, there is a certain uncouth yet irresistible river guardian with whom I must converse."

Vance grinned and said, "Is that what they call it back in the old country?"

She pinched him on his cheek and then gave him a not-so-gentle smack on the backside. "Don't tease me, young man. Remember, I found you naked."

He masked his yelp of indignation with a nervous chuckle, and then said, "All kidding aside, go easy on him, all right? He's missed you something awful."

"As I have missed him. We simply must work out a co-habitation plan. Good luck, Vincent."

"Same to you, Auntie."

He feared he might get another ass smack for that remark, but instead she threw back her head and laughed. "You may address me as such when you've won the approval of Eridanos, so get to it!"

He flinched after Ondine disappeared before his eyes. He took a moment to tune his guitar and finger comb his hair before clearing his throat to get the attention of his love and her great-grandfather. Feeling at a bit of a loss, he dropped to one knee and bowed his head low before the river god.

"I would like to offer tribute to you, and to humbly request the hand of your great-granddaughter, Lorelei, in marriage."

No reply came, and though it nearly killed him, he dared not lift his head. Maybe it was a test, or maybe Lorelei wasn't ready for marriage. *Oh hell, I didn't ask her first! Man, that's just going to piss her off, treating her like she's property up for auction.*

"Your manners serve you well, mortal. What tribute would you offer the mighty god of the Rhine?"

"I would sing for you, your…highness?"

"What, no dragon slaying?" The deep voice held mirth, which surprised him. Still, Vance recognized a test when it was put to him.

"I've already battled a modern-day dragon, a demon of my own making that I'd been fighting for far too long. Your granddaughter saved me from it. I love her. I want to spend the rest of my life showing her how much I love her. I swear to you that I will be faithful, that I will honor and cherish her, and that I accept her fully as she is and will be, just as she has accepted me."

"Look upon me, worthy human."

Vance looked up into the fearsome face and found unexpected warmth and kindness in his gaze. "Your acceptance of her, *all* of her, is what earned you the gifts I will bestow upon you. I hereby decree the curse of Melusine broken, not just for Lorelei, but also for all of my Nixies. Their siren call shall no longer harm living creatures, unless they require it for defense against those who wish them harm."

Lorelei burst into tears, but her smile told Vance how much her grandfather's gift meant to her. Finally, she could find peace and heal the hurts of her past, too. And she could sing for love and joy, spreading these magnificent feelings to those lucky enough to hear her.

"Furthermore, so long as you fulfill your vows of fidelity, honor, and love, you shall live as long as your mate."

Vance stared back, dumbfounded. Immortality? How would *that* work?

"I imagine you'll find your way. Perhaps you'll choose to "disappear" at the height of your fame? It has worked well for a few other famous bards of your era," he said with a knowing wink.

Okay, definitely asking Lorelei about that *later.*

"I imagine you'll bring her home to visit from time to time?"

That he made it a question surprised Vance, but he didn't hesitate with his answer, "Of course, your highness."

"You may call me Eridanos, son. Now, on with your tribute!"

Feeling ten feet tall with a heart full with hope and happiness, Vance played and sang, pouring out his love and gratitude for his new family, his new life. Lorelei wept, and he could've sworn that the old guy got a little misty-eyed as well. He couldn't help the tears that fell from his own eyes, nor did he care.

He'd found his home.

Epilogue

One year later

"Hey, Vance, we're on in ten."

"Be right out, Mark."

He stared at his reflection, wishing he'd taken the time to shave, but was otherwise satisfied with the man staring back at him. He'd put on a healthy thirty-five pounds, and daily swims with his Nixie had added wiry strength to his muscles. After finger combing his hair, he splashed some water over his face, toweled off, and sat down to psyche himself up for tonight's performance at the Ryman. Standing room only, much of the proceeds would go to the clinic he'd opened with his sponsor, one that specialized in treating addicts in the music industry. Along with the music, helping others get clean and sober kept him sober and grounded.

Plus, giving back some of what he'd recovered in his life felt pretty damned good.

Lorelei kept herself busy working as Jack's right-hand Nixie, guarding the waterways east of the Mississippi in their world and working with the Cumberland River cleanup in the mortal world, at least when she wasn't volunteering at Walden's Puddle Wildlife Rehabilitation and Education

Center or recording with Vance and the band. He'd been trying to get her to go solo. She had the talent, and since the nixie curse had lifted, nothing stood in her way. She'd promised to think it over. Told him that just being able to sing out loud without any fear was gift enough. That was a start, at least.

Besides, he knew she was happy. For the first time in her long, long life, she'd found purpose and contentment. She told him often how proud she was of how far he'd come, but he was bursting at the seams with pride in his lady.

"Thinking about me, Vincent?"

He didn't jump this time when she appeared in the room, but it took some effort. He just smiled at her reflection in the mirror before turning around to face her. His woman made blue jeans and a T-shirt sexier than any lingerie. The fact that she was wearing one of his T-shirts, "Vance Idol and the Rivermen" emblazoned over those high perfect breasts, made her damned near irresistible.

"Isn't materializing in my dressing room against the rules?"

"Only if you tattle on me," she replied as she walked up and wrapped her arms around his waist. "Besides, I need the practice. This is kind of a new thing for me."

They both had been adjusting to her new powers. Apparently a combination of natural maturation, his tribute, and her act of courage had triggered his Nixie's full potential, including the ability to assume fearsome forms like that of her mother, which she suppressed, and the ability to travel great distances, dematerializing and materializing more or less at will. It took a great deal of energy and practice, but she seemed to be getting the hang of it.

He closed his eyes and savored the contact, giving himself over to the feel of her strong arms and the soft hands that stroked his chest. Of all the things she'd taught him, and there had been so many, the ability to stop and savor those small moments of peace filled him with gratitude so profound he thought his heart might burst.

Naturally, Mr. Happy chose that moment to stand up at attention. Being close to his Nixie tended to have that effect on him as well, not that he was complaining.

"If you keep rubbing me like that, I'll be late getting to the stage."

"Well, we wouldn't want that," she murmured. "Go on and get ready."

"Wish you were coming on stage with us tonight."

"Maybe next time. Tonight is special, something you and the boys earned. Besides, you know how much I enjoy watching you…perform," she said, waggling her eyebrows and giving him her best come-and-get-it-boy look.

He groaned, fists clenching and unclenching at his sides as he fought the urge to stalk over and pin her against the dressing room door and have his wicked way with her. She laughed, the vixen, knowing damn well the effect she had on him and loving it. Loving him.

Life was pretty good.

"Oh, and by the way, check the second pew back and left when you get on stage. You've got some special guests coming tonight."

Vance opened his mouth to ask who it was, but she'd already gone. Shaking his head and grinning like a fool, he walked out the door and joined his band on stage.

"Hey, my man! You ready for this?"

"You know it, bro," he replied, slapping Sticks on the back. "Full house, man. Let's do this."

Mark gave him the thumbs up and went back to his sound check. Vance looked over at Josh. He was fiddling around with the microphone, brows furrowed and gaze intense. Always so serious, most people would probably read anger in his expression and tight posture. Vance knew better. He knew Joshua Rollins needed to keep a tight rein on himself. He might play it off as cool professionalism, but this night meant the world to him, and he was bottling up all of that emotion, saving it for the crowd. It was the only time he ever let it out.

The thought hit Vance hard in the gut and tightened his chest. After all, he used to do the same thing. Of course, Josh hadn't turned to drowning his sorrows with booze and pills, so he didn't have the right to get up in his buddy's grill about it. He just wished Josh could be happy. And, he wished the two of them could bridge the distance that still lingered between them.

Maybe there was one way.

He walked over to Josh and put his arm around his shoulder. To his credit, Josh didn't stiffen or pull away. Some of the hurts between them had healed.

"You doing okay, man?" Josh asked.

"Yeah, Josh, I am. I really am. So good, in fact, I think I'm going to take a little more time off and spend it with the clinic, and with Lorelei."

Josh frowned. "How's that going to work with our tour schedule?"

"Well, I kind of figured you might like to take over more of the vocals. You've got the pipes for it."

He blinked once and leveled Vance with a stare of disbelief. "You want me to be lead? For real?"

"Sure. I'm digging the studio time, but life on the road lost its charm a while back for me. I talked to some of the folks at the studio, and they're showing me the ropes on the production end. I could still record you guys and play with you local until you find another lead guitarist. What do you say?"

"I'd ask if you were back on Jack Daniel's, but something tells me you've been thinking about this for a while."

"Josh, it's your time. You've earned it, and the guys would follow you anywhere. You *deserve* it. So I guess the only question left is do you want it?"

"Yeah," Josh said, his eyes alight with excitement. "I do want it. Thanks, brother."

Before things got too weird between them, he pulled Josh in for a quick guy hug then released him before the emotions became too overwhelming.

"Come on, then, boys. Let's rock and roll!"

As the lights went down and they started in with "This is Home," which had recently reached number seventeen on the charts and continued to climb, Vance looked out into the audience for his anchors. He found Lorelei front and center, beaming up at him with her killer smile and swaying to the music in a way that let him know she'd be favoring him with a private show later on. Beside her, Jack and Ondine cheered him on, along with the rest of the crowd. Ondine had taken to spending summers in the U.S., while Jack took his sabbatical and headed to her neck of the woods in the wintertime.

He gave Ondine a wink and swiveled his hips in her direction, which earned him a smile from her and a mock scowl from Jack. Deciding not to push his luck, lest the old fish make good on his threat to swallow him whole again, Vance turned his attention to Jay. He found his sponsor in the crowd, arms crossed over his chest and sporting that special scowl that only hard-ass military guys could pull off. Jay didn't smile when Vance caught his eye, but he nodded. That was high praise coming from a guy like Jay.

A blast of cool air hit him from the right, and it sure as hell hadn't come from the stage fans or air conditioning. He grinned in spite of himself as he glanced over and caught sight of the birdman. In spite of being a royal pain in the ass, the big guy had become something like a brother-in-law. And like all overbearing relatives, he popped in whenever he damn well pleased.

Then again, he made one hell of a roadie. Vance suspected he'd been by earlier this evening. Their equipment had been unloaded, organized, and waiting for them as soon as they'd made it to the Ryman. He'd even set up coffee and refreshments for the band and the rest of the crew. Vance nodded at Bruce, who grinned and flashed his fingers in a series of numbers, of which Vance made a mental note. Backstage passes and an introduction for ladies in the audience who'd caught the Sylph's eye. Seemed like a fair trade.

He then turned his attention to the left, checking the second pew back for his mystery guests.

Sweet Jesus, how in the world did she swing it?

Staring back at him, eyes wide, tears streaming down her face, and singing right along with him was Katie Michaelson. God, she'd grown up so fast. No longer the shy, awkward teen, this woman-in-the-making floored him with her presence. She'd grown as confident as she had beautiful, and, judging from the guy beside her with a death grip on her hand, she'd grown up in other ways that brought out his protective side. He'd have to do some heavy-duty vetting later on. Katie looked more like Maggie now, and it made his heart swell and ache at the same time. Healthy and happy, Mags would've been so proud of her sister. And having Katie here was like having a piece of Maggie back, wasn't it?

He looked away, his vision blurring, and sought out Lorelei once more, his strength, his anchor, and his love. While Josh and Mark worked their guitar and bass mojo, Vance blew her a kiss and mouthed, "Thank you." And in that moment, with all those he loved most surrounding him, his heart filled to the brim with a long-sought peace and satisfaction.

This is home.

***Crosscurrents*, Southern Elemental Guardians Book 2 coming soon from D.B. Sieders…**

Freshwater mermaid Ilsa is heir apparent to the kingdom of the Rhine, though no one believes her worthy.

Including Ilsa.

So instead of embracing her role as river royalty, Ilsa opts to extend her holiday in the New World. Avoiding responsibility and frolicking with mortals has always been her M.O. until she answers a distress call from an endangered species in the waters near Chattanooga. When her close encounter with a motorboat threatens to expose the world of elemental guardians, Ilsa partners with biologist and unlikely ally Paul Pulaski to throw them off her trail.

Worlds collide and sparks ignite between Princess Ilsa and her diamond-in-the-rough skeptical scientist Paul. But can they survive monster hunters, a rival scientist with a grudge against Paul, and a dark elemental force that could destroy mortal and elemental alike?

Excerpt

Sweet Jesus. He couldn't believe it.

Yet, he could see her plain as day, stretched out beside him in the flat bed of Chuck's truck. And the feel of smooth, sleek scales covering her tailfins drove the reality straight into home plate. Curled up next to him beneath a blanket of rough tarp was a bare-breasted, beautiful, half-woman half-fish creature of myth and legend.

Mermaid.

He'd had always considered himself a rational man. Hell, skepticism was part of the whole scientist package. There had to be some sort of logical explanation for all of this. Maybe she was an actress, out on location for a movie or television shoot? Good God, she was pretty enough. Yeah, that could be it.

The costume and special effects budget must be huge with get-up this realistic.

But…where was the camera crew? Dress rehearsal? Maybe she was some sort of hard-core method actress and wanted some fins-on experience to get into character.

More likely, he thought with some annoyance, she was some stupid drunken co-ed who liked to play dress up.

The scales covering her lower half seemed so real, though. They reminded him of a snake's skin, water tight and covering powerful muscle. Fighting a case of the heebs, Paul ran a hand over her hip and down with as much clinical detachment as he could muster. He took care to avoid the juncture between her legs, since there had to be a pair of legs buried beneath the mermaid suit.

She was stacked, that much was certain. Beneath the veneer of a researcher, Paul was a red-blooded hetero male with a healthy appreciation for feminine curves. He resisted the temptation to grope her ass, though, determined not to unleash his inner caveman on an unconscious female. Continuing down, he fully expected to encounter two separate kneecaps underneath the admittedly thick material of the fin suit.

He didn't.

Holy shit!

No joints. And it wasn't like he didn't dig good and deep. Below the waist, she was not built like a human. Streamlined, and well-muscled, the fins were clearly designed for speed and strength. The biologist in him marveled at the juxtaposition of mammalian and ichthyoid body planning. Though the structure of her spine and positioning of the hind fins appeared more like a marine mammal's and would likely propel her through water using horizontal rather than vertical strokes, half of her was, for all intents and purposes, a fish.

And yet, she breathed air. He felt the expansion of her chest as she sucked air into what had to be a pair of lungs. But with that fish tail...was she amphibious?

Jerking his now trembling hand back, he took a few deep breaths of his own before brushing aside her soft blond tresses and running his fingers along her neck. Damn, how could her hair be so smooth and silky? If this creature was, well, what he thought she was, then she lived in the water. Yup, there they were. Barely discernible upon a light brush, with a firmer touch he found three ridges along the side of her neck—gill slits.

Oh man, this was huge. No, beyond huge—this was the kind of discovery that represented nothing short of a paradigm shift for biology, physiology, and judging from his sudden case of the cold clammies, he should probably throw in psychology, philosophy, and religion, too. Her existence would alter the foundation of their entire world if she was, in fact, really a mermaid. He'd need to perform a much more detailed external examination to be sure. And they'd need X-rays to assess the bone structure within that tail, blood and DNA tests, naturally, samples of the fin scales, and—

A plaintive whimper from the creature beside him jolted Paul back into the moment. On instinct, he wrapped her up in a tight embrace and tried to will some of his warmth into her body. He slid his hands gently up and down her arms, and didn't even hesitate to lower his hands to rub that strange, alien lower half. Relief washed through him as she pushed herself back against his body, murmuring words that sounded like a mixture of English and some sort of guttural, Slavic tongue.

Thank God.

Helping her would be so much easier without any communication issues.

"It's okay," he whispered, his cheek next to her ear. "It's going to be okay. I've got you."

Question was, what in the hell was he going to do with her?

ABOUT THE AUTHOR

D.B. Sieders was born and raised in East Tennessee and spent her childhood hiking in the Great Smoky Mountains, wading barefoot in creeks, and chasing salamanders, fish, and frogs. She and her family loved to tell stories while sitting around the campfire.

Those days of frog chasing sparked an interest in biology. She is a working scientist by day, but never lost her love of telling stories. Now, she's a purveyor of unconventional fantasy romance featuring strong heroines and the heroes who strive to match them. Her heroes and heroines face a healthy dose of angst as they strive for redemption and a happily ever after, which everyone deserves.

D.B. Sieders lives in Nashville, Tennessee with her husband, two children, two cats, and her very active imagination.

To learn more, visit www.DBSieders.com

63786458R00168

Made in the USA
Charleston, SC
13 November 2016